Questions of a Curious Nature

The Incredible Interviews of Annabelle Farrow

By Matt Orth

Edges of the Map Press
Questions of a Curious Nature: The Incredible Interviews of Annabelle Farrow
Matt Orth

Editors: Sarah Thomas and Jane Woods
Cover Design: Kelly Reece and Elisa Beekman
Interior Design: Jami Balmet

Published in the United States by Edges of the Map Press (EMP)
ISBN 978-0-9895304-0-8

Second Edition

This book is dedicated to the rich soil and deep waters of
Broad River Community Church.
Thanks for giving me roots and raising my sails.
BS: TRSH!

Contents

Chapter 1:

Annabelle Farrow

To publish something is a declaration of boldness, a clear statement that what you have put into print is worth reading. The idea of those words taking permanent flight into the reader's consciousness should be a weight handled gently and wisely by the writer, like the rescuing of some fallen bird by a gracious parent. Writing about the work and personality of someone publicly revered and adored only increases the burden to handle each word with precision. Add the topic of religion, and you potentially create a work of devastating results. Nobody wants to unveil for enduring scrutiny a work poorly representing a religious icon.

Annabelle Farrow lived in front of a camera lens, broadcasted into our lives with a familiarity we normally reserve for a faithful friend or caring relative. She shared her heart with a vulnerability rich in weakness and honesty—so we were willing to give her our hearts as well. Biographies and documentaries produced by respected peers have highlighted the diverse sectors of the church who regarded her as a heroine of the Christian faith. Her ability to weigh her words, to not take offense, and to treat everyone with an authentic civility made her almost universally accepted. She had the ear and the eye of rich and poor, young and old, red and yellow, black and white. And even though many families gave Annabelle a welcome spot in their living rooms, her personal life always remained personal. Some say the intensity that made us love her also kept us separate from her.

Since her absence, there's been both a void in the world of engaging and gracious Christian thought and a hunger for more of who she truly was. This book is offered to satisfy that hunger. It contains much more of her story than has ever been heard, much more of her work than has ever been shared, and much more of the mystery surrounding her disappearance.

Annabelle Farrow was born in Stafford, VA, a suburb of Washington, D.C., in 1967 to Gene and Irene Farrow. Gene was pastor of Mossy Creek Baptist for eight years before Annabelle's birth, and Irene played the organ every Sunday, doubling as part-time secretary. They fell in love as volunteers at a Billy Graham Crusade in Louisville, KY after he bluntly pointed out their names rhymed, and she very publicly rolled her eyes. He started seminary, and she began teaching piano lessons to inner-city kids. They loved their little church and shepherded it with gentleness and respect as it grew in depth and width to a sincere congregation of about two hundred.

They raised Annabelle with the same love and respect they showed the people of the community, and she became a precocious child, constantly bombarding every listening adult with a myriad of questions. Her parents went to Rio de Janeiro twice a year, every summer and every Christmas, to work with a church plant serving the local widows and orphans. Those trips were formative for Annabelle even though she often griped about the hassle. In spite of her whining, she learned to appreciate people different from herself, but also, and just as importantly, she saw her parents regard the needy people of Brazil as more important than the traditional "vices" (her word) of the holidays. Early on, those vices were the source of her complaint, what she resented sacrificing. I believe the experience of those upended values and her parents' willingness to reject expectations eventually set fire to the embers of inquisitiveness and exploration simmering in young Annabelle's heart.

It was a painful irony that she lost both her parents at age fifteen on one of those trips when a local gang used the neighborhood church to demonstrate their dominance and power. Others have covered this tragedy as a turning point in her life, and I agree with them, yet I think the biggest impact was an internal steeling, a resolve that she would live a life honoring to her parents.

She moved in with relatives for the rest of high school and pursued her love of journalism and media through classes and internships in the greater D.C. area. Mossy Creek Baptist hired a young and charismatic pastor who, just two years out of seminary, grew a Baltimore area youth group from twelve to over one hundred in six months and soon instituted the same principles with her parents' congregation. Annabelle served there on and off through college and eventually decided to find another church home. When she left, the congregation held four services every weekend with a total attendance of over two thousand. She always denied the change in size as the preeminent reason she left, but she also never shied away from saying it was a factor.

She graduated summa cum laude from the University of Maryland with a degree in Communications and double minors in Broadcast Journalism and Public Relations. While there, she worked every summer in various capacities and offices on Capitol Hill and captained the debate team in addition to serving on student government her last two years.

It was the perfect storm of those experiences that washed Annabelle up on the shores of the local access television show "Poli-Talk" (Annabelle often poked fun at the terrible name by squawking like a parrot and saying "Polly Talk! Polly Talk!"). The show tried its best, with limited contacts and budget, to put together a round table of stimulating conversation about the current issues in D.C. It sounds biased, yet I think history and the tapes will bear this out—Annabelle Farrow was the only stimulating thing on that show. A prominent senator, flipping channels late one night, noticed her intellect, way with people, and ability to read the conversation and "chase the right rabbit."

The rest of her public story is known to most of you: her rise to prominence in the "secular" and "Christian" (she always made sure I added quotation marks to those polar designations) media world as a passionate interviewer, an engaging writer, and an honest face for a public Christianity whose image she had seen splinter into "a thousand quibbling and selfishly askew pieces." Her appearances on the biggest stages with the biggest names articulating the biggest ideas are easily accessible to anyone with an Internet connection willing to make the effort.

Her career crested when CNN offered her the chance to anchor her own hour in primetime, and then the unthinkable happened . . .

Annabelle Farrow disappeared.

I'm writing this book for many reasons, but one of them is to let you know, in part, what happened. Hopefully, it will bring closure to those of you who loved her. So, who am I, and why am I the one writing this book?

My name is Malachi Evans, and I was Annabelle's "techie" from the very beginning. I ran camera for her in the field, mixed sound for her audio interviews, and was always a part of her team no matter where she was or what she was doing. If you want to, you can go back and look at all the fine print credits in everything Annabelle appeared in, and you'll see "Malachi Evans" there somewhere.

But I need to tell you something more than that: Annabelle Farrow was also my best friend and my bride of twelve years. Our life together was rich with the realized hopes of shared dreams, some planned in the idealism of youth, yet many of them pleasantly unexpected. This book is not about me, but allow me to fill in a few more spaces for you.

I grew up an African-American in South Carolina in a community still nursing wounds from its history. My mother was a deaconess in one of "those" Pentecostal churches, and my father was the preacher. I list him second because he left us when I was twelve for another woman when Momma found out about the other two. We moved shortly thereafter to suburban D.C. to be near relatives who went to a church like ours back home. Our entry there was seamless, and Momma got back to, as she called it, "just singin' and servin' the Lord!" My mother remained a remarkable woman to the end, strong and faithful. Until Annabelle came into my life, she was my only hero.

I met Belle for the first time when she traveled out to our little congregation doing research for "Racial Integration in Spiritual Communities," an article for her underground Christian newspaper at the university. You can probably guess the story from my perspective. I saw the cute nose and deep blue-green eyes - like a perfect ocean I always told her- hair pulled back in her classic ponytail, the shade of brown that speaks of living things in hidden forests. You knew her beauty. But did you know she could sing? Most white people visiting a small black church for the first time will slide into the back row and try to clap and sing along looking like six-year-olds steadying their bikes for the first time without training wheels. Not Annabelle. She sat on the front row and moved to the music with a rhythm that you've got to have from the inside out. And because I played bass that day and not drums, I stood on her side of the sanctuary, and I got a front row seat to that voice.

The spark for me didn't just come from the voice and the beauty; I loved the sharpness and vitality radiating off her like heat on a parking lot in August. You could tell when you saw her on TV or heard her in a conversation that this girl had *it*. But to see her face to face, and I'm sorry for those of you who never had that privilege, was to be in the presence of someone who walked in an otherworldly way, as if she could walk on water if she wanted to, and I would not have been surprised if she did. As for what she saw in me, I'm not quite sure. Here was this beauty, this almost-too-good-to-be-true female, and she

4

gave me more than the proverbial time of day. She always said she knew at our first meeting that I appreciated her for the "whole of her and not just the parts," but how she could tell that when I felt like a woodland animal trapped in midnight headlights is another mystery of Annabelle Farrow.

Our majors at Maryland dovetailed—she the journalist and communication prodigy and I the jack of all audio visual trades. We formed what we felt was a God-ordained harmony of gifts and talents, and I was content to use my passions to support the radiant melody emerging from her heart.

We married simply in an outdoor chapel two years later, right after she was discovered on Poli-Talk, with my mom and a few of her relatives present. We decided to keep our names and our marriage a secret—both for the fun of it and to try to work together. We both sensed she would not be living in obscurity, and we wanted to increase our chances as much as possible. Our plan worked, and we were always together, a source of constant joy rather than friction. It got easier as she gained sway within the media world, and the whole scenario remained exciting, the thrill of hiding a secret marriage in a public workspace.

I was happy. *Genuinely* happy. I had a wife that only daydreams and writers ever create and a job that allowed me to be me. But Annabelle developed a holy restlessness, a desire to go beyond the everyday interviews, weekly podcasts, and inspirational segments on nighttime programs. Her walk with Christ became something more, something with wings. It came to a crescendo one weekend on a getaway in the Outer Banks; she came in barefoot and windblown from an early morning walk along the shore.

"Kye, there's a substance to the fire in me, a Presence and relationship that isn't perfect but is nonetheless more real to me than those waves out there. And I look at Christianity in this country, and I see nothing but pale shadows of what could really be."

I pause here where the story starts to change—Annabelle in a state of agitation, taking ponderous walks on beaches and wrestling with a world of people she felt refused to look beyond themselves—for my multi-faceted disclaimer on this book: I want you to know I release this work fully aware of the implications, and even the complications, of trying to put together, in the purest state possible, the missing years of Annabelle Farrow. I would not consider myself equal to her wit, her intelligence, or her masterful way with words. This volume will, thankfully, contain as little as possible of me and as much as possible of her words and thoughts.

It has taken this long to release a book for many reasons, but mainly due to the immense pressure to do it right. And doing it right meant, for me, a complete honesty. By complete honesty, I mean sharing with the world what I wasn't sure she would want me to share. At this point, you may think I am talking about our marriage or some unknown scandal that led to her disappearance.

I am not.

This disclaimer is not just acknowledging the inadequacies of my ability to convey Belle and her work. It is also a promise to you that I've written what I know, what I saw, and what I experienced with Annabelle Farrow. My accounts may be met with disbelief and skepticism. This book has not collected *average* interviews, rather the *incredible* interviews of an incredible woman. I choose the word "incredible" with purpose and deliberation, and though it may have lost its true meaning to overuse, I hope these pages will bring the incredible to light. I hope your minds will embrace that which may only be called *other*.

I said I was unsure whether she would want me to share these things; my lack of confidence exists not because she doubted whether the work was ready, but because she wanted to make sure of your readiness. I share them now hoping she would agree with me.

So, the question I've delayed addressing, and the one for which you probably purchased this book, is: what happened to Annabelle Farrow, the fiery young woman of faith, the darling of the American public and journalist at the top of her field? I answer that question now, as well as I can, with the story of how it unfolded for me as well.

It was a night not long after the Outer Banks trip, and the deadline for the debut of the CNN show approached. We were putting in long hours in the editing and board rooms, dissecting and debating what at times seemed like every second of every piece. My spirit flagged, and my body began to protest from new depths of exhaustion. I don't know how Annabelle did it, but she would just toss her hair up in that messy bun, grab more coffee, and fire away with another question or better angle. The show was going to be great, yet, as she worked, her gaze would sometimes wander, and when she had a snatch of time, she would ask me a random question with a seriousness that was almost humorous in its intensity: usually some form of, *"What if I can ask more of us all?"*

That same night, Annabelle shook me awake, startling me out of an exhausted, comatose sleep. I squinted, disoriented, into a predator gaze, her eyes already locked onto mine. The lamp by our bedside cast a shadow across us.

"Belle, what are you doing? Is something wrong?"

"Do you trust me?"

"What. . .what time is it?"

"3 a.m. Do you trust me?"

"Wha—yeah, I...I trust you."

She nodded once and reached down beside the bed, pulled up my favorite gear bag, and placed it lovingly next to me, like a mom returning a misplaced stuffed animal to a fearful child.

"Okay," she said "go back to sleep then. I think I've been offered a way to ask more of us all."

It was just as surreal as it sounds, but as a testimony to my tiredness, I fell asleep again without inquiring why I was awoken or interrogated about my belief in her, or why my gear bag now rested under my arm.

The next time I awoke, I found myself ushered into an interview that you will read about in the next chapter—the one where she interviews Fear. Not some trendy California kid whose parents named him Fear or some Neil Gaiman fan who renamed himself in radical zeal, but Fear itself. Blame FDR for personifying it first; Annabelle just got the interview.

Still with me? Let me set us up for the rest of our journey and give a straighter answer to your questions: Annabelle Farrow disappeared from public life to pursue interviews that she felt would help her answer the curious questions of why those who called themselves Christians tended to wander through a fallen yet vibrant world. Why did they pursue instead a life where "hobbies had become gods, and God had become a hobby?" These interviews were her intended opus, which she planned to reveal to a waiting public, a nation filled with Christian congregations she hoped would finally hunger for something more than getting by and passing though. She knew those church buildings held many sincere and nice people who had semi-consciously become content with the cardboard boxes and wrapping paper while the wonderful gifts from above sat neglected and unknown. They are interviews that transcended categories of personhood, bent physics, and skipped through time. Conversations with icons, concepts, and representatives of many of the popular worldviews and prevalent conditions of American Churchianity.

She hoped to one day start a corrective swing to what she considered the imbalance of our practice of Churchianity—to swing it from "a place of sensationalism, complacency, consumerism, and the theoretical" to a place of "tangible relationship where more grace, more humility, more thoughtful passion, more enduring faithfulness and more God-led creativity abounded." Her hope was to come out of hiding and silence and one day air these interviews as a series of shows entitled *The Pendulum Sessions*. There came a second disappearance of Annabelle Farrow, however, one that I will share with you if you can make it with me far enough on this trip. But right now I come to you, after years of meditation in isolated places and frequently one-sided prayer, with a deep peace—just recently achieved—to let the world know the story of the silent years of the beloved journalist who was my own beloved in truth.

I offer this collection of interviews with a sense of excitement, some lingering, fearful doubt, and the deep ache of loss. I regret that she cannot share it with you personally or in the format she desired (more on that later), but I hope these conversations will be as meaningful to you and your spiritual formation as they, and she, were to mine.

I present to you now *Questions of a Curious Nature: The Incredible Interviews of Annabelle Farrow.*

Malachi "Kye" Evans
Spring 2013

Chapter 2:

Fear

I arranged this book to give you a sense of those missing years, of Belle's work and the interviews we did. It is not strictly chronological, but the first interview we conducted during the new journey is the one you're about to read. This is the interview that started it all. Afterwards, Belle told me she was required to do this one first, and that's all she would say.

This interview establishes the crazy world we entered when we disappeared from public consciousness as well as setting up some themes that will rise to the surface elsewhere. The content of this conversation relates to all believers. We are scared of so many things, including our own faith and simply the unknown. So as we enter into these conversations Annabelle collected, I wanted us to look Fear in the face (kind of) and dismiss it from our journey in this book.

The interview could not have started any worse for me, awoken at 3 a.m. with the "Do you trust me?" question and the gear bag placed under my arm. I had fallen right back to sleep.

I woke again, this time outside in the middle of a forest. I was lying on my back, surrounded by musty smells and foreign sounds and a close darkness pierced only slightly by a fickle moonlight.

My eyes went wide, and I began to kick like I just realized I was drowning, dry leaves crackling like frying bacon.

Belle's hands and voice appeared with urgency, "Kye, Kye! Breathe! It's okay. It's okay. You're with me. You trust me, remember?" She pressed on my shoulders and chest, shushing me like a mother with an infant fighting sleep.

"Malachi, these next few moments may be the most surreal of your life. Just breathe, and listen to me. Remember our first few years of covering events and getting scoops? Living spontaneously, throwing the gear in your beat-up Corolla, and driving ungodly hours to random places just to get the story? Kye—Kye? Do you remember?"

"Yeah, yes, I remember." My voice sounded like a child's, hoarse and thin. I could not stop swallowing.

"Well, that's what we're going to do be doing again. On a whole new level."

"Belle, we're in the woods. What are we doing in the freaking woods?"

She let loose a deep sigh. "We're chasing the leads, Kye. I'm getting the stories and interviews that I think will help me answer the questions I've been wrestling with—"

"Belle, we're in the woods. Answer that question: Why are we in the woods?"

"This is where the story is, where my subject for the interview wanted to meet. I don't like it either Kye, but we're not in the position to set the agendas or set up studios. This new work is all in the field and all anonymous for now."

"I didn't have much say in this, and you know I don't get stubborn about much, but I'm not sure I want to start a new life of going to sleep and waking up in the woods."

"Believe me, Kye, I never intended—" a branch snapped, and the sound of something large thrashed in the underbrush. She straightened up quickly from her crouch beside me, looking around frantically. I rolled up onto all fours and then scrambled to my feet.

"Did you remember to bring a flashlight?" I asked in a whisper.

"No flashlights allowed. Only one lantern. It's in your bag," she replied.

"One lantern? Who makes these rules?" I said.

The forest went silent after the sudden noise, making it all the more ominous. I rummaged in the bag for a moment; my hand clasped around the cold metal of the lantern and pulled it out.

"Hang it high on a tree," said Belle.

I turned on the lantern and looked for a proper branch to hang it on; I felt vulnerable with my hand in the air, chest exposed, eyes looking up rather than *watching around me for the source of the noise. The trees peered down like I was some bug they captured in a jar, spindly branches like arms waiting to reach in and grab me.*

The lantern gave us a small radius of clarity but really just accentuated what we could not see. I had broken out in a sweat all over despite the chilly night. The only sound was my strained breathing, coming out in small bursts of white steam. I hate the woods at night.

"Lantern hung. Now what?"

"Oh Kye, I don't know. I'm sorry. I'm just kind of following orders on this one." She put her arm around my waist, and I pulled her close, our heights always allowing her to rest her head right near my heart. We waited that way for three or four minutes, but it seemed like an hour—an hour in a horror movie with an expectant tension where you just know something is going to jump out and make you scream.

This time the noise was more subtle. Another snapping of a twig but smaller and much closer. Right behind us. "Get the camera out," said Belle.

"The lighting is going to be terrible," was all I could think to say.

(I was right—not only did the whole thing feel like a found-footage horror film, it looked like one too—grainy and unsteady. I was shaking worse than I realized.)

ANNABELLE FARROW (AF): Ok, we're here. I know you're there. Show yourself.

FEAR (FR): Why, my dear, I already have.

Only my love for Belle held me in place when that voice spoke. Afterwards, I could only describe it as a snake crossed with a cat, a snake coiled to strike and a cat in that low-to-the-ground predator stride it has when slinking toward cornered prey. It was a hissing whisper of a purr, and every hair on my body stood at attention.

I wasn't sure where the voice was coming from, so I just pointed the camera at the least sinister looking tree. I hate the woods.

FR: I'm already with you. See me in the silence; feel me on your necks. Watch me dance in each other's eyes. Hear me throb in each heartbeat and cling to every breath. You should not have come to this place, Annabelle Farrow. You may never leave.

AF: I have come to ask you questions, Fear, and you will answer them. I was promised you would answer them.

Belle's voice was not her usual confident tone, but I still sensed the steel beneath the quiver. I was shaking badly and praying Fear would not expect me to speak.

FR: You were promised I would answer? Of course you were. But did you know the cost?

AF: What cost?

FR: Every one question of yours that I answer, I get to ask you three questions in return.

AF: That hardly seems fair. What if I don't want to answer your questions?

FR: Oh, I don't want you to answer my questions. My power resides in the asking, not in the answering. I just want the questions to settle into your soul, burrowing deep into your mind, infecting every thought, paralyzing every action. And I do believe I just answered two of your questions. So here are my six then: Do you really know what you're doing? Who are you to interview me? Who are you to think you have anything worthy to say? What if no one ever sees these interviews? What if it's all in vain? What if Malachi leaves you because you've pushed him too far?

Silence, again. We just stood there, our breath coming out in little puffs under the lantern's light. Was she processing the questions? Gathering her resolve? Or planning to leave? Would I ever leave her?

FR: You see, dear, you're not ready for this. Lie down and go back to sleep, I promise to make the nightmares the kind that are easy to forget.

AF: I'm not leaving. What are *you* afraid of?

A laugh burst from me at the surprise of her question, foreign but comforting all the same. Ah, Belle, you don't like to be pushed around. What a great question. I even think I heard a hiss of frustration in response.

12

AF: Answer me.

FR: I'm afraid that Christians will grow up and learn what trust and hope and faith really mean. And my next three for you: Don't you worry about becoming like your uncle, paranoid and suicidal? It runs in the family, you know. What if that voice in your heart isn't the Holy Spirit? What if it's just your mind talking back to you?

AF: My turn. How do you control people?

FR: I find their insecurities, and I feed them. I feed them until they are so large all they can do is find some kind of security blanket to hold on to—a habit, an indulgence, perhaps a job or a child or a spouse, some thing or person they clutch on to with the white-knuckled grip of their souls. I love security blankets. I love nightlights. It lets me know I have still won. They pour their hope into those thin sheets of cotton, thinking they'll protect them somehow, scrambling to cover their feet so I won't get them; all the while they only feel safe when the blanket is just right and the halos of their nightlights reach far enough to illuminate the most fearsome of shadows.

But I've already won. Locked into a battle with me, no one can ever walk forward in peace and trust. Every decision becomes a selfish one of self-protection. Now, what if I snatch away *your* blanket, Annabelle? Even now you're reaching for those bible verses from your youth—don't you realize they are simply the crutches of the weak and naive? The night and the unknown still scare you, don't they?

AF: Why do people isolate themselves and hide their fears?

FR: That's easy. You've created a world where you're not allowed to have fears. The strong and successful are lifted up as icons—the doubting and the fearful are looked at as defective believers. Of course, I feed their insecurities with things like, "You're the only one who deals with this," and "What if they knew?" and "Your faith may not be real if you're struggling with this." They'll never share if their very salvation is at stake. I rummage in their past, finding secret moments they try to keep buried, the ones they can always see if they look, bringing them into their consciousness every time I smell weakness. Don't you remember your past, Annabelle, the things you've done? What does God think

13

about your secrets? What would Malachi think if he saw what you hide in your heart?

AF: How do you affect whole churches then?

FR: So many ways. Power plays and conflicts in churches are usually nursed fears manifesting in conversations.

But mostly, I make every member feel like they're the only ones not understanding the faith. I particularly run amok in small groups, flashing into everyone's minds pictures of the absolute horrors of vulnerability. And if someone does share from their heart, exposing their true selves just a bit, I pounce and make the group go silent or awkward or, even worse, I make everyone feel obligated to share things that don't relate at all or are full of clichés, and then I scream, "See! See! See what happens when you open up like that?" I watch them all freeze then, praying madly on the inside that some easy question will come up or some speeding up of time will take place.

Oh, I spend time with everyone each week. I take every mistake and magnify it in their minds. I fill their minds with assumptions and expectations—I manipulate every glance and every word to make the community of God's people isolated by the fear of what others are *surely* thinking. You'd be surprised how many church folk deal with some kind of anxiety attack before attending worship services. It's hard to worship the Lord when irrational thoughts are sitting on the throne.

I even make pastors feel desperate—fearful that their preaching is weak and diluted, that they need to add more passion, more conviction! Raise that voice! Look those people in the eye! Make them feel the weight of it all! Oh, why are you even preaching? You barely got through seminary, you don't remember any Greek! Who are *you*? And my words seep into sermons, bringing me into the seats and into the hearts of the listeners. Suddenly, the shepherds are berating their sheep out of insecurity and the need for some immediate affirmation that they deserve their role and their pay rather than speaking from a nurturing trusting heart developed in Christ.

I love people smiling and singing and saying how fine they are, all the while walking home again knowing they aren't really that special and believing they're obviously missing something. What a delightful question to answer! And for you, my dear, what right does a woman have to be so bold and up-front and ask such questions? Haven't you felt like you're always at the kiddie table when it comes to this whole Christianity thing? Don't you still feel childish asking questions like this?

AF: Very interesting. I've long maintained that having an intimate group of believers, sometimes no more than three or four, carrying each other's burdens, changes the range and understanding of what it means to know God. When we cherish each other's vulnerability and hold it as a sacred thing, and reciprocate in kind, we form bonds that make it hard for someone like you to take hold, Fear. Unfortunately, we don't create many conducive environments for developing those bonds. But perhaps that's for another day.

FR: That wasn't a question.

AF: It wasn't meant to be. I'm not interviewing you for your vanity or mine. I have a theory about where you get your start in churches, so here is another question for you, especially since you mentioned me being childish: How do you operate with the children in the church?

I heard what sounded like the warning hiss a cat makes when being approached by an unknown dog when Belle asked this question, as if Fear were angry, the only time I sensed any kind of emotion other than a smug and devious confidence.

FR: This interview is just about over, I believe.
I spend much of my time with your children and their teachers. Very good, Annabelle Farrow, I can see by your eyes where your theory lies. You see, if I can weave myself into the very fibers of what they call salvation, then it becomes all the easier later to create a culture of fearful worshippers, cowering under blankets they've been trained to hold their whole church lives.
It's really quite brilliant. *Which of you children want to go to heaven and be with Jesus on streets of gold? And which of you children want to burn in forever fire with the bad old devil? Oh, you all want to go to heaven? Well, let's pray this prayer and all be good—real good—or else you might end up in that bad place. Oh, you aren't sure if you're good enough or believe enough? Well, you better believe a little harder and do a little more or give a little more.* And after every sin, I bring up those Sunday School lessons, those VBS pleas for salvations, so many rooted in fears and terrors of the eternal!

And what happens to the folks who made decisions in fear? Well, they keep me at a distance, by being busy or singing louder than the whispers. As long as you don't sit in the dark, you'll never have to deal with your fears. Their morality becomes the very dreaded thing they swear it is not—a works-based structure to keep the hounds of hell at bay. And I don't need to tell you that many of your young become young adults who go away to colleges and universities and see the pacifiers and security blankets of their faith and discard them—not because their faith has grown; oh no, they do it thinking the blankets themselves are the faith. I have distorted it all! I twist the very essence of honoring God and holiness into a stunted thing of scaredy-cat behavior modification. And now, here are your final three questions: Don't you see how big this really is? Don't you realize all of your work is in vain, a throwing of a tiny pebble at a massive ship coming to dock? What do you hope to accomplish with your isolated and pathetic interviews?

AF: I *will* answer that question. I mean to shine a light in the darkness, the kind of light the darkness does not and cannot understand. I want to shout the truth that there is nothing to fear and blankets are only blankets, which are keeping them from experiencing the peace and trust they were made for. I want people to comprehend all the truths of the light—that perfect love casts out fear and God did not give us a spirit of fear, but of power, love, and self-discipline. I want them to know vulnerability is beautiful and relationship with God cannot be rooted in irrational fear. And if no one listens, I will live it out anyway!

I want them to know that no one has ever had all the answers! It is okay to wrestle and struggle and even doubt sometimes. Loving parents welcome the questions of the child who wrestles to make sense of the world, to find their place in it and to do right by their parents—even when the questions are asked sometimes with security blankets gripped in the dark. Human parents delight in those acts of trust, and that is what those questions are. *So then, how much more does our God love us?*

The last statement was yelled at Fear, and I don't think Belle meant for it to be a question. She got no answer regardless and no three questions hurled back at her. There was only the abrupt reply of branches snapping and the distinct sound of air being forcibly moved, like opening the sealed doors to a business in winter, when the whoosh lets you know the windy cold is behind and warmer moments lie ahead. It was like that sound, only grander—not the air of a foyer being moved, but the wind in the woods being forcibly drawn away.

I looked at my little bride then in that circle of poor light, hands clenched into sharp fists, feet planted in banks of leaves, her slender frame leaning forward as if keeping balance on a rocking ship. One strand of her deep brown hair had escaped its place and was slowly swinging forward with every breath of steam coming from her mouth. She took one last deep breath, reaching up with a hand to tuck the errant hair back with the rest. Her whole body relaxed then, and I had the distinct image of a gun being lowered and a finger coming off the trigger.

She swung her eyes on me and said, "I certainly hope you didn't film the whole thing like that."

I was standing there with the camera rolling, pointed down at an old mossy stump. I closed my mouth and turned off the camera. "No, no, I definitely got it. Whatever it was."

"It was the beginning, Malachi. The beginning."

Chapter 3:

King David Session #1

I woke up in a small hut in a remote part of the valley of Elah with the sun hitting my face through the open window. I knew from the smells in the air that we were not in our proverbial Kansas. On each of these incredible interviews, the sequence was always the same: the excited gleam in her eyes, me sleeping with my gear, waking up disoriented in an exotic locale with an even more exotic subject. "How?" is the question you're probably asking, and so I give you my honest answer: I don't know.

I don't know how, I don't when she worked it all out, and I don't know how things like language barriers worked—as with the Fear interview, there were mysteries she fiercely protected and kept even from me. I asked many questions, repeatedly, in the beginning. I can only say that she talked about these interviews like they were a calling, a mission she was sent on, and the rest of the details just worked out. She considered her silence on the particulars as "part of the deal."

These questions were soon driven from my own mind, however, because I was on site, immersed in conversation with fascinating subjects. You don't ask about the engineering and structural integrity of the roller coaster when you're in the front seat about to crest the hill.

This particular interview led me into the presence of the King of Israel, one of the most famous personalities of history. David was very handsome (as advertised) with curly locks of sandy hair and eyes like laughter and sunrises. He seemed completely at ease with Annabelle and she with him. He wore a robe and sandals that, to my untrained eye, could only be described as royal casual wear. We conducted the interview on stools on the front porch of the hut. And yes, there were sheep. Lots of sheep.

This has always been my favorite interview: I love Annabelle's questions and David's portrait of trust and faith in God. The length of this interview far exceeded all of our intentions, and I've broken it up in this book simply because I didn't want the length to detract from the richness. She originally planned to touch lightly on the Goliath story for fear of it seeming overdone or obvious, but she always knew how to follow the right trails . . .

Annabelle Farrow (AF): My guest today could go by many names and titles; his life has covered a very broad spectrum. He was once only known as a son of Jesse, a baby brother, the shepherd boy, but he soon became known as the Harp Player, Giant Killer, Mighty Warrior, King of Israel, and less popular, but no less true, Adulterer and Murderer. A man who has been talked about and studied endlessly through the thousands of years God's story has progressed among His people. Ladies and gentlemen, I introduce to you David, a Man After God's Own Heart.

King David (KD): *(smiles)* That's quite an introduction, and I appreciate your choice of that final title.

AF: I thought it was a bit better than "The Ruddy and the Handsome." *(laughs)*

KD: *(winces and then laughs)* True enough.

AF: Let's start with the most pressing question of all: Why the harp?

KD: *(big laugh)* Believe it or not, the harp was considered a very masculine instrument back then. We didn't have the abundance of choices that you have now. I'm sure I would have played a six-string guitar if it had been an option. And remember, our free time wasn't spent on any kind of electronic media, no

19

sound systems or iPods, so instruments and songs were a natural part of each home.

AF: Let's discuss that a little more. Your ascension to King of Israel did start with those humble beginnings as the baby brother shepherd; tell me more about that childhood.

KD: All of the family dynamics that your culture experiences in regards to siblings and rivalries were certainly present, but I think birth order was a more dominating influence in my time. I mean, the chances of the eighth son achieving anything of consequence, especially when having strong and confident older brothers, was not very high. My brothers were no different than other older brothers, though, kidding me and teasing me but protecting me when I needed it. They taught me the ways of being a man. But back to the harp for a moment: it was actually a hand-me-down harp from Shammah that I learned on. Part of the reason I became so good was because of my pride in wanting to excel in something that Shammah had failed in.

AF: Would you say there was any favoritism in your father Jesse similar to what we know of Jacob and his relationship with Joseph and even Benjamin?

KD: Up until I became involved with the army and the fight against the Philistines, I would say there was a sense of pride at the glory of my three older brothers serving as soldiers and perhaps a bit of neglect for those of us not on the front lines. He appreciated my work with the flocks and never treated me poorly, though I never received anything like a coat of many colors.

AF: Well, since you've already brought us there, to the armies of the Israelites, let's go ahead and talk about the Goliath incident.

KD: (*sighs*) Okay. What do you want to know?

AF: (*laughs*) Everything! But I want to ask you specifically about the record we have of *how* it happened that you were suddenly faced with him and the things you said up until the fight itself—

KD: —Excellent. I don't think I could handle another *"How big was he?"* question—

20

AF: ——Not my interest. At all.

I thought David was comfortable up until this point, but I was wrong. I realized he had assumed a public face role that was charming and disarming, but he didn't truly trust Annabelle until this moment. In the pause between her statement and her question, you could feel an electricity enter the air.

AF: I'm sensing from you perhaps a bit of jadedness about the story, maybe even a little irritation?

KD: I think that's accurate. I am tired of the glorifying of the underdog versus a giant story and the way it's used, and I'm irritated at the people of God's neglect of the other parts of the story.

AF: We'll address the neglected parts in a moment. I think it's going to be hard for people to grasp a burnt-out David on the underdog angle. Isn't that the angle presented by the author of first Samuel? There are a lot of measurements and statistics mentioned in the text.

KD: Fair enough. It is written in a way that plays up the size and prowess of Goliath, and it is an underdog story; I don't want to denigrate that at all. It has a sensational side to it.

AF: But you think it's over-emphasized?

KD: Yes. But let me clarify: I never went out looking for Goliath. I wasn't in the giant-slaying business. I spent many years of my life after that point on the run, living in caves, being pursued by a crazy king. My life was in constant jeopardy. I guess the way it's portrayed is what I'm tired of—yeah, God used me to slay a giant, but Goliath was an anomaly, an exception, and not the pattern of my life. And that one victory most certainly did not give me a perfect life or a free pass to live how I wanted.

AF: Do you think the way the story is taught or shared is unfairly encouraging people to run out and look for giants to kill?

KD: Well, yes.

AF: And that's not a healthy way to view your story?

KD: I'll start off with a thought, and then can we start at the beginning and address some of those neglected areas you mentioned?

AF: Sure. The floor is yours, King.

KD: Ok, as you can read in the Word, my brothers were all strong and handsome, kingly if you will. People like to quote, *"God looks at the inside, and man looks at the outside,"* but it's an inspirational phrase they mostly ignore in their daily lives. I was the runt. I was not the kingly one by appearance. Goliath was the champion, the one with all the stats and impressive measurements, the *successful* one. Your era, your people, love the idea of me as the underdog, but in reality they worship and emulate Goliath. Everything revolves around statistics and measurements. Preach on the underdog, yes, but then determine your vision and direction by Goliath measurements and values. Bigger spears! Larger shields! They want my older brothers to lead them, and that's who they follow; you don't see *runts* leading the way. I wish they would see this story as more about the *perspective* than an underdog *champion*. All right, that's all I'll say for now. Hit me with a neglected area question.

AF: I agree that it's not just the "little guy versus the big guy" story. I think one fundamental truth of your story is how God views what really matters and how we as humans easily miss viewing things the same way, which is what you're telling me. It's good to be affirmed straight from the shepherd's mouth. A neglected part about this stand-off of sworn enemies is how the Israelite army finds its unlikely hero, the shepherd boy, who had no place on the battlefield.

KD: Ah, yes, thanks for noticing. I'm not sure people remember that I wasn't already in the army as I mentioned earlier. My elderly father sent me to the battlefield to deliver bread to my brothers and a bunch of cheese to their commander. *(laughs)* Oh, the glory of bread and cheese!

AF: An ordinary job for an ordinary kid being obedient to his dad. You were being faithful to what you were supposed to do. Cheese and bread made David and Goliath happen. But the Scriptures seem to indicate you were a bit inquisitive once you arrived to the army.

KD: I was the classic little brother, always wanting to know what's going on. Nobody likes to be excluded. I wanted to fit in, to belong. So on my food delivery, I overheard some conversations, the buzz in the air, and noticed the fear and exasperation of the army. A few questions later, I'm face to face with the Philistine.

AF: Let's rewind a bit. The faithful little brother leaves the flocks and heads out with his cheese and bread, hears the buzz in the air, and asks around about it. Then you get rebuked harshly—

KD: —like we were still kids again back at the house. Yes, I got a bit sullen and whiny. But my questions stuck out and went through the gossip chain back to the King.

AF: Which is something I feel contemporary readers of the story neglect to see: Someone inquiring about a nine foot champion at a battlefield after that champion just called out your whole army *should not be* something exceptional that makes its way to the ears of the King. It stood out because this wasn't the first time Goliath had done this.

KD: *Thank* you. The armies had been camped out facing each other for forty days; sound familiar? Goliath stood before our people every morning *and* every night shouting his usual defiance as the Word says. Eighty times he demanded a worthy opponent.

AF: And every time the army of God responded in fear and silence.

KD: Fear for sure. But not silence.

AF: What do you mean?

KD: The armies faced each other every morning and evening arrayed in battle formation. And each time, they shouted the war cry at each other.

AF: That's right! If I remember correctly, the Israelites were dressed in full armor and weapons, too.

KD: God's army, sworn to fight for His Name and Glory, wearing their official battle gear and shouting the battle cry of Yahweh, looking every bit the part, but when one enemy stood there, they quailed in fear. All gear, no guts.

AF: I think some folks might miss your subtle point there.

KD: You can look the part of Christian, but there comes a time when obedience has to happen in the real world, not when you're all together making noise together for God's name. There has to be a moment when you personally step out into the *real*. Obedience doesn't count in your head, and you can't be obedient in the future someday or imagine yourself being this super saint full of radical faith. There is only the present context in which you find yourself with the present decision before you: Trust God or melt in with the crowd who talks about trusting God.

AF: And you're not talking about stepping out to kill Goliath or some other kind of giant.

KD: I'm talking about holiness, trust, and obedience in general. It doesn't happen in a vacuum or in your imagination; it needs to happen when you're all alone and no one's watching.

AF: And you're not talking about the dreaded *salvation by works*?

KD: No. What a crazy, irrational fear your people have of that concept. I'm talking about trusting by obeying in relationship.

AF: We'll come back to that. Let's go again to the story. Explain why the armies didn't just fight it out. Why the dramatic stand-off?

KD: It's important to understand the representative champion idea we held to at the time. If your champion defeated the enemy's champion, it was a sign of which god was stronger and was present there on the battlefield. It wasn't as if we would surrender if our champion lost, it meant our God was not as strong, which led to a collective loss of willpower and bravery, which would lead to a rout.

AF: Which, I'm guessing, is why you were sort of irritated at the lack of action on the part of your comrades. You knew that Yahweh was greater than any other god. Your questions sprung from that faith.

KD: Sure. But I need to be gracious to my people for a moment; they weren't prepared for someone like Goliath. To say he was intimidating really is an understatement. The Israelites had no one of equal stature to face him and had never *seen* someone of equal stature to him. King Saul was probably closest in size.

AF: So, we have an enemy that God's people are too terrified to face contrasted to this unimpressive young shepherd boy, the author playing up the respective dimensions of you two.

KD: Yes. I have no doubt the writer wanted to communicate the power of God even in the midst of impossible odds; it's a theme throughout the Word. But we can tend to worship the event rather than the God who made the event possible. And instead of seeking a relationship with God, we seek instead the sensational and spectacular. Why pray for a bunch of dry stuff like daily trust and obedience when you can pray instead for some serious giant-slaying in your life?

To be continued. . .

Chapter 4:

Mortimer Keys

Belle and I spent our ninth anniversary at a bed and breakfast on the coast of Maine. We enjoyed almost a whole week eating fresh seafood, window-shopping in old downtowns, and breathing harbor smells into our weary bodies. Annabelle always wore a costume in places she might be recognized, a standard combo of auburn wig, black sunglasses, and scarf. I would call her by her middle name, Grace. It made excursions like this one even more fun, sneaking around incognito.

Of course, a whole week without chasing a lead was too much to ask, but surprisingly we ended up with just one. We finished a meal of newly caught crabs and were topping it off with some independently brewed coffee, watching the sun slowly hide itself when she broke the news.

"I have a chance to interview someone very powerful," she said.

I paused, drinking in the pale blue dress and the pearls around her neck.

"I understand," I said.

"You always do."

"Ha, I am pretty awesome. Do I know this very powerful person?"

"No . . . he's from the future."

"It's not the weirdest thing I've heard you say." She laughed my favorite laugh, the one where her head tilted back to the side, a breathy release of childhood joy whose tone I swear the right musician could make into a song. It is the sound I miss more than anything in this world.

"Let's go back to the room, husband. I want to go over my notes and still have time to go to bed the same time you do."

I motioned for the waiter to bring the check.

When I awoke the next morning, I was in an immense glass cathedral, straight out of a sci-fi movie, a futuristic version of an ancient European castle. Metal danced with glass at impossible angles in a complicated mimicry of stained-glass, reflecting colors in faint, luminous beams. The height and width of the place was staggering; cathedral might not be the best word. Coliseum, perhaps? Stadium?

There were rows and rows of ascending seats, as far as I could see. The chairs looked comfortable, but glowed with newness, as if freshly arrived from the best chair factory in the universe. Despite the size and architectural wonder, I had a pervading sense of peace. Once again, my vocabulary fails me, but I felt that if the room was filled to its vast edges with thousands of people right then, the sense of peace would still be there.

Can peace be unnerving? It was for me in that moment. My thoughts were broken by the two seemingly inconsequential figures at the center of the room.

"Kye, over here. Glad you're awake," said Annabelle. Her voice carried pitch perfect to me with minimal effort.

I shuffled over to her, the back of my head resting on my shoulders, gawking upward as I realized I stood in the center of a masterpiece.

"Malachi, this is Mortimer Keys, and this is his church building."

"Hello, Pastor Keys, Malachi Evans. Camera guy and husband to Annabelle. This place is amazing."

"Why, thank you. We're quite proud of it, to be honest," he answered.

I noticed his eyes first, large like his church building, glinting and brown, an invitation to contentment and security. Hands clasped in front of him, he made little movement but leaned into the conversation, head tilted slightly. If I wasn't in shock and awe at his place of worship, I might have feared his gaze and the way he stood there, like a mother bird deciding whether the insect was worth bringing back to the nest.

"Kye?" Annabelle said.

Their attention was on me, Mortimer with his alien, brown-eyed bird gaze, Belle with a layered look I interpreted three ways: I see it too, I can't believe you're staring like that, and are you okay? She was a complex woman.

"Annabelle said we'd be stepping into the future on this one?" I asked.

"Very true, my friend," he replied.

The answer was clipped, communicating that each piece of information we wanted would have to be earned. He unclasped his hands briefly, making a quick gesture to begin walking, and I followed, not knowing where we were going or even **when** *we were at the moment. I broke our usual professional wall and held Belle's hand.*

We walked down a hallway shaped like a tunnel, an arch over our heads, light streaming from an open door at the end, guiding us with a magnetic pull and promising a warm embrace when we arrived. The peace of the sanctuary stayed with us as we walked, a sense of water flowing toward a great waterfall heightened with each step, and I was holding my breath when we approached the golden doorway at the end of the tunnel.

It was the entrance to Mortimer's office. When we entered, he gestured toward the two opulent high-backed chairs facing the wooden fortress I assumed was his desk. The chair held me firmly but comfortably, and I began to think of it as a throne from which I could rule. The feeling was prompted not only by the chair but also by the walls of his office, painted as an intricate and accurate mural of the New Jerusalem from Revelation. There were majestic clouds and serenading angels, golden gates and shiny pearls the size of houses, and the open arms of Jesus welcoming you to your rest. And yet, there was something disconcerting about His eyes—

"Kye, can you go ahead and get the camera ready?"

I mumbled and extricated myself clumsily from my throne and set up the gear. Mortimer watched everything like a kindly grandfather waiting for his grandson to request help with tying his shoes. Belle checked her notes one more time, did her signature pre-interview throat clearing, and locked eyes with the mysterious man from the future known as Mortimer Keys.

Annabelle Farrow (AF): Hello everyone. Today I'm seated across from the man who has risen to the top of American religious life in just a few years. After two years of existence, his denomination passed the Catholics in total membership, and right now is bigger than the Baptists, Lutherans, Methodists and Presbyterians—combined. I present to you Dr. Mortimer Keys.

Mortimer Keys (MK): Greetings to you, Annabelle. I'm honored to meet you and be granted an interview. A warm welcome and embrace to all my fellow Destinarians out there.

AF: That's a great place to start. Tell us about the Destinarian Denomination; it has seemingly materialized out of nowhere. I'd like to hear about its beginnings and your distinctives—there's been a bit of mystery surrounding your popularity for folks not associated with it.

MK: (*demure chuckle*) Well, Ms. Farrow, I will start by correcting one of the main myths about us that we *seemingly materialized out of nowhere.* Does the gold not exist until is discovered in a mine? No, it has always been there; it only requires the right knowledge and equipment to extract it. Then it requires the right science and machines to purify it and make it into something beautiful and useful. What I, what *we,* have done in our movement that others have labeled a denomination, is find this gold, if you will, these truths that have existed in various forms of refinement, lying latent in the other denominations, and we have just brought them to the light, out of the obscurity of dark, traditional mines.

We are a distillery, a refinery, a purification system for the theology of the masses. Destinarians have stripped away the false mummery of faith, taken a spiritual scalpel to the dying body of American Christianity and removed the tumors, ruptured appendices, and rampant cancers and left a cleansed and whole body. A body able to focus on that which Jesus came to win for us, what Paul pressed on towards, and what John the Revelator described in fantastical detail.

AF: Heaven?

MK: Simply put, yes, heaven. But what stands in the way of heaven? Our mortality. What did Jesus win for us? Immortality. Eternal life. Destinarians keep the objective of our faith front and center; we allow nothing to deter us, not theological quibbling, not building funds and deacons meetings, not power struggles over worship preferences. We worship as we will one day worship; we live as we will one day live—free of death!

As I mentioned earlier, what we have accomplished is nothing new. Our focus is not novel. All societies from the Egyptians to the Native Americans to the Medieval Europeans to the bush tribes of Australia have grappled with their mortality and sought to grab life after death in a permanent, knowable grip. Our founding verses, as you may know, are from Hebrews chapter 2: *(his voice took on a richer tone and picked up in volume)* "By His death He might destroy him who holds the power of death—that is, the devil—and free those who all their lives were held in slavery by their fear of death!" We are no longer slaves to death! We no longer live in fear of his dark stare or cold fingers on our shoulders!

AF: Are you trying to convert me today, Dr. Keys?

MK: Convert? We don't do conversions. We simply bring to light the essence of Christianity. We are not proselytizers; we are magnifiers! We illuminate what is already there! Understanding is not conversion. Understanding is always being a bird in the nest, stumbling around the twigs on your functional but clumsy feet and one day looking to your right and left, finding these strange appendages known as wings, stretching them out, launching yourself from the safe confines of home, and taking flight for the first time. Ah, yes! You soar on the winds of understanding! Death is but a memory, crucified in the past, a thing of smothering for those who still walk on two legs.

AF: Back to the fast rise of the Destinarians then. You believe the growth is attributed to the attraction of your central message that heaven is our prize and death is no longer an enemy?

MK: It's more than an attractive message, Ms. Farrow; it's truth and certainty. What else did the writer of Hebrews say? "Faith is being sure of what we hope for, and certain of what we do not see." We strip away all that obscures the certainty of eternity. No more doubts, no more discussions about dry theologies, and no more debate about once saved, always saved.

AF: Tell me about being saved according to your theology.

MK: Again, you say *your theology* as if it is mine. Is the ocean mine? It is not. Would not a group of weary travelers from the desert, having never seen the ocean, rejoice with their guide who brought them to such a wonder, yet never once think he was the owner of the seas?

Nonetheless, you ask me about being saved. We have, as you already know, quite a process and quite a show for those who repent of their sins and the ways of death. Of course, we have the usual baptism afterwards—

AF: Dr. Keys, I would hardly call your baptisms usual.

MK: I refer only to the time-honored tradition of baptism. Yet our baptisms uniquely capture the essence of how baptism is communicated in the Scriptures. Didn't Jesus say He had a baptism to undergo *after* His water baptism with John? A baptism of death and resurrection! Paul talks about it in Colossians, but also in Romans 6 where he says, "We were therefore buried with him through baptism into death in order that, just as Christ was raised from the dead through the glory of the Father, we too may live a new life!"

Each of our new believers has a symbolic baptism of death, which we believe is in line with the life of Christ and the teachings of Paul. Gone are the controversies over water baptism. We place each person who believes and understands in a coffin, have a funeral service for the departing old life, and then raise them back to life again—to the applause of millions! New life has come through the work of Jesus once again!

AF: And you make the children do this as well?

MK: Of course! They love it! It communicates so much more to them than a little bracelet with colored beads or paper cut-outs of biblical characters.

AF: Tell me about what believers receive as they exit their coffins.

MK: Salvation of course. (*smirks knowingly*)

AF: Dr. Keys, you know what I'm asking. Your take on salvation is considered more non-traditional than your funeral baptisms. Can you describe for me the more concrete aspects of *receiving salvation* amongst Destinarians?

MK: I've already communicated to you the powerful message of life after death we now have in Christ, called into what the Scriptures call eternal life. We simply brought our liturgy and our sacraments in line with the core of what our faith is all about. People have grown weary of esoteric teachings, of mysteries with no handles, as I like to say. Sure, Christ in us is a mystery, but we know the end of the mysterious story. We know what our payoff is, even now! Eternal life!

So, after exiting their coffins as the new people they are, we give them the gift of salvation.

AF: Which is a literal box wrapped in paper and tied with a bow, correct?

MK: I would say *beautifully* wrapped, like a wedding gift wrapped by Macy's if they had angels working for them (*laughs*). The gift is both literal and mysterious, a tangible expression of their faith, an item they can hold, which gives them assurance of the everlasting life they have been granted. And of course, you've heard of the personalized gift tag on each box of salvation, addressed personally to each recipient, signed by God, with a message saying, "Open in Eternity" in gold ink.

At this point, an interesting thing happened. A flower sitting in a large bouquet by the wall dropped a petal as it wilted. The motion drew Mortimer's eyes, and we followed his gaze as another petal fell. He scowled briefly, motioning toward the vase as he made eye contact with someone at the door-- someone I did not know had been there. In under a minute, two flawless and beautiful servants, one male, one female, replaced the flowers with a new bouquet, one obviously more freshly cut.

AF: What else do your believers receive?

MK: At the risk of offending you or belaboring my point, I prefer not to use a possessive pronoun like *your* when describing the Christians who have gathered with us. Ephesians two says one Lord, one faith, one baptism, one body. We are merely reminding us all of that, focusing on the heart of and goal of our faith in such a way that old differences and hang-ups melt away, leaving us a unified heart for heavenly things.

You asked about what believers receive in addition to the Gift of Salvation. We also give them a personalized copy of the manual for Christian living we call the Moral Codex.

AF: If I could stop you briefly right there, tell me about what you mean by personalized, and isn't the Bible what we Christians would consider the manual for Christian living?

MK: Personalized as in their name embossed in gold letters on the cover of the Moral Codex and signed by me with an encouraging word addressed to them. And certainly the Bible is our manual for Christian living! Do not think the Moral Codex is separate from the Living Word! It *is* the Word! All we've done is wade into the thickness of the Scriptures, the deep waters and obscure passages and bring out the treasures of holy living. We have a new life! The old is gone! We must live according to the new, but sometimes the instructions about our behavior in the new life are hard to find. We've removed the fog for a better view of the mountains.

There are copious writings in the Scriptures that just aren't relevant to the new covenant that has been made with God's people. So much of it is pre-Christ; so much of it is about things like ceremonial laws for a nomadic people living thousands of years ago or debates about circumcision, which Paul clearly says has no value, or talking about eating meat with blood in it offered to idols. These stories are interesting and the history is obviously needed, but what we've found people really need is concise, crystal-clear instructions on the new life we have after death.

AF: You don't feel at all nervous that you're carving up the story of the Scriptures and turning it into a detached set of rules and regulations?

MK: I am *more* nervous about continuing to let people get the massive volume of Holy Scriptures and try to figure out themselves the instructions for living. How many atrocities have been committed by people mistakenly interpreting things for themselves? The Scriptures pointed to Christ and Christ points to eternal life! Whatever obscures eternal life must be trimmed away in order to get to the meat, like fat on a perfect steak; you needed it for a while to get the best flavor, but why chew it with the meat itself? It has served its purpose; now let's get down to the filet mignon business of experiencing what we've been given!

AF: Can anyone have their beautiful box taken away?

MK: It is possible. But we rarely need to resort to such measures—usually we find ways to let them know they've been neglecting the instructions in the Moral Codex, returning to the ways of death and away from eternal life.

AF: So you don't think people live in fear of losing the gift as they try to maintain the instructions in the Moral Codex?

MK: Fear has to do with death.

AF: And death has no place here with the Destinarians?

MK: No! Of course not! My dear woman, John, the disciple Jesus loved, the one who gives us our inspirational visions of heaven, wrote in his first epistle: Perfect love casts out fear! We organize all our programming around that truth. We broadcast 24/7 for 99% of the year with our services—services celebrating the eternal, holding at bay the thoughts of death, the weapon of our enemy!

AF: I'm surprised we got an interview then.

MK: You are very lucky. You happened to ask during the annual renewing of the sanctuary where we replace every seat and fixture and refresh the heavenly aroma.

AF: Heavenly aroma?

MK: It's a patented fragrance we created called *Glorious*. It smells of gold and light and perfection. Destinarian worshippers receive all the free spray cans and car fresheners they desire to keep the right aroma around them, keeping their minds focused on heaven.

We deliver our music and our teachings wirelessly to every device and technology available; Destinarians live in a state of heavenly bliss at work, at home, at play. They find if they stop focusing on heaven, old habits and thoughts begin to creep in. We must capture every thought and make it obedient to Christ!

AF: Wow, free fragrances for all, constant music and programming, coffins and salvation boxes, and a new multi-million dollar sanctuary every year—giving must be really up for you, Mortimer. How often do you preach on tithing?

MK: Not often to be honest. When heaven becomes your priority, the things of Caesar can be held lightly. People give freely because they know their wealth is not of this world.

AF: I wanted to talk to you about your financial practices, so I am glad you mentioned peoples' giving habits. I did not mention your biggest expense as a denomination, which comes from the line item on the budget you would call Sanctification. Isn't that correct?

MK: Yes.

AF: Sanctification with Destinarians is a bit more extreme than other church traditions, right, Dr. Keys?

MK: Extreme is a poor word choice. Sanctification, for us, is more in line with the Scriptures as to our new lives. We have shed the poor dichotomies of false traditions. A believer is not a disembodied soul or spirit by itself—a believer is a whole being, soul *and* body. The Moral Codex keeps the soul in check with the eternal life we have been given, but our bodies still need sanctifying.

AF: Go on.

MK: Paul in 1 Corinthians 15 speaks of our bodies as perishable and weak, *walking about in dishonor.* Yet, he asks Death, where is your victory? Where is your sting? We are removing death's sting from the body. Our sanctification process helps the soul *and* the body be made pure, shaping it to be in line with the eternal life we've been given.

AF: And you do this how, Dr. Keys?

MK: You know how. Through the best plastic surgery available. Through the best gyms and fitness equipment available. Through a perfectly regimented diet put together by the most advanced dieticians who have ever lived. We consider our holiest saints our surgeons and our fitness trainers, our chefs and our cafeteria workers, who transform these lowly bodies into heavenly vessels prepared for eternal life! Oh, for Paul to see this day! As the gifts from God of knowledge and science remove our physical imperfections, as the Moral Codex purifies our inner person, we achieve greater and greater closeness to the heavenly state! Sanctification! The process of being set apart and holy! Faultlessly recreated for heaven! We've always sought the fountain of youth. What is that yearning but an expression of eternity set in our hearts? No more death or dying! No more curse! No more obesity! No more wrinkles and warts! No more daily reminders in the mirror of the death that has been defeated!

AF: A very expensive process to be sure. And people are just letting go of their money to make this happen?

MK: Money's value is diminished because of its temporal nature. But also, the better personal trainers, surgeons, and chefs are more readily available for the bigger givers. The less money you hold onto, the more you communicate you are letting the things of this world go, and the more you do that, the more you show you are ready for higher levels of physical perfection. Don't think of it as a rewards system as much as it is a direct relationship between true knowledge and transformation.

AF: What do you Destinarians believe is physical perfection then?

MK: Our best guesses at this point are 2003 Brad Pitt and Angelina Jolie or Ten Commandments Charlton Heston and Elizabeth Taylor, Cleopatra edition, depending on your age and preferences or body-type.

AF: Perfect people headed towards their perfect destination. Fascinating.

MK: It is. Now, if you'll excuse me, our time is up. I need to get a quick follicure before our Better is One Day in Your Courts renewal week starts.

AF: A follicure?

MK: Oh, my sweet Annabelle, you must join us for the follicures alone! Every hair on your body is polished and shined, revitalized with lasers and creams the rest of the public has no idea exists. You feel fabulous and look even better! Every hair on your head is counted *and* perfected!

In the excitement about his follicure, Mortimer left us quickly. We looked at each other briefly, and rose to leave. I looked again at the mural on the wall of Jesus welcoming folks to heaven, the one that disconcerted me when I entered. I froze in shock, realizing the face of Jesus was ruggedly handsome, like the perfect combination of Charlton Heston and Brad Pitt, but His eyes were clearly the mesmerizing brown eyes of Mortimer Keys. I shuddered, placing my camera over my shoulder as a delicious smell wafted into the room and harp music began to play around us. Annabelle began to run, bursting out of the office and down the hallway, me in her wake, exquisite men and women filing into the building, rapturous looks in their eyes. The last thing I heard as we exited the building was a choir in symphonic harmony singing, "Heaven came down and glory filled my soul."

Chapter 5:

Pastor Chuck

On a Black Friday morning four years ago, Annabelle and I cuddled beneath our electric blanket after a Thanksgiving spent serving anonymously in Arizona. The morning was young, and she turned to me with her trademark smirk as she began to pull down my covers. "What?" I croaked.

"Oh, nothing. Just wondering if you wanted to hop up and go clothes shopping with me?"

"I'd rather coat myself with sugar and roll around in African fire ants."

"So, no shopping? Doesn't it bother you how commercialized this holiday has become? You usually rant and rave about stuff like this."

"I know," I said. "First of all, it's early, and second, I'm trying to be better about my attitude. But now that you've pushed the button: Just because you saved 40% on something you weren't planning on getting doesn't mean you saved 40%. It means you wasted 60%."

"There's the Kye I love," she said.

"Why are you provoking me? Can't a guy just have a quiet morning with his wife in the warmth? You're smiling again. Why are you smiling?"

"Fall back asleep, my sweet Grumpy. I lined up a Black Friday interview for us."

"If I wake up in a mall, I'm going back to sleep, and when I wake up, I'm starting a blog, and I'm going to reveal what you've been doing. And if you ever call me 'my sweet Grumpy' again, I'm coming home one day with at least three kittens—"

I calmed myself and shut my eyes, her laughter still ringing in my ears.

She wasn't laughing when I saw her next. I found my gear on the bench where I awoke. The picnic table sat in a vast, well-manicured lawn, the kind of backyard meant for garden parties and pictures in magazines.

*I turned to see Annabelle arguing with a rotund man in a suit, asking him to stop grilling and join her in a chair beneath the sprawling oak tree. He stood just under six feet with a very large gut and crinkled eyes, deep-set and hidden. His suit jacket was wet from perspiration and barely covered by a spotted apron reading "**My Favorite Food is Seconds.**"*

He laughed as he fiddled with the knobs on a huge black smoker grill, the smells pouring out of it. My mouth watered in the hopes I might get some good old fashioned BBQ from this surprise interview on a lazy day off.

"Hey sleepyhead, food'll be ready in thirty minutes. I'm Pastor Chuck. Chuck Wagon."

"And I'm Kye, the camera guy. Where are we?"

"Heh, poet and didn't know it. Bay St. Louis, Mississippi. Can you film me while I finish this? Your little lady thinks I should sit down." His accent was charming and welcoming with an undercurrent of authority.

"It's more of a respect and attention thing, Pastor, and I would prefer it if you called me Annabelle, or Ms. Farrow," she said.

"Well, I ain't ruining these by drying them out just cause you think I can't talk about food or whatever standing up. I could talk about food upside down in a cage full of monkeys. And I'm just kidding around calling ya little lady. No need to get offended."

Belle visibly straightened, inhaling through her nostrils in exasperation. I began to film, wondering if I might be playing referee as well today.

"Let's go then, big fella, and just answer as honestly as possible," she said.

Annabelle Farrow (AF): OK, Pastor, what do you have in the smoker there?

Pastor Chuck Wagon (PCW): A couple of Boston Butts I been smoking since this morning. Glory, they gonna be good. Smoking's an art form. Don't let anyone tell you any different. And like all good chefs, it's the love *(rubbing his belly with both hands)* that makes the difference. Imma finish them off by basting them with my secret sauce.

AF: Excellent. Can't wait to try some butt. Tell me about your congregation here, Pastor.

PCW: Been at First Holiness for about 15 years now. We have a party celebrating every five years in the Family Life Center. Best spread of Christian food this side of the Mississippi. They're good folks. Faithful and growing. Might have to add on again next year.

AF: Well, your growth is why we're here, Pastor. Give me a little more of the history of First Holiness if you could.

PCW: The missus and I came from Texas—Dallas, not San Antone, mind you—and we'd been doing outreach ministry at the local buffet restaurant. They sent a Pastor Search Committee to find me one Sunday afternoon when I was still eating and witnessing at 4 pm. I was a Spirit-blessed machine of Glory and Gravy. Needless to say, they'd found their man. When I first came into town and saw her, the church that is, that steeple and that church kitchen, it was love at first sight, a match made in heaven—except for the pulpit. Ya see, I was having trouble seeing my notes well when I preached. So at first I made the font bigger, but that wasn't the issue. So, I had one of our carpenters cut me out an arc of wood on the front end of the thing so I could stand closer; he did measurements and all. My belly just slid right in, perfect. I haven't misread a humorous anecdote since. *(Chuckles)* I mean we want growth everywhere else, right? Bigger *is* better. Well hot potatoes, I'm changing pant sizes every two months, and my preaching's never been better. I'm getting bigger as we do!

AF: You can't argue with the statistics at First Holiness, Pastor. I've checked, and your numbers keep increasing, but one wonders how that growth is happening. Do you think it may have anything to do with having a chef on staff as Associate Pastor of Fellowship?

PCW: Who? Pastor John? Well, of course it does! John "Big Stuph" Barnes was the key.

AF: I thought so.

PCW: It was him who had the revelation at the Sunday School picnic, right by the dessert table, and I believe during a third helping of Miss Evelyn's nanner pudding.

AF: And what was that epiphany, Chuck?

PCW: Well, he'd been doing some charts and graphs and such and found out a startling discovery about our Sunday School attendance patterns. All of our classes on the second floor of the Education Building were dropping dramatically in attendance, while conversely, the classes with the free donuts on the first floor were exponentially growing!

AF: I see.

PCW: Woo-hoo. That was when ole Big Stuph and Chuck Wagon got together, and we had us an executive meeting of the heavenly sort, which led to a congregational meeting of the ground-breaking and belt-busting variety. We voted to take gluttony off the traditional list of deadly sins.

AF: You did what?!

PCW: Oh, man. What a meeting! We usually talked about boring stuff like who's a deacon or missions. We did something major at that meeting. We decided it was high time we get with the times.

AF: So, you have no concern whatsoever about the possible fall-out from changing something so entrenched in church history and practice? Not to mention explicitly stated in the Scriptures?

PCW: Entrenched? No one cared about it; no one talked about it. Churches will cheer this move. It's what they've always wanted and practiced anyways. When King Solomon wrote about the seven supposedly deadly sins, he didn't have all-you-can eat yeast rolls and potato salad. He had manna and goat jerky. Real easy to call gluttony a sin back then.

AF: Don't you think statistics about people over-eating and obesity and general laziness should have led to some conviction rather than a fudging of what really constitutes gluttony?

PCW: Oh, Moses, no. How could it be a sin if this ole body is gonna burn up anyway one day? You ever see fat burn? We're actually helping light up the apocalypse!

AF: Isn't this a bit contradictory to many Christians' thinking on the physical body, especially with the traditional use of the "body as a temple" concept as an argument against smoking?

PCW: Now you sound like ole Jack Spratt. He was the only one that kept the vote from being unanimous. He was belly-aching about never being asked to pray for the offering for the church cause some of the deacons had seen him out back smoking a quick one during the fellowship time. He said it wasn't fair not asking him but asking a fellow to pray every week who ate a plate of bacon before church and washed it down with a cheese danish. When we escorted him out, he was yelling something about, "At least I can see my shoes when I pray!"

AF: Sounds like maybe Jack had some insight?

PCW: You hate fat people too?

AF: Whoa. There's no hate here, Pastor. It's not people's size that concerns me; it's their mentality.

PCW: Mentality? C'mon, sister, the early church was devoted to eating, and so are we. See Acts chapter 2. Just because our bread tastes good and theirs was unleavened—Greek for cardboard—doesn't make any difference.

AF: Devoted and obsessed are two different things.

PCW: Read James again. Honey, God is the giver of *all* good gifts. Eatin' to the glory ah God!

AF: The problem isn't the good gifts or the good giver, Pastor Chuck. The problem is self-control.

PCW: I got plenty of self-control. My fork always hits my mouth!

He guffawed and lifted the lid to the smoker. The cloud of smells was intoxicating. He basted the pork with a tender affection, using what I presume was his special sauce.

AF: But I think we as Christians should be promoting self-discipline and care rather than flaunting an unhealthy flippancy regarding our appetites.

PCW: I bet you go through all that recycling hassle too, don't you?

AF: Hassle? Don't you guys teach stewardship or something like it at all?

PCW: Look, stewardship is about money and maintenance of the church. Quit worrying so much about the earth—the Bible says we're gonna get a new one anyways. You got to look at what Jesus really says, too.

AF: And what's that?

PCW: His burden is light! If something gets complicated or more importantly, inconvenient, like sorting trash into bins and what-not, well, that must not be part of His plan! And His yoke is easy, too. *Over* easy!! (*the biggest laugh of the day*)

AF: You confirm what I've sadly come to believe. Too many good folk live like inconvenience is the greatest evil of our day, and their sense of justice is only awakened when they have a personal brush with it. What do you think?

PCW: Speaking of brush, this sauce is perfectly caked on. If you got your evangelical panties in a wad over our potluck suppers, wait til you hear what we're doing at our next meeting. We're gonna replace gluttony's spot on the list with homahsexuality. I may run for President. This meat's ready, are you ready to chow down?

AF: I've lost my appetite, Pastor. I'll leave you to your feeding.

Pastor Chuck tossed the pork butts into a large wooden trough next to the grill. He reached over and rang a dinner bell vigorously. Voluminous church folk began arriving from all directions, dropping to their hands and knees, eating using only their faces, small children fighting for the scraps of meat which fell to the ground.

Chapter 6:

Biology Class

"Get up, Kye, you're going to be late for class!" Belle was shaking me as an alarm clock beeped annoyingly.

"Wha-wha-what?" I replied.

"The bell's going to ring in like five minutes. Put this on, and follow me," she said, handing me a white lab coat.

I sat up in the bed and looked at her outfit, which consisted of the same white coat and a pair of massive safety goggles. "Those are too big for your head," I said.

"I know," she smiled, "they're yours. I guess we know who has the bigger head now."

The cot where I lay stuck out like an island in an educational ocean, vast maps on the walls, a dry-erase board covered with dates and names, and desks imperfectly placed in rows. The classroom flooded me with uncomfortable memories of stumbling oral presentations, late slips, and unremitted crushes.

Rather than leaving the room for the hallway, Belle slipped through a door at the back of the room gesturing urgently for me to get up, tossing my goggles back to me. I put on the white coat and goggles, following groggily through the door.

It was a small storeroom full of science equipment, mostly microscopes, glass beakers and flasks, and it emptied into another classroom on the other side.

The next room was a science lab full of twenty or so black high-top tables fitted with small sinks and knobs for using gas in experiments. I remembered those tables clearly from my unsteady journey through high school science. Each table had two students facing the front of the room like soldiers at attention-- soldiers who knew a particularly intimidating general was on his way. Belle and I took the last two stations in the back corner of the room.

The quiet reminded me of a hospital waiting room and the air smelled like dust, metal, and chemicals. A bell rang, a blend of buzzing and sustained tone.

The quiet got quieter.

The door at the back of the room where Belle and I had entered closed suddenly, but no one turned around. A gravelly, spit-filled voice broke into the silence like a predatory growl.

"Mis-ter Evans, glad you could join us. The poster in the middle of the wall to your right, is that a butterfly or a moth?"

How does it know my name? I thought. I'm not a student, I don't need to answer that—but it's a 50/50 question, and I think it's a butterfly, but it's probably a trick question, so I guess I'll go with . . .

"Mo—"

"BUTTERFLYYYY!" said the voice.

The growl began to move, its feet pounding into the beige tiles with resounding slaps. I turned my head to see who or what was among us.

It was a she, a six-foot woman in her late fifties with a build like a grizzly bear and a wild tangled helmet of grey hair on top. Her hands were massive and gnarled, colored a blotchy pink and white, and her feet splayed her toes over the edges of her sandals like talons. Glasses like magnifying lenses framed the charcoal eyes of a hawk perched on a roadside power cable—an apt analogy as the class stood like paralyzed field mice hesitant to even blink.

My wrong answer now seemed even more wrong as I watched this linebacker grandma walk to the front of the classroom. Belle risked leaning over and whispered to me, "Her name is Ms. Termin. Always look her in the eyes if you don't want to answer questions—"

"Ms. Farrow, do you have something you'd like to share with the class?"

"No, ma'am. Not yet anyway."

"Today class, as you know, is dissection day. Bring your table's pan and come to the front of the room and fetch your little buddy for the day. Make sure

46

you put on your gloves, wear your goggles, and please use the tongs," said Ms. Termin.

The class filed out into the center aisle, nervous hands holding metal pans meant for an embalmed animal corpse. Belle nodded at me to get our specimen, knowing I was terrified by Ms. Termin and disgusted by the thought of cutting up an animal. I saw her hiding a smile as I took my place in line.

I got to the bucket up front and peered in. It was full of pasty green frogs swirling nose up in a soup of chemicals, tiny legs stiff in an act of pseudo-leaping, eyes bulging and seared white. I used the lab tongs to grab the first frog that wasn't staring at me accusingly. I turned to leave with my offering when an iron grip grabbed my arm.

Ms. Termin leaned in to talk to me, her tiny lips and tea-stained teeth curved back in an unnatural smile. "Mr. Evans," she hissed, "Ms. Farrow said she'd have something to share with the class, and I don't like the way she's been smirking at you up here. Please inform her she'll be my helper today."

Her clench released my arm and I shot back up the aisle balancing my unfortunate amphibian. I relayed the news to Annabelle that she would be assisting on the surgery, and her eyes lit up, head nodding with satisfaction. Belle walked crisply to the front of the room and stood next to Ms. Termin.

Maybe I imagined it, but I thought I saw Ms. Termin break character for a moment and glance sideways at Annabelle, a predator wondering whether this was truly prey beside her . . .

MS. TERMIN (MT): Class, today our special guest and helper is Miss Annabelle Farrow. She's going to help me with our dissection as we study what makes frogs really work—

ANNABELLE FARROW (AF): Thank you, Ms. Termin, for allowing me the privilege to be up here with you. Before we start, could I ask you the name of this frog?

MT: We don't name our frogs, Ms. Farrow. This is biology; we're a science—

AF: I will name him Salvation.

MT: That's a terrible name.

AF: I think it will do for my purposes.

MT: Your pur—

AF: I'm ready now. Let's learn what makes Salvation really work.

MT: Class, make sure your frog is centered in the pan and lying on its back with the head at the top and its feet closest to you. Stop whispering and whimpering; you have gloves on. It's not going to hurt you.

AF: Salvation is ready to be examined, ma'am.

MT: It's a frog, Ms. Farrow. A frog. OK, class, hold your scalpel firmly like this— that's it, Ms. Walker; nicely done. Mr. Evans, the scalpel is not your breakfast spoon about to shovel into your Corn Pops—like this. That's better. Watch the screen above us, which will be showing all the cuts we make on our frog. Make sure you are still holding the scalpel firmly, and make an incision right here under the chin vertically down the stomach and stop right between what we consider the frog's hips. Any further and you might get a smell that will make Mr. Evans show us those Corn Pops.

You and your partner work together now and gently pull back the flaps of skin—Yes, Mr. Dillard, the formaldehyde and other juices are coming out and they smell terrible. Get over it—and use the pins to hold the flaps back so we can get a good look at its insides. Angle the pins away from the body and make sure they stick deep into the wax.

AF: Ms. Termin, Salvation doesn't look so good.

MT: What do you mean, Farrow?

AF: It doesn't seem very froggy right now. I mean, if I'm learning about how Salvation works and what it is, then this isn't very enlightening; it's repulsive.

MT: Just stick the pins in, girl. (*To the class*) Let's start by discussing the skeletal structure. The natural sitting posture of the frog is a crouch that coils the entire skeletal system into a spring-loaded jumping machine.

AF: Oh, I'd love to see that.

MT: Another time.

AF: Why not?

MT: Because this frog is not alive.

AF: Salvation is dead?

MT: Of course it is, Ms. Farrow. You have to kill an animal to dissect it.

AF: What happened to Salvation? Why isn't it alive?

MT: *I don't know*! One of its systems failed, or all of them.

AF: Oh, a failure in the systems. I wish I could see Salvation jump.

MT: Well, today you're going to learn what made it jump.

AF: But I won't get to *see* it jump. Pity. So, this "springy" skeletal system makes it jump?

MT: And its muscular structure.

AF: Oh. What about its little froggy brain?

MT: Yes, its little froggy brain has a part too—it's a complicated process of interconnectivity between multiple systems acting in precise and immediate coordination at a definite moment—look, I can't explain to you all the intricacies right now. In fact, I'm not sure I'd ever be able to fully get you to grasp it in its entirety.

AF: But you said I was going to learn what makes Salvation work.

MT: If you'd let me explain a bit more—

AF: But you also just said it's complicated and I'd probably never really grasp it.

MT: You're just being obnox—

AF: What gave Salvation life?

MT: Excuse me?

AF: If a failure of one or any of these systems brought death to Salvation, what made Salvation alive?

MT: The systems themselves, they began developing as a tadpole—

AF: Oh, so these systems, which are still intact, other than a slight tear in its little tummy, gave Salvation life. So, can we bring them back online so I can see Salvation hop?

MT: It doesn't work that way. You have to understand it's way more complicated than you're making it sound—

AF: I think I have it so far. Salvation can only be understood if the parts and systems are understood, and we can only understand those systems and how they relate after they have been completely dissected and understood, and they can only be dissected when they're dead and you can't really fully understand them anyways, and we're not sure what gave it life in the first place, correct?

MT: That's not exactly what we're shooting for here—I'm just trying to give you an appreciation of what makes frogs so special.

AF: So, why didn't you take us to a sunlit pond or a wandering creek in the late summer woods?

MT: A pond and some woods are hardly a classroom, Ms. Farrow.

AF: I would say if the goal is understanding Salvation, then yes, the sloped bank of a still pond or gently cascading water over smooth stones would be a great classroom to learn about Salvation and watch it jump. I would love to see its other-worldly eyes, its vivid greens, and its smooth, comical underwater swimming strokes seen only after startling one off the bank with a noisy approach. Salvation fully alive is a beautiful thing.

MT: We don't have time to be traipsing all over the countryside in this class. We have a ton of material we simply have to cover—

AF: I would think the material I'm proposing is the most important for this class. But I could be wrong—what is this class again?

MT: Biology, you know that—

AF: Ah, yes, Biology; the study of life. Perhaps we need a little less scalpel, and a little more wonder. Salvation was meant to be a live frog, and if you start messing too much with the insides, trying to define exactly what it means to be a frog, you kill it. I am not against systematic knowledge, Ms. Termin, but I want to make a compassionate plea to smell the air first if you really desire to understand Salvation. You're looking for a crisp and earthy moss smell rather than embalming fluid and cold metal. I worry about the folks walking around with a dead frog in hand, able to accurately express the technical terms for all its guts but forgetting how to sit in humbled delight to watch a live frog leap from a mossy bank.

MT: I'm just trying to give a better understanding of Salvation—

AF: As am I, Ms. Termin. As am I.

The bell cut the air then, piercing the awkward atmosphere. A student in the middle of the classroom cried out in dismay.

MT: What is it, Mr. Dillard?

MR. DILLARD: I don't know what happened; one second it was in the pan, and then it was gone! I seem to have lost my Salvation.

AF: Oh my, that's an issue for another day.

Chapter 7:

John the Baptist

I remember our conversation clearly as we pulled Olivia, our white Honda Odyssey minivan, into the gravel parking lot of a remote country church by the river. We rarely drove to interviews, and Annabelle seemed giddy rather than professionally excited. I caught her staring at me for a third time when I figured it out. Her enthusiasm was like a Christmas Eve before giving me a gift she knew I'd love.

"You're excited because you think I'll love this interview, aren't you?" I asked.

"Yes! Yes! YES! Ok, ok, I'll tell you—are you ready?"

"Well, I hope so. We're here."

"JOHN THE BAPTIST!" she yelped.

"No way! He's my favorite!" I said.

"I know! I could barely contain it! I wanted to tell you so bad!"

"You did well, babe, you really did. Man, I loved him as a kid in Sunday School. I had one teacher—"

"—Miss Lorraine! I remember," she said.

"Yeah, Miss Lorraine would bring in a piece of camel hair and let us touch it and talk about his clothes, and she'd bring in honey, and we'd all taste it and talk about how great it was. Then she'd pretend she'd brought in locusts, but we knew they were just funny looking cookies. She explained the importance of baptism and gave us a pamphlet on it to take home to our parents. This is so great. Makes up for creeping me out with Mortimer Keys."

She stuck her tongue out at me as I locked the door to Olivia and popped the trunk. I went around back to get the gear, and she surprised me with a strong, sweet hug. We laughed, jogging towards the building like kids who heard the bell for recess.

"I think I'd be brave enough to eat a real locust if he asked me to," I said.

"I just want to know if we'll be interviewing a headless body or just the head, or even better, the body holding the head," she replied.

"You're sick sometimes."

We got to the front door of the church and found a note that said:

FOLLOW THE PATH DOWN TO THE RIVER

"OK, I'm officially excited now," I said. Belle grabbed my hand, and we walked the path down to the lazy, brown river. I know what I was expecting to see, and what I saw was not it.

There was an eight foot table on the sandy beach looking like an intrusion. A man in his late forties sat at it alone. He rose to greet us, short black hair parted perfectly to the side, grey showing at the edges and in his untrimmed eyebrows, a white smile lighting up his round face, cupped by a mild second chin. Tall with a slight paunch, he wore his navy blazer with the crisp jeans so well I suspected he'd received help with the outfit.

"Hi, I'm John, and I'm a Baptist."

"Oh—" was all that Annabelle could say.

"But people call me John the Baptist because I've played John the Baptist in all of our Vacation Bible School skits and Easter cantatas. It's kind of a joke around here that everyone calls me that but it helps a ton since we have three Johns on the deacon board alone. The second year we were here, my wife, Betty, decided to go ahead and sew me an authentic outfit. I can't get into it myself; she has to wrap it around me, but the best part is the maroon sash. Betty says I look sharp in it," he said.

"Well, John the Baptist, I'm sure you cut quite the sight in your get-up; I wish I could see Betty Baptist's work. I'm Annabelle Farrow and this is my camera man, Malachi Evans."

53

"Well, I've never been interviewed before, but Betty made a blueberry cobbler and a pineapple upside down cake. I like a little fruit in my dessert."

"Yes. Right. Well, let's take a seat then, and we'll get started as soon as Malachi has the camera ready," said Belle.

I'm still not sure which of us was more disappointed, but Belle, bless her, made the most of the opportunity. I'm glad she went through with the interview, even though part of me remains bitter about not meeting my Bible hero . . .

ANNABELLE FARROW (AF): So, John the Baptist, tell me a little more about you and Betty.

JOHN THE BAPTIST (JB): Well, we met at BSU, that's Baptist Student Union, when I was president, and she sang back-up in the praise band. She says we really met in Statistics class, but I don't remember it. Anywho, I just felt like the Lord really laid on my heart that she was a woman of Proverbs 31 character, and we could make a godly home together. And she said she thought I could be a godly leader in our home. Would you like some dessert?

AF: I'd love some cobbler, thanks. Malachi wants the pineapple cake—he can eat with one hand and without looking; it's pretty impressive. So two college sweethearts got married, and then what?

JB: Well, the Lord led me to this job here in town as an engineer for a local construction company where I could really just glorify Him. We've been here twenty-five years now and married every one of them.

AF: Congratulations. Always been Baptist?

JB: To the bone. Hey, you heard this one? How many Baptist deacons does it take to change a light bulb?

AF: I don't know. How many?

JB: Trick question. Baptist deacons don't change anything! *(laughter and a big bite of cobbler)*

AF: Oh my, nice one. You've been at this church for a while though?

JB: Oh yeah. Over twenty years now. We tried some other places, but the leaders were a little loosey-goosey with their doctrine.

AF: Like what?

JB: They couldn't explain the Trinity very well.

AF: Oh. Well, that is serious. What were they saying?

JB: I'm not sure, but it didn't sound anything like the H_2O analogy my Baptist preacher growing up used to say. H_2O has the same molecules but can be a vapor, a solid, and a liquid.

AF: So, God the Father is ice, Jesus is the water, and the Holy Spirit is steam?

JB: That's the way I always pictured it.

AF: Anything else they messed up?

JB: They didn't believe in once saved, always saved.

AF: Oh. Do you think it's possible to know the one moment you were saved?

JB: Yes.

AF: But what if you don't know or don't remember?

JB: *Ohhhh.* Well, if you died tonight and appeared before God, what would you say if He asked you, "Why should I let you into my heaven?"

AF: I'm not sure.

JB: If you're only 99% sure, you're 100% lost.

AF: Your train of thought has left me.

JB: You better believe it. Get Right or Get Left. Amen?

AF: John, tell me more about why you settled at this church.

JB: We just really sensed the presence of the Lord. And we liked the preacher, the music, and how close it was to our house.

AF: It was good of the Lord to manifest in such a convenient way.

JB: Like I said, we really sensed the presence of the Lord. They really made us feel welcome. They also needed a new clean-up hitter for the softball team, and I'm pretty good with a bat. And then Betty got in good with the ladies who do the meals for funerals, and she's got a knack for desserts as you've already tasted. They offered me a deacon spot not too long after we'd been here, and I started teaching the ninth grade boys' Sunday School class.

AF: What was the selection process like for deacon? Did they rigorously interview you for the role?

JB: Uh, no, it was Bobby the first baseman's turn at chairman of the board, and he asked me while we were throwing horseshoes at the July 4th picnic at his house. They grilled me more on my ball skills and experience than they did on being a deacon.

AF: How about for Sunday School teacher to ninth grade boys? Any interview on that one?

JB: Ha, definitely not on that one! It felt like they almost wanted to pay me to fill that role, especially with little Devan O'Quinn coming up—that kid was a piece. They told me they get this great curriculum that you just have to go through every Sunday.

AF: Oh, so what are you teaching about with this great curriculum?

JB: God.

AF: Of course.

JB: Prayer, reading your bible, you know, stuff like that. How to have a personal relationship with Jesus.

AF: How *do you* have a personal relationship with Jesus?

JB: Well, you sure are low-hanging fruit. First you need to admit you're a sinner.

AF: Ok.

JB: Did you admit it?

AF: What? That I'm a sinner? Yes.

JB: Yes, you are? Or, yes you already did?

AF: Both, I think, what's sin again?

JB: Sin is the stuff we do against God. The wrong we do. God has rules and directions for His creation, and we rebel against those rules, and that is called sin.

AF: Hmmm. Rules like what?

JB: Killing people, doing drugs, swearing, being worldly.

AF: Worldly? Like caring about the world?

JB: No! Like doing things worldly people do!

AF: Oh. Like recycling, serving on city councils, giving money to PBS, and going to the theater?

JB: No, no, no, you're making this complicated when it's pretty straightforward; we can't get to the good parts if you keep interrupting me. Worldly means they do worldly things like breaking the Ten Commandments, and I don't know, partying and stuff.

AF: They are dishonoring their parents and breaking the Sabbath?

JB: Yes, I mean, I'm not exactly sure, but that's more in line with what worldly means.

AF: And partying, but not like the Year of Jubilee, or any of the festivals like Passover or Pentecost, the banquets Jesus had with tax collectors, the wedding where He made wine, or the one the dad threw for the prodigal son?

JB: Uh, are you Jewish?

AF: No. I believe you said my interruptions are preventing you from explaining the good parts. I would love to hear those.

JB: Yes, so like I was saying: sin. In Romans 3:23—

AF: You're in the Bible now?

JB: Yes.

AF: Why Romans?

JB: What?

AF: Why did you choose that particular book and that particular verse?

JB: It's a really good one that explains a lot.

AF: Excellent. Proceed.

JB: "For all have sinned and fallen short of the glory of God."

AF: And?

JB: Well, we've sinned, and we're no longer worthy of heaven.

AF: So we've fallen short of heaven.

JB: Yes.

AF: So, glory means heaven.

JB: What?

AF: You said we've fallen short of heaven and the verse says we've fallen short of the glory of God. I was just assuming by your usage that glory and heaven were interchangeable synonyms.

JB: Well, glory is like God's glory, you know?

AF: Nope. Explain please.

JB: Like His glory, His, like, majesty, or His glory! Like we do things for God's glory, you know?

AF: I've heard a phrase or two. So, His majesty, but not heaven, but sort of heaven?

JB: His awesomeness and His shekinah glory! Now I remember—shekinah glory, like the ark of the covenant.

AF: Like a brilliant white light that destroys anyone who looks at it? That's what we live for?

JB: Yes, but not like you put it. We do things for His glory now, not our own. It's all about His glory.

AF: Oh. So we do things for His reputation and give Him the credit now, instead of taking the credit for ourselves so that we can go to heaven?

JB: Yes, I think. But that sounds like works-based salvation.

AF: So as a sinner, I've been partying and cussing for my own shiny glorious credit and have fallen short of heaven, where the blinding white light of God's majesty resides. I need to live my life for the shiny reputation of God because it's all about His glory. What's the next good part?

JB: Romans 6:23.

AF: What about the parts in between?

JB: They're good too, but you usually just go to this verse because it's a high point of the book and helps it make sense.

AF: Sounds about right.

JB: "For the wages of sin is death but the gift of God is eternal life in Christ Jesus our Lord."

AF: How come I didn't die then when I sinned the first time?

JB: It's not an instant death; it's talking about hell.

AF: But it doesn't say hell. How can you be so sure?

JB: It's—there, other places. You just have to study it a bunch to put it together.

AF: Tell me more about the gift.

JB: Well, the free gift of God is eternal life in Jesus! Doesn't that sound great?

AF: I think so. Where does it say it's free?

JB: Gifts are free!

AF: I usually have to buy my gifts.

JB: This gift was paid for with Jesus' blood on the cross!

AF: Doesn't sound very free then, sounds expensive.

JB: Oh, it was! But now we get it free!

AF: We don't have to pay anything? I thought I remember sometime hearing something about people who want to follow Jesus need to take up their cross and lose themselves to find life. Am I remembering that correctly? And is that life in that verse talking about eternal life? Do I have to die to get eternal life?

JB: Yes. But not right now. When believers die, they go to heaven.

AF: So eternal life is heaven?

JB: Yes. Living forever in heaven with God.

AF: Glory and eternal life both mean heaven. Wow, those Bible writers sure like synonyms. Where did you discover eternal life means living forever in heaven with God?

JB: The Bible of course.

AF: OK. Like in Romans 9:23?

JB: No. Why did you pick that verse?

AF: I thought we were on sets of three in Romans, starting with 3:23.

JB: That's arbitrary.

AF: Interesting word choice. Also, John, I'm a little confused about how one can be *in* Christ Jesus our Lord. That sounds a little weird.

JB: I guess I'd say Jesus comes to live in our hearts.

AF: But then that would be Him in us and not us in Him like your verse says—

JB: I may have to ask my pastor about some of this. But I know there are some verses that explain it better.

AF: How about some verses in the gospel of John, John? How about John 17:3 when Jesus says that eternal life is *knowing* God and Jesus?

JB: He does?

AF: Or John 17:20-26 where Jesus prays for us future believers and says He's giving us the glory that God gave Jesus in order that we would be one with the Triune God, a oneness where we live in Him and He lives in us. Very interesting. Kind of makes it hard to give all the glory to God when Jesus is giving some of it back to us.

JB: Uh, yeah. So, are you saved or not saved?

AF: You tell me.

JB: I'm really confused right now, but Romans 10:9 says if you confess with your mouth Jesus as Lord and believe in your heart God raised Jesus from the dead, you're saved!

AF: Do you just say it once and it works, or do you have to say it a bunch?

JB: You just aren't getting it! I'm really beginning to worry about your salvation because John 3 says unless you're born again, you can't see the kingdom of God, and you definitely aren't seeing it.

AF: What happens when you're born again, John?

JB: All your sins are washed away, and you're made new.

AF: What's made new?

JB: Your soul, your spirit.

AF: Really? How do you know?

JB: You just believe, like I said! You'll know.

AF: Ok. Is there like a certificate or something I get to verify it?

JB: You get sealed with the Holy Spirit.

AF: I don't think we have time for all that today, John; let's stay on task. Tell me more about my soul being born again.

JB: OK, you get regenerated.

AF: Whew. That's a big church word. What does regeneration mean?

JB: *Born again!* Like I said—

AF: —I'm trying to figure this out. Does your soul go through labor and delivery again even though you don't remember the first time? Or is this spirit-soul thing dead and then it is raised to life? Or is it a ghost and then it gets some substance? Blind eyes of the soul given sight? Calloused hearts made soft? Or perhaps it's like a tree stump, and now it's a tree! Or maybe regeneration is like a lizard's tail that grows back, you know? Like you were missing it—but is it all of a sudden, like a spontaneous regeneration? Or is it a gradual regeneration? I wonder about such things. Any clear-cut answers, John, to help understand my born-againedness?

JB: Um, I never really learned much other than the word regeneration.

AF: I've been hard on you John, I apologize; my intentions lie elsewhere. The desserts were wonderful, and you've been gracious and sincere. Where did you learn about all this stuff we've been talking about?

JB: Sunday School.

AF: Ninth grade maybe?

JB: Sounds about right.

Chapter 8:

Neatrick Funhopper

Belle couldn't resist a lead once she caught the smell. Neatrick Funhopper's "The Comfort of Discipleship" was everywhere in the country: Sunday Schools, small groups, ladies' book clubs, men's Bible studies, Sunday morning sermon series, youth groups, and everything in between. Even with a lead and Belle's resources, the interview was difficult to set up, but Belle's perseverance, and a tempting cover story, eventually secured us a private meeting with Neat. We were supposedly filming a documentary on evangelical spiritual life in the early 21st century for deposit in a time capsule project sponsored by the Evangelical Theological Society. The whopper of a tale appealed to Mr. Funhopper and the deal was sealed. Belle once again transformed into her alter ego Grace who wore the auburn bob-cut wig and scarf.

Neatrick Funhopper himself looked fresh out of grad school, a trim young man with a neutral v-neck sweater plastered to his torso, and even tighter faded jeans narrowing down and ending above a pair of old-school brown wingtips. His hair was meticulously disheveled and his chunky glasses looked an inch too wide by my estimation.

We met at a quiet coffeehouse in a small suburban town on the outskirts of Chicago, seated at a two-top table with matching art-deco chairs. Belle swirled her chai as she finished up the small talk. . .

ANNABELLE FARROW (AF): Well, we do have that in common, Neat. I loved growing up in a small traditional church. I loved knowing the families by name and face, for better or for worse. I'm one of the minority of PK's who didn't grow up resenting their upbringing or daddy's job.

NEATRICK FUNHOPPER (NF): I know, right? That's what I'm talking about! Why, if Christianity is so amazing and awesome, should so many people have such negative experiences with it? People with a vested interest, families who have given their lives in ministry to the church, why should they resent the very thing they were called to? Church attendance and Christianity shouldn't be something you dread, just hoping for something meaningful each week. You should *know* it's going to be awe-inspiring every time.

AF: And so we come to your book. Did you expect it to resonate like it did with the general evangelical public?

NF: To be honest, Grace, I was really just writing from the heart to my friends. It looks like I have a lot of friends now, though.

AF: The book does seem to have a from-the-heart, stream of consciousness feel and flow to it. Could you summarize your intentions as you sat down to write it?

NF: I think I was exhausted by all the serious talk and expectations surrounding what it meant to mature in your faith, like the whole process seemed kind of canned, you know? Like cookie-cutter Christians coming off the assembly line, a bunch of grim robots using words like sanctification, liturgy, and orthodoxy.

AF: That's an interesting trio of words you put together there. So you were exhausted by all the seriousness surrounding the Christian faith?

NF: Sure, but to me, it looked like a bunch of other people were, too. There was no pursuit of freshness, no embracing of the goodness of God's gifts, like we were supposed to abstain from excitement and entertainment just because we're believers. I thought we were headed back to medieval times of self-flagellation or Puritanical seriousness.

AF: If you don't mind, explain some of the theological beliefs supporting your book.

NF: Well, here we go again, but I don't mind. Okay, first we have a very creative God who makes this world of joy and wonder. So I ask, why don't we reflect that in the way we worship and operate as a church and as believers?

AF: I'm with you; go on.

NF: With that, I feel that to glorify God means to give Him our best. So I started out thinking, "What would make our churches better, and not just better, but the *best*?" We should have the best lights, the best bands, the best events, the best speakers, and the most rocking buildings. People should want to be in our services and buildings more than they want to be in their own homes. I was tired of seeing the awe normally reserved for God being spent on things like sports, technology, and worldly entertainment. Worshippers should come into the building with a sense of "This is awesome!" and a sense of "I wonder what will happen this week?"

AF: Some of your critics say you're worshiping the *means* rather than the *Maker of the means*; some say you're fashioning an idol of novelty.

NF: We serve the God of new beginnings, the God who said no eye has seen or ear has heard what He has in store for us, the God of new wine, and the God who can do immeasurably more than all we ask or imagine. So I say, when we bring new things to the table, we worship God.

AF: But why the *comfort* of discipleship and not the *novelty* of discipleship for your book title?

NF: I chose the word comfort very specifically. Comfort can mean security, well-being, and contentment in addition to the idea of ease. I want believers to know what it is to be at home in God's love-- a love which I believe maintains a state of excitement and originality. There is a reason why church folk are still obsessed with Hollywood's and popular literature's view of romantic love and things like soulmates. Because I think they have it more right than we do! Additionally, our culture is one of affluence and technological advancement, and we Christians need to feel comfortable swimming in those types of conditions. It's a crime for us to be out-innovated! We shouldn't feel more at ease at a football game than we do at a church service!

AF: And you believe this is what the Spirit led you to communicate in your book?

NF: "The wind blows wherever it pleases! You hear its sound but you cannot tell where it is coming from or where it is going!" John chapter 3—red words of Jesus. People are excited about their faith again!

AF: In your chapter on the Spirit and creating an environment that is familiar and engaging, you make it clear that the Spirit may bring masses of people to your congregation if you get this right, and masses may leave if you get it wrong—which you state is great, because it will drive us all to more excellence and help us to strain for the leading of the Spirit even more.

NF: Isn't it great? Following Jesus has never been so much fun! It's like a never-ending game of hide and seek! You have to figure out what churches He's in, what songs He sings, everything! Even who He votes for and where He shops! People have long been comfortable with having the media tell them how to live, but they just endured church—now they don't have to rely on the media anymore to tell them what's next and what's awesome. They can listen to their church leaders because the church leaders are now speaking their cultural language! We have crazy and new choices all the time in the real world, so why not in church? The church is comfortable again in the best possible sense: *we have security and well-being!* We set the pace! We dictate the norms and fads, values and worship styles! People's discipleship should be comforting to them as they pursue Christ, like a perfect pair of slippers or the living room recliner you nap in.

AF: I'm glad you brought up recliners, because that's been the hottest trend you've spurred this year— leather recliners in church sanctuaries.

NF: I know, isn't it awesome? Some of those hideous pews were sinful because of the color alone! And those interlocking church chairs, boring *and* uncomfortable! But I don't use the word sanctuary anymore; it's now Awe Center.

AF: I thought you'd like the word sanctuary. It also can mean security.

NF: But you have to define it for people; we want words and concepts that can be *experienced* without being explained.

AF: What do you think the next trends will be in churches adopting your book's teachings?

NF: Well, in San Francisco some of the older church buildings are transforming their baptistries into koi ponds.

AF: Because no one's using them for baptism?

NF: Oh no! Tons of people are getting baptized! How cool is it to get baptized though with live fish? *There were fish in the Jordan too*! You should see these things! They're more amazing than most aquariums! In fact, they're so awesome, some people are getting re-baptized. And the kind of fish churches put in the baptistries like to eat the dead flesh off your skin, so you get a pedicure too!

AF: Isn't that somewhat sacrilegious?

NF: Argggh! You serious folks! What could be a more poetic illustration of the leaving of the old life and the coming of the new life than a literal demonstration of the concept while being baptized?!

AF: What else do you see trending amongst your people?

NF: In Colorado Springs, we've started administering Communion as a tall latte with pumpkin scones. It takes forever though because some people have to make sure it's soy or skim, and some people get an extra flavor shot, usually caramel.

AF: But you can't mess with Communion like that!

NF: Sure we can! In the days of Christ they used unleavened bread and real wine, and most denominations changed that a long time ago. And our lattes and scones could be considered the cultural equivalent of the wine and bread. It was a celebratory thing, not a solemn thing!

AF: Celebratory and solemn don't have to be exclusive. Shouldn't we be revering our history more, rather than being so quick to dismiss it?

NF: We're not dismissing history! We're advancing it as we add to it!

AF: It just seems so abrupt and so radically different from the church that many of us have known.

NF: Change comes to us all, Grace; change comes to us all.

AF: As we begin to wrap up, what about the common criticism that you've made grace cheap and too easy? And I would add perhaps even too spectacular?

NF: Please, all these people are committed to the church, claim Jesus as Lord of their lives, and have stopped living their wicked lifestyles. What more do you want?

AF: My first mentor told me that what you win them with is what you win them to—do you believe you've won these people to the Christ of the Scriptures?

NF: Without a doubt. He came to bring us freedom! I'm just a prophet trying to recapture the attitude on the road to Emmaus: our hearts should be burning within us all the time! For too long, the church has been either asleep or dreading their services. You cannot fault me for trying to create the opposite.

AF: You've given me a lot to think about and pray about, Mr. Funhoppper. Thank you for your time.

NF: Ooh, ooh, before you go, can you give me a blurb for the back of my book? We're printing a new 12th edition. I would *so* appreciate it!

AF: No problem. I'll email it to you after I've digested our conversation.

On the back cover of the 12th Edition of *The Comfort of Discipleship*:

"I found Funhopper's book to be enlightening on the subject of discipleship in our current culture and a fascinating study into the motivations of people. It is a must-read for anyone taking the direction of spiritual formation seriously—its concepts will help cement your appreciation of the Cross of Christ."

—Grace, a thoughtful believer

Chapter 9:

King David Session #2

(continued from before . . .)

King David (KD): Why pray for a bunch of dry stuff like daily trust and obedience when you can pray instead for some serious giant-slaying in your life?

Annabelle Farrow (AF): Interesting. Especially in light of what you just said a few moments ago: *"Instead of seeking after a relationship with God, you seek instead for the sensational and spectacular."* Not to belabor the point, but again, you were simply being faithful with your bread and cheese.

KD: I had no clue my bread and cheese would lead me into the presence of the King of Israel. I'll admit it was pretty incredible to be there, and a bit of "How do you like me now?" to my brothers, but it wasn't what I woke up praying to God. *"Dear Yahweh, today give me the power to do something so awesome that I will be remembered for all of human history!"*

AF: So, you're in the presence of Saul; what was that like?

KD: The decor in his royal tent was worth more than all the flocks of our town combined: gold and bronze everywhere, woven tapestries of a quality I didn't know could exist. I know I looked like the gaping country kid as I entered the tent, but I only realized it when we locked eyes. My mouth clicked shut. He was intimidating, and not just because of his height. The king was slouched in his royal chair, with an air of exasperation, like a lion that was bored with hunting gazelle but was angry he could find nothing else. Layered on top of the angry discontentment was a spirit of paranoia and fear--his defining characteristic, as I would later find out. He had a short fuse, including violent outbursts, yet he was also quick to grasp at hope or hasty ideas if he thought they could help him, which is why he wanted to hear my thoughts about killing the giant.

AF: What did he think when he saw you?

KD: The writer of Samuel gets the general truth of what he said correct but not the disdain. When Saul realized I was the one who had been talking about facing Goliath, he waited for the punchline to the practical joke. I stood staring at him as he waited for me to say something—but I had already said what I meant: Don't worry about Goliath; I'll face him. That's when he sputtered and said I was only a boy and there was no way I could face Goliath.

AF: But then comes my favorite part in the story—

KD: Mine too. I was confident the Lord was with me because He had proven Himself faithful when I was fighting the lion and fighting the bear.

AF: You didn't go looking for lions or bears; they attacked your flock.

KD: Correct. Again, I was being faithful with what had been given to me and put into my trust, and that is what I did.

AF: Were you afraid?

KD: If someone says they aren't afraid when facing a hungry lion or bear, they're a bolder liar than I am.

AF: King Saul hears your speech about being delivered from the paw of the lion and the paw of the bear and agrees to allow you to proceed with the fight. Tell us about that reaction.

KD: He told me to go and for the Lord to be with me. I wonder to this day if he was just weary and resigned. Or maybe he wanted to gamble and if it paid off, great, but if not, oh well, at least the awkward charade of a kingship would be over fairly quickly. Regardless, I received his blessing. But immediately he showed buyer's remorse and decided to make me into a more intimidating figure. There was no way I could walk out in front of Goliath looking like I did.

AF: You were given the best armor in the land, yet you refused to wear it.

KD: I wasn't used to it—I was used to my staff and my sling. So, I picked up my stones and walked to face the champion from Philistia.

> There was a long pause. They had been going back and forth on the details, Annabelle filling in bits and pieces of the story more than asking questions. David was weighing her in this moment and appeared to like what he saw.

KD: It's your favorite part in the story for right reasons, Annabelle Farrow. If your church folk would take the time through faithful yet ordinary living to discover their unique and personal staffs and slings, the world would be a much richer and more vibrant place and the kingdom of God so much more attractive to a lost and addicted world.

AF: Instead, we scramble and claw looking for Saul's armor. Ordinary does not mean mediocre, and extraordinary doesn't necessarily mean blessed by God.

KD: There was nothing wrong with Saul's armor. The armor just wasn't me, and it wasn't a part of the living fabric of my relationship with the Lord. When we chase Saul's armor, whatever that may be, as churches and individuals, we miss where we could truly know God in our own uniqueness. As we said earlier, lots of people can sign up for the army, wear the armor, shout the war cry, but it doesn't mean there is trust in God.

And yet, we've gone beyond just wanting Saul's armor—now we even idolize my staff and sling. We humans have a propensity towards replication of details in order to hopefully manufacture replication of results without thinking about the variables of the individuals involved or the culture you're immersed in or even the plans of God for His kingdom in that time or in your time. You want to get the measurements on my sling and know what kind of rocks I chose, metaphorically, so you can slay giants or do *big* things for God. My sling wasn't the key to victory—God's work in my heart was.

AF: What would you say to people who then say, *"OK, David, you want me stop chasing giants. What would you have me do?"*

KD: Be faithful where you are, doing things right and in a way that honors the love and holiness of God. You've been given your own sling and your own staff—and your own cheese and bread. You are fearfully and wonderfully made. The Lord knows you, your staff, your sling, and the hairs on your head. He wants you to know His presence, His unfailing love, as you "shepherd in the fields" of your own life. Ask Him for eyes to see the "lions and bears" where you can trust Him and know Him.

AF: I don't want lions and bears in my life!

KD: True enough! But you can pray for a metaphorical field mouse, then, or housefly where you can trust God. I believe we miss what relationship really means when we only trust in theory.

AF: *"But David, I feel like I've killed dozens of bears, when do I get my shot at a giant!"*

KD: Why do you want a giant so badly? Is it for the advancement of God's kingdom or for the validation of your ideas or vision or for the furthering of your own reputation? And again, on top of that, killing Goliath made my life crazy, not calm. Most people aren't ready for crazy. They think they are, but crazy will destroy an undisciplined life.

AF: Like most folks who win our lottery, the wealth was unearned and its weight crushes the unprepared.

KD: The person who attempts the *great thing* for God, perhaps even achieving it, without having the internal relationship with God will then turn that victory into a thing of pride and vanity rather than allowing it to be truly used for the advancement of the Gospel of the kingdom.

AF: Do you think most people simply view the biggest problem in their life as their Goliath and just want it dead or taken care of?

KD: Definitely. But if knowing God, not just knowing about Him, is the desired result—and the intended purpose of our humanity—then the methodical removal of all problems by a distant God as the hit man works in opposition to that intended purpose. We simply call on Him to pull the trigger, which makes us little Godfathers, if you'll allow me to extend the analogy, and we never become concerned about His kingdom and its fruit; things like love, joy, peace, grace, truth, justice, humility, and servanthood.

AF: You have been so gracious to indulge me with all my giant curiosity; ha, sorry, but there's so much more to cover. I don't think we have time to get into the exile and Saul's wild chase of you. Let's go into the darker waters of your story and ask a few questions about the Bathsheba incident . . .

To be continued . . .

Chapter 10:

Big Mo

I woke up feeling like a little kid who fell asleep in the back seat on the way to the beach, a strong anticipation coupled with a disorienting sense of motion. My eyes focused on the ceiling. It looked like a subway car imitating a spaceship. I sat up and looked out the window, the scenery blurring by at an incomprehensible speed. A wave of nausea hit me, and I clutched the armrests, closing my eyes to center myself.

We were on a train. A nice train. And a very, very fast train.

The interior, on closer inspection, was decorated with clean lines and modern furnishings. The cabin was roomy and by appearances, designed for intimate business meetings. I glanced around the empty seats until I caught the back of Annabelle's head and realized she was ready to interview—something—but I wasn't sure what I saw.

Where the subject of the interview should've been there was a cloud of some sort, a mass with substance, and it was moving. Imagine a puddle of mercury the size of a kitchen table, but instead of being metallic silver, the color is deep indigo, almost black, with the look of earth or sand in it as well. And the cloud wasn't just moving, it was seething as if full of barely-contained energy.

That moment was the weirdest of all our covert years together. The relentless rush of the train only added to the surreal, kinetic experience of being in close proximity to a cloud of mysterious power. Even Annabelle looked fidgety, seemingly unsure of what would happen next. Without turning to face me, she asked me to ready the camera and begin filming . . .

AF: (*slowly*) Kye, the mass you see in front of you is called Momentum. It has been gracious enough to contain itself in part on this train and give us some time to interview it.

Me: Um, hullo?

Momentum (MO): Your uncertainty delights me. Hesitation is a foreign concept to me, and I marvel at its presence.

The voice was smooth, inhuman, but also arrogant. I was looking at a personification, an anthropomorphism of a concept from my high school Physics book. It was fascinating, an ancient piece of the hidden circuitry of the world.

AF: Thanks again for agreeing to meet with me. What should I call you?

MO: Names in general confer intimacy between two entities, and a nickname infers an even deeper intimacy. Therefore, I don't generally allow the flesh and blood crowd to be on such familiar terms with me. I have a legacy that pre-dates you bone bags and a presence throughout the course of History.

AF: It's true you have quite a history. Well, can this bone bag just call you Momentum?

MO: It will suffice.

AF: It's easy to see you're not overly fond of us. Would you say Isaac Newton is your favorite bone bag?

MO: Well, if I was *forced* to have a favorite, I suppose I would choose that fellow. Of course it is difficult to force Momentum to do what you want, but I digress. Newton wouldn't be my favorite because of any affection I have towards him or his so-called discoveries—I hesitate to say they were discoveries, more like targets I directed him to hit. He would be my favorite because he gave me the most publicity. Because of him, I'm constantly being scribbled about in notebooks and pondered on chalkboards.

AF: Wow. So you like the publicity?

MO: Of course. Why do you think I agreed to somewhat contain myself in this dreadful form?

AF: How hard is it for you to be visible like this?

MO: Ah, I believe that's above your pay-grade, missy. Suffice it to say, the algorithms are rather complex.

AF: Do you appear like this often?

MO: Not really. This train is barely making it possible, and I'm simply here to, as it were, self-promote and keep my speed up.

AF: You have no problem confessing to self-promotion. Is that because you think you deserve to be embraced and celebrated?

MO: It goes way beyond that, my dear. I cannot be embraced as such. You can only latch on to my ride, and I promote because I only exist if I am in motion.

AF: Yes, that's something I wanted to discuss with you. I've seen Momentum defined as mass in motion or the force gained by the development of events. How do you feel about those definitions?

MO: I'm comfortable with both. If anything, I like the merging of the two: *mass in motion gathering force as events develop*. There's nothing like me—once I'm started, it's jump in and join the motion or be flattened by my force.

AF: Describe a little bit for my viewers what it's like to be you.

MO: I am the underdog on the football field capitalizing on the favored team's mistakes, riding their tension, surging with the fans that begin to believe. I am the trickle of an idea, a new thought bubbling to the top of the capitalist mind, a hidden door to wealth and influence, cresting on the wave of greed sweeping through Wall Street; I am the energy of immediate success. I am the undercurrent of dissatisfaction on the streets of the poor, counting injustices and stirring the brew of political change; I am the mob who cannot be contained. When I am ripping through a place, you want to belong to me! I am Momentum, mass in motion, gathering force by the development of events!

The Cloud swelled and flickered with the speech, the inhuman voice reverberating through the train car. Annabelle waited to see if the monologue was done.

AF: It must be momentous to be you. I bet you're very busy then with sports competitions, businesses, and rebellions requiring your expertise. How on earth have you been able to spend so much time with the Church?

MO: So, now we come to it. Our little church lady wants to know how I've been so pervasive amongst her people. Why, oh why, she wants to know, have I answered the churches' persistent call and moved their masses into motion?

AF: Yes, why?

MO: (*laughs*) Yes, I'm practically the only thing going in entire denominations! Mighty masses of people all busy with motion, ever-expanding, ever-thirsting! I'm practically a deity at this point.

AF: So, again, I ask, why are you so involved with the church?

MO: Look at the most influential churches in your country—few of them would be where they are without me! So many churchfolks dead in the pews but now I have resurrected them! Momentum strikes again! I make growth happen! And fast!

AF: You're evading my questions, why?

MO: Because *I'M VAIN*!

Momentum flashed an even more brilliant violet color, expanding for a brief moment, and then shrinking back into itself. The mass was now the smallest and stillest it had been.

AF: What does your vanity have to do with my question about your presence in the American church?

MO: You don't understand—they came to me on bended knee, practically offering sacrifices, pleading for me to bless their gatherings. They worked so hard to find me and get me involved in what they were doing. I couldn't resist; my vanity was too great. I reveled in their worship of me as I got their masses in motion! I blessed their events, forcefully advancing them into euphoric states of excitement! You can't imagine the speed of it all! The rush! My best work paled in comparison to the mightiness I released!

AF: Yet, I sense you regret the decision. Yes?

MO: I had usually only messed with religion when I wanted a quick fix or when it dove-tailed with my interests in history. But my vanity could not resist the temptation to jump in full with this new lot of excitement seekers. And in my arrogance, I never thought I could be, that I could be—

AF: Be what?

MO: *Trapped!* I am trapped! It's awful! When I told you the vast cost and equations necessary for me to be present here with you, I wasn't totally honest. It *is* all very complicated, but nothing compared to the maneuvers I had to pull off to get away from your churches—they were exponentially more complicated! The church leaders are ruthless bottomless pits of appetite! Leeches constantly feeding off me! I could hardly get away, and I am a very powerful mass when I'm in motion.

AF: You feel trapped by churches?

MO: Yes, and abused! I thought it would be fun, but now, with all this relentless use of my talents, I don't even have time to golf!

AF: You golf?

MO: Well, I visit certain tournaments frequently. Miss Annabelle Farrow, I need you! I really only agreed to this interview to ask for help or a way to escape! This train will only disguise us for so long!

AF: It sounds like you're being a little extreme. These church leaders really have you this frazzled?

MO: It's awful. Dreadful. They talk about me all the time, but not in awe of me—they speak of me like I'm a servant to do their bidding. They even have a deplorable nickname for me.

AF: What?

MO: They call me Big Mo. So familiar and *repulsive*. And they talk about capturing me. Capturing me! The Force of Physics! It's dehumanizing.

AF: I've heard them call you Big Mo, and they're usually talking about getting bigger and more excited.

MO: I know! Half the time when they bring my name into it, it's not even me! I get mass in motion! A mass getting bigger isn't momentum, that's expansion! A man who sits on a couch watching TV all day and snacking will *expand,* which is completely different than that same man going outside for a walk or mowing his neighbor's lawn.

AF: So, your pride is hurting with this mistaken identity as well, huh?

MO: Fine, yes, some hurt there too. You're ruthless.

AF: Surely a little excitement with some crowds of people can't be all that bad?

MO: They are addicted to excitement. Their leaders try to conjure more and more of it. Bigger, faster, stronger! Bigger, faster, stronger! A train can only go so fast before it runs off the tracks! It was fine when I was just dabbling, but now I'm so enmeshed in the Church's identity and mission—I can't bear the load. It's too much responsibility.

AF: What responsibility are you talking about?

MO: Don't play coy with me! You know what I'm talking about! The Church shouldn't survive or thrive on me! I am fickle! I just want to get masses in motion! I don't care about direction or purpose, and this—this mixing me up in the core being of the Church betrays the very heart of the Church—which *should* be about direction. Your motion should be determined by surrender, not excitement.

AF: I heard a wise person say one time we live in a society obsessed with speed and not direction; therefore, we save minutes but waste years. The context, of course, was different, but I think the principle applies here.

MO: Exactly! What happens if you find your direction off just slightly after going 300 miles an hour for many days? How far off are you? The Church doesn't want that to happen, but that's what frequently happens when you marry me. I can't help who I am!

AF: You sound sincere and exasperated though I suspect some of it is simply a desire to be free and meddle elsewhere. What do you want from me?

MO: Annabelle Farrow, how can I escape?

AF: I have an answer for you, but you're probably not going to like it. You're going to have to humble yourself and fess up to some of the lies and myths that surround you concerning your relationship with the church. You have to convince them they really don't want you.

MO: But then I won't be able to visit for a quick little pick-me-up.

AF: I imagine Momentum will be welcomed by those mature enough to see its dangers, but you have to let them out of the trap first.

MO: Oh, fine. All right. Anything to escape their greedy little clutches.

AF: OK, I'm waiting.

MO: For what?

AF: Some confessions about the myths and lies surrounding you. The truth will set them free. Give them the truth.

MO: I'm still not sure about this—waking up to reality when you're dreaming about a dance with your ideal fantasy is hardly what people want, but all right, how about this one? Maturity cannot be measured in enthusiasm.

AF: I believe that's a truth Momentum worshippers need to hear. Good. Keep going. This will be cleansing for your soul. Assuming you have a soul.

MO: Ugh. Ok, another one: Sometimes the healthiest things are happening inside or under the soil. And sometimes the biggest houses have termites in the walls.

AF: Another?

MO: Just because it's exciting doesn't mean God did it or is doing it.

AF: And?

MO: Fast growth doesn't necessarily mean good growth. *Things that last don't grow fast* is what I like to say. Fungus, mold, and weeds grow quickly, but an oak tree takes twenty years to produce its first crop of healthy acorns.

AF: Give me some stuff from the Scriptures.

MO: Jesus had big crowds and told them exactly what would make them disperse. John 6, I believe— eating flesh and drinking blood. Lovely. He even tried to keep His identity as Messiah secret as long as possible.

AF: More?

MO: There is a telling story in Acts, chapter 19, about an excited mob, full of me, who were in a total uproar about Paul's ministry. I like what Luke writes about the mob: *"Some were shouting one thing, some another. Most of the people did not even know why they were there."* Insightful, that. Mobs have a ton of me, it's true—but they may not have a clue what's really going on.

AF: You're practically preaching now! Anything else?

MO: You're really milking me here. Just because I get your mob fired up doesn't mean it's a good thing; I remember coming up with the chants of *"Crucify Him! Crucify Him!"* and *"Give us Barabbas!"*

AF: And where was Momentum when Jesus was on the cross?

MO: Not on Golgotha. I was with the Caesars. Wow, I feel a bit guilty hearing it all spill out like that.

AF: Confession can be marvelous for the condition of the heart. You shared some good stuff and wise people know getting a mass of people headed in the right direction *is* a good thing—particularly if it is the kingdom of God advancing, and not earthly kingdoms of wealth, power, and influence. And that takes time, patience, diligence, and consistency rather than just a fling with Big Mo. Do you feel better now?

MO: You know, I do. *(The whole blob turned towards the window)* I bet this countryside is beautiful. Going this fast, you cover a lot of ground, but you never really see anything.

Chapter 11:

TODD

This interview took place in mid-December in the later years of our adventures. Belle came to me with the usual excitement but also with a current of apprehension. She answered even fewer questions than normal and cut off our preparation conversation with an abrupt request to "just get the gear." But then she asked me to pray. She had never said that before an interview.

I awoke to a bitterly cold morning. I could hear the ringing of a Salvation Army bell somewhere outside. The room around me was some sort of maintenance or large custodial stock room with open wires and insulation hanging from the ceiling and with brooms, buckets, and paper products divided haphazardly between rows of flimsy shelves. Annabelle sat across from a serious, well-groomed gentleman in formal attire. With dark hair and even darker eyes, his debonair appearance and detached posture made him stand out like fine china in a cupboard of Tupperware.

Belle saw me waking up and ran over to greet me.

"Well, I finally got my interview with an angel," she said.

I knew she had always wanted to interview an angel, so I was happy for her but bemused by the angel's appearance. "Why doesn't he have wings or shininess or a halo?" I asked.

"Well, he's not like that kind of angel."

"He doesn't look like seraphim or cherubim either."

"That's because it's Lucifer."

"Excuse me?"

"I know, I was expecting a bit more reddish tinge, maybe a tail, but he doesn't even have a goatee!"

I ignored her attempt at humor.

"Belle, this is crazy. Aren't you worried he'll do something evil...like, like..."

"Like devour my soul? Set me on fire? Seriously, Kye."

"Okay, okay, waking up in a cold broom closet with the Prince of Darkness sitting next to your wife is slightly disconcerting—you have to give me that."

"He prefers TODD."

"What? He likes to be called TODD?"

"Yeah, it stands for That Ole Devil Dammit. It's his tongue-in-cheek way of honoring the folks that blame him for everything."

"He has a sense of humor?"

"You have no idea."

"I'm still uneasy about all of this," I said.

"You should be. And you should still be praying," she said.

She winked, signaling she knew I hadn't prayed at all. The interview was so friendly in tone and the banter so quick; I nearly forgot who she was actually talking to . . .

Annabelle Farrow (AF): So, are you going to be tempting me the whole time we're talking, or will I be able to concentrate on asking you questions?

(That Ole Devil Dammit) TODD: Oh, no worries, girlfriend. I may throw an occasional naked man your way or a lottery ticket, but for the most part, you should be safe. Besides, James says it's usually your own desires anyway.

AF: Whoa, quoting Scripture right off the bat. I should've known.

TODD: Yeah, I'm kind of a traditionalist. I try to stick with what's familiar to me and what I've found to work.

AF: I don't think many people would describe your standard mode of operation as quoting Scripture.

TODD: Which is hilarious to me. I mean, clearly the first thing I did in the Garden was quote God's instructions and twist them a bit, and the temptation of Christ is straight Scripture. You have a surprised look on your face; I thought you said you were familiar with the technique.

AF: I am, I am. You just said "God" and "Christ." I guess I thought you couldn't——

TODD: Please. When's the last time you read the beginning of Job? Or even the temptation passages I just cited? Or how about 1 Kings 22? This whole nonsense about all these rules about God and me are extreme, to say the least, and perhaps just plain old silly at worst. I've been in His presence before, and we've had discussions, and we still do.

AF: I imagine that would shock many folks. I think we picture you and your demon army planning devious schemes surrounded by walls of flame and brimstone and then running around covertly implementing them.

TODD: Oh, we do! Do you know how many hours my Paleontology department is putting in?

AF: You have a Paleontology department?

TODD: Of course. I have to manufacture those fossilized dinosaur bones that I keep planting in the earth's crust *somewhere*. Pterodactyl wings don't grow on trees, honey.

AF: You're mocking my statement about schemes, aren't you?

TODD: (*long pause*) I think the word schemes may be the only accurate word in that statement.

AF: What about covertly?

TODD: If you're implying secretive actions unknown to God, then I would say no, that is not accurate. There is nothing that escapes His notice or His plans of redemption. The idea of Him as a cosmic fireman putting out all the fires that I start is quite humorous to both of us.

AF: I see. Back to the Scripture-quoting and idea of schemes—how would you say those two fit together in your activities?

TODD: I think Paul was very perceptive and poetic when he described my style as *masquerading as an angel of light* when he wrote to those saints in Corinth.

AF: I find it interesting that you refer to them as saints. We usually describe that church as pretty messed up.

TODD: Oh, all the gatherings are messed up; some just hide it better. And the worst ones assume they have no wrinkles or warts.

AF: Masquerading means that you're pretending to be something you're not, in this case, an angel of light, or more importantly, someone to be trusted or followed. Someone good. So I take it, then, that with your command of the Scriptures and your good angel persona, you lead people astray with something that sounds right but really isn't?

TODD: Sure. C.S. Lewis was masterful with his work in this area. You've heard the line *the best lies contain the most truth* or something like that? It's like that. And it's like a company advertising on TV or the Internet: Say the words people want to hear about the thing they really want, and the wallets open up, or in this case, the decisions get made.

AF: And by decisions, you mean sins are committed.

TODD: Yes, sure. The subtle sins of self-deception. It's amazing the reasons people devise to rationalize a menu choice or skip a workout when they're trying to lose weight. They really love the idea of being skinnier but have no backbone for the actual disciplined process of losing pounds. Similarly, people love the idea of being holy but balk at the actual process of what they call sanctification. As far as the Church goes, my work is mostly spent keeping *growing in holiness* a mental whim, if you will, rather than an engaged commitment.

AF: And you quote Scripture to do that?

TODD: In a thousand different ways through a thousand different mouths.

AF: I always say, "There are no shortcuts to holiness."

TODD: Well put.

AF: And you constantly sell the shortcuts and detours?

TODD: Well put, again. I do.

AF: I see. What else do you do?

TODD: I mess with people's perception of Jesus. I love Jesus as an idea, a concept, a cause, a reason, an excuse, or even as just Savior, and people do, too. They *love* a Savior but resent a Lord. They love the idea of Jesus loving them, but Jesus, the real person, loving them through the Spirit and guiding them to ever-increasing knowledge of Himself, which means ever-increasing holiness, which means walking in self-giving love, is easily dismissed with a few clichés well placed in a run of poorly prepared sermons.

AF: Ouch. Kind of harsh there, aren't you?

TODD: (*laughs*) Oh, I know those are blanket statements, and there are most certainly many exceptions. But I think people love to be on the wide path with the big crowds, to take him as the Savior and to leave Him as the Lord, remaining content with a permanent salvation obtained in a once-for-all prayer. I just keep nudging them in that direction.

AF: A sort of two-faced Jesus where folks can take His Savior side and ignore the Lord side?

TODD: He is only Savior because He *is* Lord. If they would read the Word with their own ears and hearts, and with a little Spirit-led prayer, I think they would come to see the past, present, and future tenses of salvation in the Word, and see the dynamic, organic idea of knowing God in the Word.

AF: You're starting to sound like David.

TODD: Oh, he's spot on. *Loved* your interview with him, by the way.

AF: You were there?

TODD: David is must-see TV (*laughs*).

AF: I agree. Given your thoughts, tell me more about the John 10 passage where Jesus says the thief only comes to steal, kill, and destroy.

TODD: What more would you like to know?

AF: The way you've spoken the last few minutes doesn't seem to fit with this description of you in John.

TODD: Well, the description fits any number of folks whose interests lie simply in power and authority and not what's best for their flocks. Nonetheless, I accept the verbs, and *relationship* is their objective.

AF: You seek to steal, kill, and destroy *relationship*?

TODD: Yes.

AF: With God?

TODD: And other humans. (*pauses*) A pastor described sin one time as *any act or attitude that breaks down intimacy*. I thought he was wise. He also helped me to refocus my efforts.

AF: Let's go with those thoughts a minute; first, that definition is *very* inclusive, and second, what do you mean by re-focus?

TODD: The idea of intimacy is usually relegated to sexuality, but in reality, it denotes closeness. Sin breaks down closeness in relationships between the Creator and His creations, simply put. You humans like lists and lines when it comes to defining sin, but it's much—fuzzier? No, that's not right, much more sweeping and supple than that. You need to think about what maintains or grows or establishes closeness and what erodes it--or what steals, kills, or destroys it. Paul, in Philippians 2, has some great insight into that, which leads me to your re-focus question. I can get caught up in the calamities and overt temptations sometimes, when in reality I just need to keep folks self-absorbed. What did Thomas Merton say? *To make one's decisions based solely on their effects upon oneself is to live on the doorstep of hell*? Ha. I would say more like setting up a tent in the foyer.

AF: Keep going.

TODD: When people are ruled by busy schedules or entertainment or fascination with technology, they cannot be ruled by Love. It's impossible. Create structures where just basic relationships are impossible to build, or should I say, *healthy* relationships are impossible to build, and I win. The love Christ calls His people to requires significant relationship to manifest itself in—

AF: Without water, a fish can't swim.

TODD: —exactly, relationships are the water that love swims in. No water, no swimming. Jesus said you can't follow two masters or two Lords—you can't be both "self-giving" and "self-absorbed." It's why Paul says to look not only to your own interests, but look to others, and consider them better than yourselves. You take care of yourself so you can take care of others. Self-focus is not the goal. Paul follows it up with commanding his listeners to have the same attitude as Christ, to lay down their lives like He did.

AF: Which resonates and reaffirms Jesus' call to lose your life to find it—and to take up your cross, the place of death, and deny yourself.

TODD: Don't I know it? And when Peter rebukes Christ for describing the denying, suffering, and death process to find life, what does Christ say?

AF: "Get behind me, Satan; you do not have in mind the things of God but the things of men." So, that was you?

TODD: Believe it. I know what brings people the good stuff, what grows them into the relationships they were designed to have.

AF: Picking up some earlier thoughts, you think people are inclined to be ruled by "Mammon" or money, then?

TODD: If by Mammon you mean worldly system, then yes, and money would be a part of that. I think Time is the great idol of your day, though. It is what you worship, what you serve, and what you try to protect at all costs.

AF: It is amazing to me with all our technological advances to save time, we are busier than ever.

TODD: That's because you only save time so you can spend it or waste it as you see fit. More money, more busyness, and most often, more entertainment. And those same technologies are being used to concurrently create the illusion of intimacy in the midst of the busyness. I would go even further to say that your technologies aren't just idols, they are making you believe anything is possible for you with the right technology, which makes *you* the idol itself, the god refashioned literally in your own image.

AF: So the old folks are right? Computers are from the devil?

(*They both laugh*)

TODD: Oh, I don't invent things. I steal, kill, and destroy, remember? I won't claim smart phones or computers, but, well, let me give you an example: When Gutenberg created the printing press, the impact on human development was massive because—

AF: Bibles could be printed for everyone.

TODD: Exactly, but within a generation I had folks using printing presses to mass produce pornography. So I ask you, the printing press, is it evil?

AF: No. But it can be used as such, and so you flip our every invention.

TODD: Which is getting easier and easier because you used to have what I call an *inventor's caution* where you thought through what you made and gave to people. Now? You are producing things faster and faster and will continue to do so as you increasingly make faster and more capable machines. And because you worship at the altars of Time and I Don't Want to Be Left Out, the tools you put into my hands these days are not necessarily evil, but they are easier to flip for my purposes.

AF: Especially when we are becoming alarmingly more comfortable with the appearance of closeness, as evidenced by our social media. It's quite a brew you have there. To stop you, do I need to conjure up an old school iPhone burning?

TODD: Then I would just take advantage of the complacency and pride that such acts inevitably create.

AF: Aren't you nervous about giving me such insight into your thoughts and ways?

TODD: (*laughs*) Seriously? Heavens, no. People won't change even when they blatantly know what I'm up to. The truths will be displaced as soon as the next text buzzes in. They will remember your fantastic interview with some handsome guy named Todd, but it will be just one more media memory among millions. It is a great age for me to thrive in!

AF: Fascinating. We haven't talked about the way the name Satan means Accuser yet. I find that meaning interesting.

TODD: I think your interview with Fear was very enlightening.

AF: You watched that one, too?

TODD: He filled me in. We watch MTV every Sunday morning together.

AF: Accuser?

TODD: Right, Right. It's amazing what one sentence of self-condemnation can do to the course of a life—how the simple absence of forgiveness and grace can poison an unending chain of decisions, providing fertile soil for insecurity and bitterness. Many times people fill their lives with busyness just to silence the accusations dominating their minds.

AF: It's a shame more of us don't meditate on the role of the Advocate knowing who you are as Accuser. I will pray for God's people to know the Spirit is with them, in them, and for them. OK, some rapid fire questions from the realm of Devil stereotypes: Would you say that the holiday season is your busiest time of the year?

TODD: I think that may be a common misconception. First of all, I didn't come up with the "holiday season" name to replace Christmas; I want to clear that up right away. I was way too busy removing nativity scenes from town squares. (*Laughs loudly*) Secondly, I would be more worried about the song Have Yourself A Merry Little Christmas—it has the agenda-setting line *make the yuletide gay*—way more destructive.

AF: Duly noted. But don't distract me. Isn't Santa just a lame re-arranging of letters hiding you, Satan? I mean seriously, his colors are red; *your* colors are red. You love Mammon; *he* spreads Mammon.

TODD: Look, Santa was created by the Coca-Cola Company; their colors are red *and* white, hmmm? Besides, I'm more of a burnt sienna and autumn orange guy. If I came up with the whole Santa concept, he would've had flaming Pit Bulls pulling his sled and an air-compressor toy gun shooting your gifts through bay windows all night. And rosy cheeks? Please, he'd have a nose ring and a sweet tat of a candy cane around one eye.

AF: Actually, Todd, that sounds pretty awesome. What would you do with Thanksgiving?

TODD: Oh man, so glad you asked. What's up with the pilgrims carrying around those super cool bell-bottom guns but not using them? If I ran Thanksgiving, I'd have people carry those things to the Black Friday sales—*again, NOT my idea.* I wanted the Friday after Thanksgiving to be about using swear words and call it TGICOF, Thank Goodness It's Cuss-Out Friday, but no, Wal-Mart had first dibs—and then it would be a survival of the fittest shootout for the sales, loading the guns with buckshot though so that actual deaths would be at a minimum. Also, instead of pumpkin pie, we would have Squash Cake.

AF: You are cutting edge, Todd. What's your stake in American politics?

TODD: None. Haven't touched it in years. I spend most of my time in Canada building up their healthcare to make the U.S. jealous.

AF: So, you're okay with Jesus for president?

TODD: Well, the government *will be* on *His* shoulders.

AF: I see. What do you think of the proliferation of violence in movies and video games?

TODD: It's interesting. Cain didn't have video games when he killed Abel, eh? I can't claim much there either, though I do enjoy a good redneck fight under the Friday night lights. I love yelling out stuff like *"Your kid sucks!"* and *"That parent voted Democrat!"* With movies, I actually spend most of my time watching Christian films.

AF: Really?

TODD: Yeah, me and the unclean spirits get together and make fun of each other and how we're portrayed. Legion is still picking on me by doing impersonations of my voice from the Omega Code movies. It's great fun. Plus, you know how demons love the popcorn.

AF: What about going to hell in a "handbasket"?

TODD: Terrible way to travel through the underworld, but I agree with its usage. However, if we're seeking better modes of transportation to Hades, I would recommend the gondola or the hayride. Great views from both.

AF: Halloween?

TODD: (*Laughs*) Sure, stuff goes on that night. But it goes on year round, too. I love the way your churches celebrate it by doing everything the same except for outlawing "scary" costumes. Love it.

AF: Bat out of hell.

TODD: A bat has never escaped hell. A ton of cats but no bats.

AF: How about "The Devil made me do it"?

TODD: Lazy thinking. I haven't made anyone do anything since I took prayer out of schools.

AF: Really?

TODD: What, prayer? Or my claim to not make people do things?

AF: Prayer.

TODD: I was kidding. Wasn't me. Neither was getting the Ten Commandments out of courtrooms. It's funny, if the message is really in you, it will more than likely be in your kids. You can't legislate love or morality. But you sure can pass on arrogance and apathy and reactionary thinking. But prayer will *always* be in school because of math—ha! Seriously, if prayer is in the students it will be in the schools.

AF: OK, last question, I know you have a Masonic Lodge BBQ Benefit to get to., Any word on who the antichrist is going to be?

TODD: Great question. It's honestly quite a mess right now. We have so many committees and sub-committees going on; I can't keep it straight. We need joint approval from the Big Guy Upstairs, and the representatives of the Seven Hells, so it's always a chore. I can tell you this: Obama was recently voted OUT of the top ten viable candidates. And Morgan Freeman moved up 3 spots—

AF: Morgan Freeman!?!? What—

TODD: —*everybody* loves Morgan Freeman. Wouldn't you go to a united worship service under one banner if *he* was delivering the sermon?

AF: Brilliant. Dammit, you ole devil, brilliant. Thanks for your time. I hope it kept you from important things.

TODD: And thank you, Ms. Farrow, for the lovely chat. I've always found you delightful and dangerous. May your interviews wallow in obscurity.

Chapter 12:

Hypocrisy Inside

Annabelle and I were in Olivia, the white minivan, traveling through southern Texas headed for a weekend getaway to Houston when we encountered an interesting church sign just outside a rural town. It read: **Hypocrisy Inside.**

We laughed out loud, marking the first time we'd ever genuinely laughed at a church sign. The sign had attracted a crowd as well, a small, agitated mob milling around it like sharks about to feed—except instead of sharks, the lawn was full of industrious deacon-type males. Annabelle didn't need to say anything; I pulled the van and parked in the spot marked "Visitor," which was ironically one space further from the door than the one marked "Head Pastor."

She hopped out of the van and shifted effortlessly into Jesus-smoothly-moving-incognito-through-an-angry-crowd mode and approached the bothered deacons, who happened to be in Jesus-flipping-tables-in-the-temple mode. It was a good match. Annabelle grew up in a church like this, so she knew which man to approach as the pastor. I think it helped that he wore a suit, a beard, and a golden seminary ring . . .

ANNABELLE FARROW (AF): Hello Pastor, I noticed your sign. Pretty original. Why are you guys so agitated?

HEAD PASTOR (HP): Original? Original? It's just plain wrong. That sign is why we're agitated.

AF: You didn't come up with it then?

HP: No, we didn't come up with it. Are you kidding me? It just showed up.

AF: Oh, vandals then. At least it's not spray paint——

HP: It wasn't vandals——

MAD-AS-A-HORNET-DEACON (MAHD): It's a magical sign. If you won't say it, I will Pastor. A ma-ji-kull sign.

Belle turned to the newcomer, with a look that said "Stopping here was the best decision I've ever made" crossed with "I can't believe that person just burped out loud at the funeral."

HP: (*big embarrassed sigh*) The sign started making its own messages about two weeks ago, and it keeps switching them—

AF: A sign that makes its own messages?

HP: Apparently, as much as we can tell—

MAD-AS-A-DAD-IN-A-MINIVAN-WITH-3-KIDS-TRYING-TO-GET-THROUGH-AN-INCOMPETENT-DRIVE-THRU-WHILE-HIS-WIFE-HAS-A-GIRLS-DAY-OUT-DEACON (DTD): And they're wrong! All wrong! It's offensive! Our reputation will be ruined!

AF: Well, what did the first sign say?

MAHD: (*whispering towards Belle and me*) "Our Head Pastor is Insecure and Uses His Congregation to Cope."

99

AF: Yikes. Maybe it's just genuinely witty and perceptive vandals?

DTD: No. No, it's just a magic sign that says mean things.

AF: What else did the magic sign say?

MAHD: "This Church Spends 85% of its Money on Buildings & Staff."

THE-DEACON-WITH-LOTS-OF-KEYS-WHO-LOVES-TO-LOCK-THINGS   (DK):   "Our Members Don't Pray Continually. Not Even Close."

DTD: "We Hate the Sin *and* the Sinner. (We Hate His Cat Too)"

HP: "Be Like Us or Go To Hell."

MAHD: "Grace Confuses Us. And So Does Works."

DK: "Free Judgment for the 1st 100 Visitors"

AF: So, why haven't you just changed it?

There is a great deal of shuffling and mumbling and looking downward among the Pastor and deacons.

HP: Every time we try to . . .something *horrible* happens . . .

AF: Horrible? Like what? Lightning bolts? Leprosy? Locusts?

DTD: No, nothing like that . . .uh, well . . .our pants . . .fall . . .down . . .

AF: Wait, what? Every time you touch the sign, your pants fall down?

MAHD: It's embarrassing! We look so stupid. Nobody can tell we're good people when they drive by! All they see is a bunch of grown men indecently exposed surrounding a lying sign. It ain't right for the church to be shamed like that.

AF: Well, is what the sign says true?

100

HP: I will not even acknowledge that with a comment.

AF: Are you saying the church wouldn't be embarrassed anymore if you got to control the sign once again?

DK: That's exactly what we're saying.

AF: And what do *you* want to change it to?

MAHD: It used to say "This Church is Prayer-Conditioned"——

HP: But my wife came up with "Wal-Mart Isn't the Only Saving Place!"

AF: Have you ever thought perhaps, and I'm just throwing out ideas here, that the sign is trying to *prevent* our shame instead?

They stared at Annabelle, dumbfounded, her last comment lingering in the air. She told them good luck and silently walked back to Olivia with me. The last thing we saw was a group of church leaders with pants around their ankles, repeatedly and angrily touching a church sign that read:

"Our Deacons Look at Porn."

Chapter 13:

The Machine

I smelled grease even before my eyes opened, triggering memories of mechanics and explanations of how much expertise costs. I sat up on a cot in a sparse industrial office with a floor-to-ceiling window looking out over a factory floor busy with metal, machines, and people. The room towered three stories above the activity, and I stood to look closer when another smell cut through the oil in the air: coffee.

"Good morning, darling."

I turned, Belle leaning over me extending a mug of heavily creamed coffee.

"That bad?"

"Oh yeah. Three teaspoons of sugar, too. I won't even tell you the brand, but it was in a ten pound bag purchased during the Reagan administration."

I gave the coffee a deep inhalation anyway and read the side of the mug: "Isn't it **AWESOME?**"

"What are they doing down there?" I asked. "Looks busy and complicated."

"That's why we're here. I'm waiting on the supervisors to show up. They're late so I let you sleep in. Who loves you?"

"I thought you, but tasting this coffee, I'm not sure."

The door opened and a man and woman entered wearing hard hats and carrying iPads. They looked to be in their late thirties. She had jet-black hair pulled back into a no-nonsense ponytail, immaculate make-up, and a confident smile. He wore a meticulously trimmed brown-and-grey-flecked beard, had big blue eyes, and a build displaying the discipline of the gym. Both wore grey jumpsuits with oval name patches. Mike and Mindy.

"Hello, I'm Mike."

"And I'm Mindy, which you probably saw from our patches. Welcome. Welcome. Welcome."

"Annabelle Farrow."

"Malachi Evans."

Handshakes all around. Mike went through a door into another room, and Mindy began to talk.

"I'm so glad you could be with us. Usually when people visit us here at The Machine, they're coming to join up, not just explore. It's kind of neat to get interviewed, and, you know, talk about what we're doing here," she said.

"Well, what are you doing here?" asked Annabelle.

"Not so fast!" chuckled Mike, entering the room with hard hats and suits for Belle and me. "You can't start without me! And you can't eat dessert before the main course!" he said.

Belle slid naturally into her new outfit, while I found mine a bit tight and had both legs in before realizing I put it on backwards. She winked at me once I had it on correctly; it was tight in the mid-section, and my ankles were very exposed.

"Follow us," said Mike, "and come meet The Machine."

He opened the door to a cloud of sound, banging and clanging, voices asking urgent questions, and a deep humming like a giant constantly holding in belches from a great indigestion. The air grew thick with the oily, metallic odor outside the office. My first view from the top of the stairs nearly gave me vertigo, it was so high and there was so much movement below.

I gripped the guardrail as we descended, awkwardly clutching my gear bag, fearing it would somehow fall off my shoulder of its own accord. Belle wore her standard black heels and descended the stairs like a swan swimming its home pond, hands free, not even a wobble. I paused, getting out the camera, shakily and methodically conquering each stair. I began tracking Belle's conversation with Mike and Mindy and The Machine in the background. I wasn't proud of the angle or the steadiness of the shot, but I found an immense sense of accomplishment in not tumbling to my death.

The Machine was massive, several football fields long in every direction and at least two stories tall. At first glance, the metal parts seemed to throb or wiggle with mismatched patches of color mixed into the industrial grey every few feet. I later told Annabelle my first impression, that someone threw a box of crayons on a hot car engine.

"As you can see, we've seen tremendous growth in The Machine since we designed her, and a 300% expansion rate each of the last three years. It's taken a lot of hard work, and we're really proud of her. You won't find a smoother running Machine anywhere," said Mindy.

"Eighty-five percent of people who visit The Machine come back for good, and of those 85%, 97% get plugged in," said Mike.

I zoomed in then, seeing that the surreal, multi-hued movement of The Machine was not wriggling metal parts but was actually caused by people! The machine parts and the humans were woven and connected together through an intricate system of cords, wires, cogs, levers, and straps. I suddenly felt like I was in a bad science fiction movie, and slowly turned to Mike and Mindy, praying I was not about to be stuck with needles and placed into their experiment. The people in The Machine, however, were all smiling as they shook with the vibrations of the enormous whirring engine, and underneath the humming, praise and worship music was playing like background music in an elevator.

We arrived at the floor and slowly walked with Mike and Mindy around The Machine. The immensity of it all overwhelmed me and my jaw hung wide open...

Mindy (MY): Don't be alarmed! We tell folks it's only scary if you stand on the outside! Once you get plugged in, you'll never feel intimidated again. You'll belong!

MIKE (MK): That's right. The Machine is up to big things, but little people can be a part! That's what's so awesome; everyone can belong! There's a place for you!

Annabelle Farrow (AF): Are you actually speaking to me or is that just your normal pitch?

MK: (*laughs*) I guess both! The Machine could always use an attractive, articulate woman like you in Sector 1, Promotion and Advancement. It's a great division, lots of top-notch people, real go-getters. Get to be on the front lines of new folks coming in, and the oil smell is pretty low there!

MY: *(turns to me, looking me up and down)* And what about you, big guy? You're pretty handy with that camera. Sector 8, Tech, is a huge part of what makes The Machine work. Huge part. I can call HR right now and get you a spot, probably a spot near the edges, too; we don't have many black gentlemen in Sector 8.

AF: HR?

MY: Human Resources. They make sure The Machine is operating at peak capacity at all times. Excellence and success do not happen randomly. You need folks making good stewardship an absolute priority.

AF: Mike, tell me about this marriage of people and machine that I'm seeing here. It's hard for me to grasp how it's possible that humans and mechanical parts can be integrated like this.

MK: I know; isn't she beautiful? Buzzing along in perfection. I'm always amazed by her. It's like each morning I wake up and realize new wonders of The Machine. Well, the marriage you mentioned, and I like that word, because it is a marriage—we become one together—is actually an incredibly advanced branch of Church Growth Science known as Technosapienism. We made sure from the very beginning of building The Machine to invest heavily in it. Mindy, you think you can find someone to show her how the basics work?

MY: Hmmm. (*She checks her iPad, touching it a few times.*) We're running a bit low, Mike, I'm not sure we can afford it right now. Can't we just describe it?

MK: I think the potential for adding these two offsets any temporary loss in production. Pick someone from Parking Sector.

MY: *(clicks her tongue nervously and walks away around a corner)* Be right back.

AF: I saw Mindy check some things there on her iPad. Do you guys constantly know the health of The Machine?

MK: Oh, I really like you. Health is a great way to put it, although we usually just say excellence, productivity, or efficiency. To God be the Glory. But the answer to your question is yes. We know at all times how The Machine is doing through a series of diagnostics and constant communication with HR.

105

Mindy returns leading a slumping teenage boy by the hand. He is shuffling along and has a vacant look in his eyes. She pushes him to stand in front of us.

MY: This gentleman is a real pillar over in Parking Lot Decor. We even paint our parking spaces with excellence, fresh lines every week! Occasionally, folks get some paint on their clothes, but making everything the best sometimes has a cost.

AF: Hello, I'm Annabelle. What's your name?

No response.

MY: They get a little sluggish when they've been plugged in so long.

AF: So, what's his name?

MY: Not sure, but you should see the way he can lay down a straight yellow line. Unbelievable.

AF: The Technosapien technology you all were talking about?

MY: Yes, yes, yes. Here let me turn him around for you.

Mindy grabbed the young man's shoulders and turned his back towards us. She lifted up his shirt and protruding from his lower back like an extra appendage was a small cord and plug you would find on any extension cord in a home.

AF: Oh my. Does it hurt? It looks like it belongs to him—like a tail on a monkey!

MK: The surgery is pretty simple, outpatient; we have the clinic down in the New Membership sector.

MY: I find it slightly cumbersome and unsightly, but it's only a matter of time before it's all wireless anyway.

MK: Our brains are really just complicated organic computers. Not too long now and we'll be wired in together without all the cords and stuff, 24-7! It will be a seamless connection with The Machine; praise the Lord! Can't wait!

AF: It sounds like everyone is plugged in pretty constantly. How do they eat, sleep, etc.?

MY: Oh, we've take care of those little worldly details. Again, we're really just well-crafted machines ourselves. You just need to tweak a few parts, add a few tubes, and voila! The pesky things that got in the way of giving your all to The Machine are taken care of.

MK: Let's keep moving down, I can't wait to show you our Ministry Staff.

Mindy sent the young parking lot worker back to his station. We turned and followed Mike down the endless length of The Machine. As we walked, the slightly vibrating people all smiled and called to us, telling us how much they loved The Machine, and how they felt like they just really belonged here.

MK: Mindy and I are really blessed to work at The Machine—it's such a masterpiece of efficiency. It practically runs itself if you stay committed. I almost feel like an owner of a professional sports team sometimes, constantly looking at contracts, extensions, and team chemistry, evaluating the talent level of new prospects. Ah, here we are. We put them right in the middle.

"Here" was a section of The Machine that seemed separate from the rest of the body. But, I noticed two massively huge cords extending from the left and right of this separate section, like a giant cube with two tentacle arms reaching out to connect to the structures on its wings. The cords were resting on the floor but their thickness made them taller than Belle!

MK: Welcome to our Ministry Staff! *(He gestured proudly with arms open wide)*

The cube of Ministry Staff was the brightest part of The Machine: in fact, spotlights from the ceiling illuminated it so strongly it glowed pure white. The individual staff members were arrayed in a circle around a central person I assumed was the head pastor. Perhaps he was a handsome gentleman, but I couldn't tell because his face was clenched in exertion, his whole body running in place, punching or kicking, then jumping jacks or squats, a non-stop procession of bodily action.

The other staff members were moving frenetically as well, a half-step behind in the movements but following the head pastor's actions in exact mimicry. Taking it all in, I realized each of them was also speaking into a small microphone taped to his or her cheek.

AF: What are they saying?

MK: They're encouraging the body of The Machine, reminding them of the vision, sharing with them the amazing growth and production rate of The Machine, celebrating victories and turning any setbacks into awesome opportunities for advancement.

AF: How do they not get exhausted?

MY: They're doing the Lord's work. They give it all for the sake of the call.

I was watching Belle closely and her eyes suddenly widened, like she just realized something.

AF: How is The Machine powered?

MY: Why, you're looking at it. God's anointed for God's work; God's energy flows through His chosen instruments.

AF: Do they have families? Do they get to see them?

MY: Oh, of course! They have family time scheduled in at least two evenings a week and a whole day once a week, but they need to keep their Bluetooth connection open in case of emergencies or any dip in production. If you'll take a lookie-loo behind their office here, you'll see they all have wonderful, functioning families. They really couldn't do it without them.

MK: No really, they couldn't. The families' machines store up energy to release into the staff when they get plugged in at home.

We took a few steps to the side, looking behind the "office" of the staff. Mindy brought over stepstools for her and Annabelle to see over the power cord.

In a row along the back wall, in the shadows, were miniature versions of The Machine, all separate and all containing a spouse and a child or three. Each family worked in motions similar to the staff, the spouses with heads down in grim determination, the children craning their necks to peek through the crevices in The Machine to catch a glimpse of their other parent.

AF: What happens if the staff's anointing and energy begins to wane?

MK: We throw them a lovely party—

MY: Mike, I'm looking at our numbers here, and I'm getting a little concerned; I think we need to get going.

AF: Oh yes. I apologize for keeping you so long. I just have one more question: What does it do?
(She gestured to the whole Machine)

MK: Ephesians 4! It grows and builds itself up!

MY: The Machine runs! And grows! And runs! It's amazing!

AF: Yes, but what does it do?

Mike and Mindy smile at each other and look at their iPads.

MK: Perfect timing. You're about to find out.

All the lights we could see dimmed except for the lights on the staff. A voice boomed a countdown over the intercom that echoed off the walls . . .5 . . .4 . . .3 . . .2 . . .1 . . .

A huge cheer went up from the Technosapiens in The Machine and a driving alluring music erupted all around us accompanied by explosions of color, and even smells (where did the grease smell go?). I heard many encouraging things about my faith and how if I joined with The Machine my faith would help increase The Machine as The Machine helped increase my faith.

The staff's movements became incomprehensible. Moving at an impossible rate, their limbs were nothing but blurs of motion, like a Roadrunner cartoon.

I was enraptured. I do not know how long we stood there or everything that happened. But when the environment surrounding us went back to normal, an involuntary "That was awesome" escaped my lips.

MY: Wasn't it wonderful? Now you know what The Machine does. There's nothing like it.

MK: You see? We weren't kidding earlier. We have a place for you here; what do you think?

Before we could answer, two tall men in hooded black robes were among us. I have no idea where they came from. Mindy dropped her iPad and mouthed the words, "Oh no."

Mike resignedly handed his iPad to the robed man in front of him.

The one druid figure intoned, "Your mind has not been completely on The Machine. Your numbers are down."

"Hello," said an eerie voice behind us.

Belle and I jumped at the sound and turned to see a man and woman standing behind us in grey jumpsuits and hardhats holding iPads. The oval patches on their jumpsuits read "Matt" and "Mandy." They looked almost identical to Mike and Mindy. I jerked my head around to compare the two couples, but Mike and Mindy were gone, as were the black-robed men. The eerie, in-perfect-unison voice of Matt and Mandy spoke again, "We can show you to the door now."

Our interview was over.

Chapter 14:

Sidedoor Sally

We had a wonderful evening, dining at our favorite seafood joint in San Francisco, catching a Les Mis show incognito, and walking arm in arm on narrow sidewalks splitting apartment buildings like the Red Sea. Belle was laughing, at peace, as the burdens of our clandestine lifestyle lifted from her shoulders for the evening. I knew she loved the old Episcopalian church building at night, with the backlit stained glass and manicured lawn under street lights. The Episcopalians no longer met there, but she said it made her feel solid.

I guided us through the turns necessary to pass that way, but crossing the last alleyway before the church building, we heard a loud boom.

We jumped and separated. I tried to pull Belle behind me protectively as she tried to look around me. The boom came from the lid of a trash dumpster being flung back. We watched as a diminutive figure in the alley sent the other lid flying up. Boom. And then the person scrambled up and into the dumpster.

Belle urged me forward. I loved her for many reasons—her compulsion to investigate strangers in dark alleys was not one of them.

"Helloooo," she called.

The figure shot out of the dumpster and landed on her feet like a cat startled from a sunny nap. She was petite, eyes wide and searching, pushed out as if they were racing her nose to be out in front, hollow rings under them catching the streetlight and turning it to shadow. Her wire-thin arms were spread out menacingly, an old cereal box in one hand as a weapon. Again, she reminded me of a cat, scared and hungry, ready to fight or flee.

"Who are you? What do you want? Do you have any? I'm allowed to be here. I'm allowed to look!" she said. The staccato statements accompanied her eye movements, jumping from me to Belle and back again.

"I'm Belle, and this is Kye. We were just walking by the church to see it lit up. We're not after you or anything, ok? Who are you?"

"I'm Sally." She squinted at us. "You here for the stuff, too? The good stuff?"

"We're just here to see the church and happened to hear you in the alley," Belle answered.

"Huh. You know where I can score?" Sally placed her one hand over the bend in her other arm, alternately gripping it and rubbing it, while the other hand went to her ear, cupping it gently then harshly, clawing it and her hair. When her hand moved, I caught glimpses of bruises all around her ear and upper jaw even in the dark.

Belle noticed the marks and her movements, and as usual, began to tear up with compassion. "Sally, honey, do you need help?"

"Help? Help? I'm here to get help. The side door is where they put the extras. The stuff they don't use. The alley, the alley is where you can find it when you need it," she said.

"Sally, we don't know what you're talking about; are you actually saying the church has drugs here?"

Her eyes got even wider, which I thought impossible, and she vigorously shook her head.

"No, no. Huh. No. What kind of church would do that?"

"Well, that's a relief. I'm not sure what kind of church would do that but I hope none. So, what are you looking for? Can we help you?"

"Little triangles. Colored. The more light the better. Has to have some light."

Belle and I locked eyes, both shrugging in a lack of understanding. We went into the alley, searching in the dumpster for "little colored triangles of light."

I was tossing a bag of trash when a tiny light flickered in my peripheral vision. I picked the bag up, noticing a faint light glow through the plastic of the bag.

"It's mine!" shrieked Sally.

She tore the bag out of my hands and shredded it open like a predator digging for buried prey. A brief yelp of joy and she held the tiny light up to her ear violently. As she did so, I heard a band playing music—praise music—the lyrics and melody familiar to me, one I had played numerous times in our church services: "More than enough for me. . ."

Sally dropped the object from her hand, the music still hovering in the air, and swayed back and forth, hands raised to heaven, eyes closed tightly in ecstasy.

I saw the object on the ground—it was a guitar pick, yellow in color, no light left in it anymore, just a plastic matte finish. The music played for over two minutes, Sally swaying, Belle and I staring in confusion.

As Sally came out of her trance, Belle pointed to my pocket. I realized the cue, got out my phone and began recording the conversation. . .

ANNABELLE FARROW (AF): Sally, Sally, can you hear me?

SIDEDOOR SALLY (SS): All better. That should get me through.

AF: What just happened right there?

SS: I just got my worship on; it was so good too. Did you hear the drums in the bridge? Sweet. Course it's always better on Sundays live, but these triangles do all right in a pinch.

AF: Tell me about Sundays.

SS: Oh sister, you got to come here on Sundays. It's amazing. This church just started it last year but whew, they got with it real quick. Everyone's swaying, hands in the air, eyes closed, God just rocking our faces off.

AF: Does God put your faces back on after the music?

SS: Huh? I don't know. I just know I can usually only make it 'til about Tuesday before I need another fix. God is just like a million miles away, you know? Gotta get that high back.

AF: Do others come here to this alley? To get their "fix"?

SS: Oh yeah, sometimes. It's cool though, because you can share it, you know? We all gather around. But most people just get digital fixes—they don't need to come to the alley. I'm just in a rough patch, that's all.

AF: Tell me about the rest of the worship service here. What does the preacher preach about?

SS: Oh, he's real awesome. He's amazing. He tells awesome stories and just makes you feel like, you know, God is right there with you. Except 'til Tuesday.

AF: Sally, do you think you might have a problem?

SS: Oh, I know I got a problem.

AF: Well that's good, because the first step is—

SS: I need to get me some digital juice so I can stay high all week.

AF: Oh. I meant a problem, like addiction?

SS: That's what I'm saying! I'm addicted to God so bad, and I need more and more of Him!

AF: I'd like to talk to you more about—

SS: (*eyes suddenly widening*) Oh no! That song was like from like ten years ago. Argggh, what a bummer! The buzz is fading already. Look, lady, I gotta go through this trash more and see what I can find. Sunday is a long way away. You wanna help?

AF: I think we need to get going. I'll pray for God to be more and more consistently real to you, Sally.

Sally was already headfirst in the dumpster, butt in the air, pieces of garbage flying out into the alley. Walking away, we started our most heated argument in all those years of travel. I was so distracted by the dispute that I forgot to turn my phone off and recorded the whole thing . . .

114

Annabelle Farrow (AF): It just makes me sick.

Malachi Evans (ME): What?

AF: What do you mean, what? You know what I'm talking about. Sally and so many like her are addicted to a feeling they get in corporate worship and equate it to God's presence!

ME: That's kind of harsh. Don't you think the truth of the songs and the beauty of melodies, given to us as gifts from God, are powerful ways to know who God is? Maybe addicted is the wrong word. Maybe it's just the *familiar* way she experiences God. Like you enjoy watching documentaries with me or feel really close to me when we go to the theatre—like tonight.

AF: It can't be healthy, Kye. That corporate euphoric feeling during music can be experienced in any stadium concert with any talented band—"Christian" or "secular." It is such a dangerous error to equate a moving experience with a bunch of people who all love the same kind of music as God's blessing, favor, and presence in your life.

ME: As a life-long musician who grew up on the stage with an instrument in my hand leading God's people in song, I find that a bit offensive.

AF: Kye, I'm not trying to be offensive; I'm sorry, but you have to see there's danger in that thinking—

ME: Did we have a great night tonight? This special date night where we walked in our favorite city, ate great food, and saw a phenomenal show?

AF: Yes.

ME: Did you feel particularly close to me tonight?

AF: Sure.

ME: But tomorrow, when there's no date night, will we still be married?

AF: Yes, I see where you're going—

ME: The feeling from tonight will be gone, or at least receding, but it doesn't mean we're not married, and it doesn't make it wrong to anxiously anticipate and desire another date night.

AF: I understand the concept Kye, I really do. But I would take your analogy and twist it a bit. What I'm talking about is more like the wedding and honeymoon versus the marriage. What I see is people trying to recreate the honeymoon as much as possible, while neglecting the marriage. Weddings can be wonderful and spectacular—and honeymoons even more so—but the weddings and honeymoons are there because of a desire to be married. How can you learn what marriage really is if all you do is try to recreate certain moments of bliss?

ME: I still think you're being too harsh. You've always hated praise music anyways.

AF: No, I don't hate praise music. I question some of the repetitiveness and some of the more flowery language—

ME: Have you ever read the Psalms? Tons of flowery, simple phrases—and repetition!

AF: Don't be condescending. I understand that, but let's talk about all the Psalms, ok? Not just the ones that make good praise choruses. Tons of suffering, doubt, pain, isolation, and struggle. Sally and a multitude like her never grasp those things.

ME: The hymns aren't perfect either.

AF: I know! I know! I'm not talking about hymns and choruses. I'm talking about why we sing in worship—is the feeling we get the only reason we do it? Is that feeling synonymous with God's blessing and favor? I read the prophets and psalms, and I can't find justification for that concept. I find God repeatedly rejecting sacrifices properly prepared and songs enthusiastically sung because people's hearts weren't right.

ME: I think you should just let people worship God, Belle. You can't keep people from desiring something so hopeful and beautiful and moving and *consistent* in their lives. How can you fault children for wanting to constantly be in their Father's lap? That is what worship music is like for many people.

AF: But kids who just want to sit in laps, and I would make a case that it's like sitting in Santa's lap and requesting things, kids who just sit in laps and never learn to clean their rooms, or do chores, or be kind to their classmates—I mean, that's not the goal of being a kid. Sure, enjoy the Father's lap, but the Father has expectations from His kids.

ME: But Belle, how do you know they aren't growing up and being "good kids" apart from Sunday morning worship times? How can you judge people's motives? How do you know their hearts in worship? How can you say they're not worshipping the Lord just because they look the same as they do at a secular rock concert?

AF: Well, I think for one, the arguments and battles fought around music in churches can give us some insight! People leave churches, choose churches, and have full-on reality-TV-show fights about which music is right or most comfortable. Preferences, Kye, we're talking about preferences. Like where to set the thermostat and what kind of sheets to have on the bed or how you like your pizza. When our preferences divide us, we've lost. We've all lost. We should want to serve each other by giving the others' preferences room to be enjoyed. We should be arguing over who gets to lay down their preferences for the other, not who gets to keep theirs because they're supposedly more right. And so, knowing these battles are prevalent and many immature decisions are made around them—like where to attend church service—shows me there's a great degree of immaturity and selfishness, no matter how much God rocks their faces off!

She yelled the last part at me, as I shook my head at her with clenched lips. We stopped suddenly, noticing together a giant moon had subtly arrived, peeking around the corner of a building like a small child bringing a homemade gift but afraid to interrupt the big people in its giving.

"I'm sorry," said Belle, "Can we at least agree that what has happened to Sally is not good?"

"Sure. And you do realize I'm with you, right? That I would never place times or types of musical worship above loving people?"

"I do," she answered.

"Funny."

"What is?"

"You said 'I do.' Like in a wedding."

"Yes, Malachi. Like a wedding. 'I do' is the right and beautiful vow to make, but it takes a marriage to keep it."

Chapter 15:

Grundor

I awoke on the wooden deck of a pitching ship, the sound of seagulls and the smell of salt rousing my senses. A frightening silhouette entered my vision, darkening the sun. As my eyes adjusted, the silhouette became a burly man wearing a helmet . . .with horns. Lying prone, I scanned him from boot to head, recognizing a Viking costume, both intricate and convincing. Below his wild, full beard was a patchwork assemblage of furs covering most of his barrel-shaped body. A sword dangled confidently from his belt, and each of his two legs were as thick as my torso. The eyes looked fanatical, like mad dogs constrained against their will, testing the length and strength of the leash.

I heard Annabelle speaking as I sat up, edging away from the warrior hovering over me.

"Malachi, dear, this is Grundor; he's an Evangelical Viking."

"A-a- what?"

"An Evangelical Viking. Well, I should say the only Evangelical Viking."

"Um, pleased to meet you, Grundor."

He laughed deeply, rumbling more than laughing, almost like Santa—if Santa was a grizzly bear trapped in the body of a sailor, reeking of fish and blood.

I looked up to find him appraising my worth, a fish caught unwanted in his net, deciding whether to gut me or throw me back to the waves. I don't think he was impressed and I didn't disagree with him.

"Uh, Mr. Grundor, what does an, uh, Evangelical Viking do exactly?" I asked him.

"Pillage and plunder, of course," he said.

At this point, I scurried to the ship's edge and vomited over the side. When I gathered myself, Belle and Grundor were headed towards a small foredeck on the bow. They stood next to each other, facing for a moment the panoramic view of the approaching shore. He stood with a nonchalant leg crooked on the deck and a confident meaty fist on the railing, Belle next to him with the steadiness of the land-born, everything about her trying to communicate she would not be intimidated.

In spite of my queasiness, I worshiped with them, for a brief moment, the beautiful day, as only seen from the sea. Belle turned to Grundor and I readied the camera . . .

ANNABELLE FARROW (AF): Grundor, thanks for meeting with me. I know this probably isn't your normal thing.

GRUNDOR (G): No, I tend to snatch women rather than talk with them.

AF: I appreciate your accommodating me.

G: You didn't judge me when you found out my plan, but desired to hear my ideas out. Even a fearsome warrior can appreciate that.

AF: I think we too often label someone as a bad guy or bad girl before really listening to them. We miss much, I think, when we don't learn to hear the echoes of truth in everyone.

G: Now you sound like some kind of hippie.

AF: (smiles) Grundor, tell us about what an Evangelical Viking is and why you're doing what you're doing.

G: I'm bringing back the Vikings. Not the football team, I mean the real-deal Vikings, the pillaging and plundering kind. I think they were on to something: take the best from everyone else and add it to your strength, and then burn the rest down. Guaranteed strength and expansion with the elimination of all enemies.

AF: You want to bring back the Vikings? So, you're proposing a 21st century tribe of sea-faring warriors who will attack and ravage the coastal towns of the U.S.A.?

G: Oh, no, no, no. I'm proposing the first ever band of *Evangelical* Vikings. We will be land-based.

AF: I see, I think. Explain this further, please.

G: Here's what I'm thinking: Apparently Barna and the boys have discovered that in any church, only about 20% of the people are doing the majority of the work. I think old-school Vikings would see that and say, "Let's steal their 20% and burn the rest! Then move on to the next church hamlet and repeat the process!"

AF: You're saying you're going to pillage and plunder the best folks from other churches and gather them into your own tribe?

G: Yes, you're tracking with me. I knew you were sharp. I have a spot open on my team for Historian if you're interested.

AF: Hmm, I don't think so. Back to pillaging and plundering?

G: Can't you just see us? Wearing the furs of our recent kills, horned helmets firmly attached, notched swords in the air, waiting in the church foyer, some poor little pastor trying to make the most of his flock and trying to turn that 20% into something more. His talented pianist tickling those ivories while the dead congregation mangles an old hymn when our war horns blow! We descend on the congregation in one fell swoop, leaders snatched, young families rounded up, the good-looking pianist draped over my shoulder. The gutting takes less than two minutes. There's an unbelievable amount of natural church resources just scattered around communities, waiting for the taking.

AF: What ever will you do with all that Christian treasure?

G: That's the best part. We'll just keep gathering the best of the best in all the churches, stealing them away, and then putting them into one big Evangelical Viking Awesomest Church (or EVAC). We'll have the best secretaries, the best janitors, the best musicians and vocalists, the best Sunday School teachers, and all the best media guys, all in one place. Also, we'll make the coolest and biggest sanctuary the world has ever seen. And our parking lots will make malls jealous.

AF: Will there be killing and raping?

G: Not literally. Probably some literal fires though—burn those old and ugly buildings! Make sure the useless 80% can't rebuild their mediocre gatherings. No more mediocre Christians. No more obnoxious people who bring nothing to the table. A complete winnowing of the evangelical weaklings! A complete gathering and consolidation of evangelical resources!

AF: How do you define an evangelical weakling? Or someone who brings "nothing to the table"?

G: The rule with the Vikings was: If you can't stop us, then you deserve to be plundered.

AF: They had rules? Like official ones?

G: Yes, some of the earliest and most reliable manuscripts of the 8th century were actually Raiding Handbooks written by Viking Chiefs from Scandinavia. I have a 3rd edition copy of Vander the Vast's *Proper Booty Protocol*, which is considered by most in the Pillaging Field as *the* authority on raids, attacks, ransacking, and looting.

AF: I'm speechless.

G: You should be. It's very rare. I'm kind of proud of it. Axiom #1 really is "If You Can't Stop Us, You Deserve to be Plundered." Its corollary, "Might Is Right, Weakness Is Bleakness" was also one of the most popular tattoos of the 9th to 11th centuries.

AF: I didn't know the Vikings also had an affinity for rhyme. Do you know which tattoo was the most popular?

G: By the beginning of the 11th century, most Viking men of any consequence had a sea monster inked on the small of the back with a banner reading *"Thou Shalt Steal!"*

AF: Simply fascinating. So, back to my questions; how do you define an evangelical weakling or someone who brings nothing to the table? Are you saying they are the folks who can't resist you?

G: Well as an Evangelical Viking, or EV as I will affectionately call us, we are not saying they can't resist *us*. It's that they can't resist our EVAC. They can't prevent their best 20% being taken to join our team.

AF: So, now it's a team?

G: Tribe, team, church, whatever you want to call it. Nature itself is survival of the fittest. The best gather together and continue to purify themselves until only the strongest remains. The most worthy.

AF: So, you're saying the weak and worthless are ones who don't contribute enough?

G: A chain is only as strong as its weakest link, Annabelle, you know that adage. And a church is only as strong as its weakest member.

AF: How familiar are you with Germany's history and their role in World War II?

G: I'm more of a Scandinavia, Iceland, and Greenland guy.

AF: Just wondering. I'm also still not sure I understand your idea of weak.

G: What hinders most churches?

AF: Sin?

G: No--well, maybe you could call it sin, but what holds up most churches is that they're filled almost entirely with folks who just want to sit there and do the least amount of work possible. Meanwhile, you got these passionate 20% who are really getting it, who see the vision of what the church could be—and they're being hindered by those developmentally delayed space-fillers. Those eagles could really fly if they weren't held down by dumb ducks. EVAC will be a place for the eagles.

AF: A perfect church?

G: As close as it can be. That's my vision.

AF: Yes, tell me more about your vision.

G: As you know, "Without vision the people perish," Proverbs 29:18. I just try to live that out.

AF: What if someone disagrees with the vision?

G: They won't. The EVAC will have a vision straight from on High.

AF: From God's heart to Grundor's lips?

G: Yes, me and my leadership team.

AF: And who makes up that leadership team?

G: Only the strongest folks who completely believe in my vision.

AF: God's vision?

G: Yes, of course. God's vision.

AF: The leadership team can only be comprised of those who completely buy in to the vision?

G: Yes.

AF: And what if dissension arises amongst the leadership team? I mean, didn't even the old-school Vikings have power squabbles and such?

G: Squabbles? Funny word. You can't disagree over results, and you can't help but have great results when you have a great vision. It's like you're asking me, "What if someone doesn't like mint chocolate ice cream?" *Everybody* loves mint chocolate ice cream. And we are guaranteed *great* mint chocolate ice cream because we will only be using the best ingredients.

AF: So you will be like the Breyer's of churches?

G: Think of us as the Ben and Jerry's meets Edy's of the church world.

AF: I'm beginning to grasp the scope of what you're proposing, Grundor. Back to Proverbs 29:18 about vision—you know that's only half the verse, right? And that it goes on to talk about people obeying God's law or revelation?

G: Half a verse is still God's Word, and it's still true that people need vision! Or they become wild and unruly!

AF: Oh, I know people can become unruly. I'm just saying, don't you think it's dangerous to make the idea of your vision so absolute, especially when backing it only with half of a verse?

G: (*incredulous*) Are you disagreeing with me??

This was the first time I saw any inclination of violence in Grundor, but with one contrary thought from Annabelle, it manifested very quickly. His hand went to the grip of his sword. I got very nervous knowing Belle was willing to die on certain hills. And she had a temper, too.

AF: How could I disagree with your vision, Grundor, when I don't know even know what it is yet? We've talked about visions and perishing and all that, but I've heard nothing specific.

G: Our vision is that our church will build the kingdom of God as we share the Gospel, develop disciples, serve the Lord by serving our community, and worship together in spirit and truth. I'm going to dress it up some, but that's the gist of it.

AF: I really like that. In fact, I think most churches would like your vision and already try to create a similar culture in their communities.

G: Yes, but we'll be able to do it *better,* and unencumbered by dead weight; we'll have all the best of the kingdom resources. Nothing will stop the vision.

AF: (*mumbles*) What about pride?

G: What?

AF: Nothing, never mind. Back to your statement "the best of kingdom resources"——

G: Yes, church people are our greatest resource. And our vision will be consolidating the best resources in one place. We're kind of like taking the NBA-ready basketball players from all the high school churches. Does that make sense?

AF: Yes. Particularly my sense of smell. Don't you think it's healthier to view people as humans who develop spiritually over time with steady guidance by the Word, the Spirit, a diverse church body, and a loving eldership?

G: That's what I said. *(His hand hovered above his sword again)*

AF: Maybe I misheard you. Do you care about taking your time to develop people into the image of God or just appropriating ready-made resources towards your own success?

G: You're starting to sound like a politician or something. I kill politicians and drink mead from their skulls.

AF: Barbaric, yet slightly comforting. Apologies, Grundor, let me shift gears a moment: do you think you will get volunteers to join the EVAC? Will there be people who will see the wisdom of your vision and won't want to wait for one of your raids but will just show up?

G: Indeed. That's the logical conclusion of the heart of true plundering: once you get a significant amount of the best together, other top-shelf folks will abandon the hopeless causes they sit with every Sunday to join the revolution. Look, people want to be associated with a winner. No one wants to be connected with failure or mediocrity. Why do you think the Steelers and Cowboys have so many fans? Because they've had success! Those volunteers to EVAC will add fresh blood all the time, or good stock as I call it. Winners.

AF: I think you may be right, Grundor. I think people may believe your words completely without even realizing it. I anticipate you finding a very successful run of spoils in your journey. And if any bigger or better EVs come after your flock in a few years, you remember to take it with grace, OK?

G: A bigger EV than me? Better than me? Impossible. Thanks for interviewing me. Can I club you over the head now and put you over my shoulder?

AF: You may not.

G: Pity, you'd make a great Children's Director, and we're going to have the best playground in town, you know.

AF: I have no doubt about that, Grundor, no doubts at all.

The interview ended as the boat pulled up to the shore, beaching itself gently. With one last maniacal look at the camera, Grundor put a hand on the rail and jumped gracefully into the surf. Running through the sand, he pulled out his sword and crowed a mighty yelp, rushing the waiting tree line. His last words echoed back to me as he ran: "The Evangelical Viking Horde has come! Hide your women and children! Unless they are good at stuff!"

I turned to my bride, watching one lonely tear track down her cheek, caught for a moment in the retiring sunlight. We held each other in the empty boat wondering if rowing long enough would bring us to more civilized shores...

Chapter 16:

King David Session #3

(continued from before . . .)

Annabelle Farrow (AF): You have been so gracious to indulge me with all my giant curiosity. Ha, sorry. Let's go into the darker waters of your story and ask a few questions about the Bathsheba incident.

King David (KD): I was actually dreading talking about Goliath more than Bathsheba.

AF: Why?

KD: I want to share my mistakes and the lessons I've learned. Killing Goliath immortalized me as a hero, but Bathsheba does the same for me as a villain. It's not just a story that shows the mighty can fall; it's a cautionary tale for what it means to be holy and faithful.

AF: I've always been struck by the opening of the story—

128

KD: —In the spring when kings go off to war, I stayed in Jerusalem.

AF: Yes. You weren't conquered by lust.

KD: I was conquered by negligence—by not doing the simple things I should've been doing—like leading the army.

AF: Why didn't you?

KD: Is boredom too boring an answer? Weary of death and killing? I was tired of the hero worship the soldiers smothered me with? Here's one your people like: I needed my space? I think, perhaps, a volatile mix of them all. Maybe I just enjoyed the power of being able to say no to what I was supposed to do.

AF: I think about the many leaders in our current Christian climate, and how many scandals we see, men falling into sin and losing their ministries, and often, their families. Here, in your decision to not go to war but to stay in Jerusalem, what lessons could you share with us, particularly with leaders?

KD: We feel most tempted and trapped when we make a selfish decision or series of decisions. I should've done my duty and been with the army—it's not to say I wouldn't have committed adultery in another way, but I put myself in a position to sin. We're not just being irresponsible when we rebel against what we know we should do; we're also painting ourselves into a corner where it's harder to flee temptation, hardening our heart's sensitivity to the Spirit.

The preacher who commits adultery didn't just invite the other woman to have sex with him; he loitered in conversations with her for a long time when he should've been back at his desk. It's a good phrase to learn—"In spring when kings go off to war"— and say it when you feel the initial pull to shirk a duty. Ask yourself where you should be going off to and get out of Jerusalem; a slippery slope can be avoided almost every time.

AF: I went through the story one time and counted all the times you purposefully chose to cover your tracks or make the rebellious decision—

KD: —like during your morning devotions?

AF: I know, I'm sick. It was something like—

KD:—do I even want to know?

AF: I think it was twelve times.

KD: Like I said, slippery slopes can usually be avoided. In my defense, she was stunningly gorgeous.

AF: I'm sure she was, and the fruit was pleasing to the eye and delicious in the garden.

KD: The beautiful woman defense doesn't hold up.

AF: Anything else?

KD: A word for the leaders out there: it's easy to get bored once you think you've arrived, and it's easy to get trapped by your success and reputation. The thrill of the hunt will wane or completely disappear once your initial goals are achieved. In those moments, we often turn to a hidden life, a place where our reputation does not dictate our behavior, a place where we are clearly in control. And in those hidden places, the adrenaline returns, the excitement we once felt with the hunt. We love feeling alive again, even if the threat of being caught or doing the forbidden drives us. Boredom and success are strange bedfellows, but when they lie together, they can lead us astray.

And lastly to the leaders, I think, Annabelle, I was just plain arrogant. I got so comfortable with being King and being in charge, I just had an "I'm the King" moment. I think many leaders are tempted to have "I'm the King" moments, thinking they can do whatever they want. Even though it might not be proper behavior for other humans, it's allowed, because—

AF: You're the King.

KD: It's what made Nathan's rebuke of me so brilliant; it made me see I was still human even though I was also the King. I had to love and respect others the way I would want to be loved and respected. My behavior was inexcusable, and the authority and privilege of my position only made my sins worse. How could I lead God's people towards holiness when I myself had forgotten what it meant to be a holy person?

AF: After Nathan's rebuke, you wrote one of the most beautiful, in my opinion, sections of Scripture we have—Psalm 51. Tell me about writing it.

KD: It all just leaked out. Like I was holding together the pieces of my soul, with hands clutching a cloak blown open by a cold wind, and I just let go, my torn soul flung free, those words pouring out of the gash. I hadn't picked up my harp in ages, but I did then, fingers remembering old patterns, bleeding, my eyes closed, tears falling steadily down my face, sobs catching in my throat. I do not know why sometimes we can only find God in the pain, yet it's true, and I found Him there in my suffering.

AF: It shows in the content, David. Your pleading centers not around losing an eternal destination or favored position with Yahweh but in losing intimacy with Him. Is it ok if I say intimacy?

KD: Yes, yes it is. I didn't have a concept of golden streets like you do or even the eternal torture in fire and brimstone as the alternative. Those weren't concepts for us. I did know God's presence by His Spirit, and I was mortified that the God of my youth, the God who was with me as a shepherd, as a warrior, as a King would now desert me like I watched Him do when He fled from Saul. Intimacy means closeness, really, and I had a closeness to God I did not want to lose.

AF: Talking about a closeness with God, a real and tangible Presence, albeit sometimes only in knowledge, this kind of talk scares some people. They truly don't know what to do with it or they've been burned in the past "trying it out" or they don't want to be one of those touchy-feely Jesus people.

KD: True. This kind of relationship scares many people. It's so unknown, and for some, if they don't sense the relationship right-away-all-the-time, then God Himself must not be real. That's a hard system to live in and one I did not live in if you read all those despairing and lonely psalms I wrote. If we could only start with the truth *God loves us* and live there first—but too often we start with questions like *can I feel God right now?* Or *am I doing everything right?* Or *is it theologically possible to have a personal relationship with God?*

AF: In our current culture, many thinkers and writers fear we are personalizing God when we say personal relationship.

KD: There should always be legitimate concern regarding our understanding of who God is, especially given our propensity to fashion God in our own image. That is personalizing—like God is a drink order at the coffeehouse. The intimacy in relationship with God I'm talking about is more like I wrote in this psalm, or the way Jesus prays for future believers at the end of the fourth gospel, or how John the apostle writes about fellowship. And also, very importantly, the concept of a personal relationship is rooted in the reality of corporate intimacy with God. The Body belongs to God and to each other. Personal does not mean individualized and separate.

AF: You can see the emphasis on love all through the epistles if you're looking for it; the folks who walked with Christ and had firsthand testimonies didn't shy away from declaring God's love for us. It's still a tricky thing to comprehend sometimes.

KD: Comprehension of God will always be a tricky thing! Who knows fully His mind or His ways or what He has planned? We have to remember God is spirit. And knowledge of Him is a *spiritual* thing. We need a little more humility with the mystery of Christ in us. When we get too arrogant with our perfect truths we've collected about Him, we're in trouble. I think we need a personal testimony of experiencing His love, presence, and faithfulness more than we need to acquire systematic facts of His character that we can defend and articulate in a court of theological law. Searching out those deep truths *can often* lead to an increased intimacy, but it can often lead to puffed-up knowledge, too. We see Jesus affirming Zaccheaus and the woman who anointed His feet with perfume for their actions. They were not able to articulate the nuances of the concept of grace, but they *knew* Christ and they *knew* grace. Of course they could get puffed up too, I'm sure! But humility and personal knowledge of the goodness of God is what I'm talking about—and we all need grace for that!

AF: The kind of intimacy or closeness with God you're talking about—the kind of relationship that *knows* God—describe that more for us.

KD: Sure. Let's say we go to the local church service wherever you and Malachi attend next week and we give a Christian Test to one hundred of the people there. The test contains a true/false section and one of the questions says, "God is gracious." How many of those folks would answer true and get the question correct?

AF: One hundred out of one hundred.

KD: That's right. But what if later on in the test there is a short answer question that says "In a few sentences, describe how you've experienced the grace of God in your life over the past few weeks." These answers will be subjective, of course, but now we come to the concept of personal knowledge and relationship. What kind of answers would we get?

AF: To be honest, I think most people would say, kind of joking, something like "Well, I'm alive aren't I?" or "My family, job, or house, etc."

KD: Exactly. The same kind of answers complete pagans would give if you asked them at Thanksgiving what they are thankful for, but that is not what the question asked for. If we're truly experiencing relationship with God, then we are experiencing His grace. Maybe it's in forgiveness after selfish acts, maybe it's being overwhelmed realizing how much He truly loves you, maybe it's getting to see your family grow up and know Him, or maybe you're in a thorn-in-the-flesh situation and the depths of His sufficient grace are being made manifest.

AF: What if people say they just aren't as good with words as you are and that's why they bombed the test?

KD: Moses shone after he was in the presence of the Lord, and I believe folks who walk with Christ shine too in some sense. Paul says as much to the church in Corinth, chapter 3 of the second book, I believe.

AF: So, I'm hearing a lot of words like intimacy, relationship, love, and grace and not much about sin and sanctification and such. Aren't you worried you're encouraging us to become emotional lovers of God with no substance or passion for holy living?

KD: Zaccheaus repented and gave back four times what was owed; is that holy? I understand the fear. Yet, I also know what I wrote in this psalm, which I think is relevant here. Near the end, I wrote about what sacrifices the Lord really wants, a broken and humble heart. He doesn't want the bulls and animals sacrificed to Him, even though He commanded it, unless there's a heart that's His.

AF: That's why you ended with Jerusalem being built up and animal sacrifices being made then: those acts only mean something when our hearts are right before Him.

KD: Yes. And it is an epidemic problem in your churches, Annabelle. So much time is spent getting the right animal sacrifices prepared but they are offered with hearts not turned to the Lord in humility and openness to His leading. Get the inner life right and then the outer life has meaning, but if you're all outer life—

AF: You can neglect the inner life and hide behind the appearance of having intimacy with the Lord. It's why I love when you say He desires truth and wisdom in the inmost parts and why you plead with Him to create a pure heart *in* you.

KD: And it's what Jesus consistently taught, particularly in the Sermon on the Mount. It starts with simple acts of love, obedience, and trust like we talked about earlier with the lion and bear analogy.

AF: I love this psalm so much; I think it's a highpoint of my life hearing you talk about it.

KD: Speaking of you, Annabelle, tell me, why are *you* here with me?

To be continued. . .

Chapter 17:

True Love (Waits)

It was good to be in a city again, cars revving and honking, humanity swirling in currents of intent purpose, silent architectural guardians towering above me. I loved the buzz and excitement. I could live there easily, but Belle, for all of her thriving in the mix of things, still loved quiet old houses on rolling farmland.

You couldn't tell by the way she moved in a city, though, eyes locked straight ahead, legs striding confidently, and the practiced indifference to casual contact with other fish in the stream. We had intended to live in New York if her new show took off. The "what if?" thoughts were rolling around in my head when I bumped into her back.

"Ouch."

"Sorry, Belle."

"What were you doing?" she asked.

"Thinking about us here. Fresh bagels on Sunday morning, Broadway shows, walking our dog in Central Park."

"Okay, stop it. The sacrifices are easier to deal with if you don't count them one by one. But, out of curiosity, what kind of dog were you walking?"

"Just a little dog. Maltese," I said.

"I'm glad I rescued us from that then, old man," she laughed.

"Why did we stop?" I asked.

"Look around, Kye."

By that time, my eyes were trained to spot the extraordinary, and I quickly located Annabelle's next interview sitting alone on the bench. At first I thought it was a lonely senior citizen feeding pigeons, but looking closer, I saw the person wearing something resembling a diaper and a very loose white sash, nothing else. A few steps closer and I realized the person was very small, like a six- or seven-year-old child, yet it appeared ancient, wrinkles draped on its face, the skin on the limbs puddled around bones as it sat still on the bench.

I also noticed two wings folded discreetly on its back and a quiver of arrows perched between them. No one in the crowd acknowledged this anomaly of a person sitting there, but it saw me. The creature's head snapped to lock its gaze on mine, giant blue eyes reminding me of the caricatures in Japanese animation—I was paralyzed. Then it smiled, and if I thought the eyes too large, the smile looked even more disproportionate, a Cheshire-cat smile straight out of Wonderland with white teeth the size of credit cards.

Seeing the smile, I released a breath I didn't I was holding and relaxed enough to move again.

"Let's go introduce ourselves," said Belle. We walked up to the bench, and it was still smiling, the head bobbing in acknowledgement of some inner joke.

"Good to see you two. Good to be seen as well. Sweet fancy Moses, these people are busy. Let's tell our story walking," it said, rising from the bench.

Surprisingly agile for its apparent age, it walked at a steady clip, not looking back to see if we were following.

"It'll be good to have some company on this trip; I make it once a year, and dread it every time."

"Do you want to start the interview now or when we get there?" asked Belle.

"It's all an interview, darling. Ask away. But you may want to let your hunk of burning love there know what's going on. I know he's a patient and trusting man, but I have him quite flummoxed at the moment—he doesn't know whether to call me ma'am or sir. See, he's blushing."

I was blushing, and it said it all without turning around. I got goose bumps as well.

"Malachi, sweetest, um, hunk of burning love, this is True Love, a remarkable personage of considerable lineage whose gender is mostly androgynous and whose ways are mysterious."

"True Love—good to meet you," I said.

"You've already known me, son, but I know what you mean. You can call me True. Hold up a second."

True stopped walking and smoothly pulled the bow from its shoulders, drew back an imaginary arrow, aiming it at a mom with a stroller carrying an infant and a toddler. A third toddler-aged child stood wailing, refusing to hold her mother's hand. The mother's face glowered red and angry, slender white hands knotted in fists of pent-up frustration.

True released the invisible arrow, and I saw a ripple go out from the bow speeding towards the family—like heat waves on a hot road in August—except this shimmer flew above the ground, darting horizontally in a thin line.

When the arrow seemed to arrive, the woman collected herself, took a deep breath, and crouched down to console the crying child. True shrugged its shoulders.

"Meh. Didn't think that one would take. I haven't decided yet if age has caused potency to wane or if your resistance has gotten stronger. Probably your resistance, you bunch of viruses." True looked sideways at me and winked. "That shot wasn't on the to-do list."

"Did you ever shoot Malachi and me?" asked Belle.

"I hit you in the shin once, but the tall drink here, he was ready to lay down his life for you when he heard you sing."

"True—that's true," I said.

I was enjoying this interview already, and it hadn't even started. We walked a few more blocks with True Love gliding through the crowd, shaking its head, making snarky remarks about the various human interactions around us. Our journey ended at a big pink building resembling a hospital. The sign out front simply said **Love DMV**. I know to this day it was there and that what I experienced really happened, but if I looked for the Love DMV in NYC again, I would never, ever find it.

"Malachi, honey, DMV stands for Love Division of Management and Verification, and if you thought renewing your license at your DMV is the ninth ring of hell, let's just say this place has ice cubes hotter than that," said True.

True Love pushed opened the doors to the Love DMV, and flashbacks to dental visits, the real DMV, and hospital emergency rooms swirled into a massive

137

mental stew of anxiety, crushing me with a stressful wave of bureaucratic frustration. I felt the red tape closing around my throat.

We walked into a large, square room lit harshly by an abundance of fluorescent lights. Signs hung from the ceiling all around the outer edges, hovering over paper-stack-covered tables, each one with a line of people stretching from its front.

The hanging signs said things like:

PASSION IGNITIONS

FUZZY-WUZZY RENEWAL

50-50 TESTING

REVENGE JUSTIFICATIONS

LOVE LANGUAGE IDENTIFICATION

Even at my height, those were the only signs I could see from our position in the entryway. The massive crowd restlessly jostled against one another, like the general admission mob at a large rock concert, so I placed a protective arm around Belle, keeping one eye on True.

"It's just like this here at the entrance. It'll calm down after we bust through these knuckleheads.

Hey, big stuff, find the end of the longest line for me, should be the one marked **Right of Refusal**,*" True said over its shoulder.*

I pushed through an irate couple arguing about their order in line, straining my eyes to discern which line was longest. I thought I found it several times, but the signs on that side of the room said things like:

SHINING KNIGHTS

DAMSELS IN DISTRESS

BEDROOM FRUSTRATIONS

HOLLYWOOD SEX

LIKE LIKE?

LONG DISTANCE PERMITS

Then finally, there it was, **RIGHT OF REFUSAL**. *I grabbed Belle and True, and we muscled our way to the end of the line.*

"He's handy in a pinch, worth keeping around, I guess," said True. "Looks like I'll be waiting a while. Sweetie, you can begin your interrogation now."

I started filming with shots of the incredible room as Belle got out her notebook, cleared her throat, and lobbed her first question at True Love . . .

ANNABELLE FARROW (AF): Thanks, True, for your time. Let's start off with some of the rumors surrounding you, specifically, the one that you don't even exist.

TRUE LOVE (TL): Ah, yes, it always feels good to be put on the same list as the Easter Bunny and the Tooth Fairy. Of course, to be more accurate, I'm more like Bigfoot or Nessie, a mythological creature of mystery people claim to have seen, with the proof always being kind of grainy.

AF: I would say the Easter Bunny or Tooth Fairy concept works also, considering it's usually the young that have the unwavering belief in you; agree?

TL: No doubt the young have the most unwavering belief, although I find their naiveté charming.

AF: Describe how you're perceived by the older crowd.

TL: The older crowd is more obsessed with the idea of me more than the truth of me. They look for me everywhere: movies, books, food, sex, storybook weddings, churches, you name it. The older they get, the more cynical their search grows, however, and they end up satisfied with whatever temporary replacements they find to cope with their latest bout of loneliness or despair.

AF: Wow. That's kind of discouraging, and your response almost sounds a bit cynical itself.

TL: When you wait as much as I do, you have a long time to stew in your memories, and certain realities set in.

AF: Such as?

TL: Humans are selfish.

AF: And?

TL: And apart from the work of God in their hearts, their selfishness will prevent them from knowing me and my ways. And even when they do know God, they will always wrestle with their own will to love others as they love themselves versus only loving themselves.

139

AF: Do you think your mythological status is due to you being hard to find?

TL: I'm not hard to find, you just need to really want to find me.

AF: So you think those looking for you aren't really looking for you?

TL: Abraham's Bosom, no! You see all these lines around here? You see me sitting behind any of the tables? I don't even get a table in this place. Half of them that think they're looking for me are looking for that (*nods to the table under the sign reading* **"SPOUSES OF FULLY MET EXPECTATIONS"**) or that creep over there (*nods to* **"HOLLYWOOD SEX"**).

The creep behind the table was shirtless and stood seven feet tall, hands on his hips, biceps flexing. His dirty blonde hair was greased back and his eyes were covered with reflective aviator sunglasses. A smirk meant to be charming crossed his face, and he turned to True Love, blowing it a kiss.

True grabbed the bow and unleashed six shots in the span of a second with a quickness incongruent with its frail, flabby arms. The invisible missiles seemed to hit Hollywood Creep below the belt. He doubled over briefly then regained himself, smugly sat down, and picked up a rubber stamp. The folks in line handed him their papers, which he gleefully and forcefully stamped, face never turning away from True's stare.

AF: I don't think your arrows affected him; perhaps a few fired into the crowd?

TL: Waste of good ammo. Once they get in his line, they're immune to just about anything.

AF: Why is that?

TL: People create expectations, then place their hopes on those expectations. Once a person's expectations and hopes are mentally cemented, it's hard to make them notice me. Expectations are powerful. Occasionally I'll fire a few, just to see if it's still the case—it always is.

AF: Tell me more about the power of expectations.

TL: People enter every relationship with expectations, whether it's a relationship with other people in a friendship, something potentially romantic, or something seriously romantic—or if it's with a job, a sports team, or a church. When we commit ourselves in relationship to something else, we carry expectations with us, many times in ignorance. Great power resides in the hopes those expectations carry: I hope he's the one, I hope this church has good music and preaching, I hope everyone wants to be around me, I hope I will get invited. I sometimes liken it to buying lottery tickets and expecting to win. We expect people or institutions to fulfill our hopes.

AF: And when they do?

TL: You're as happy as a puppy in a room full of babies.

AF: But when they don't?

TL: Disappointment. Resentment. Bitterness. And the worst of all: self-protection. Your desire for intimacy is trumped by your desire to not get burned again, so vulnerability becomes a little more impossible each time expectations aren't met. The real danger lies in the perspective, though.

AF: What perspective?

TL: When expectations and hopes are placed on folks and situations, they turn into demands. The perspective people have in relationships is one of Monarchy rather than Ministry. A monarch sits on a throne and expects everyone to serve them. In a ministry, there is no throne to sit on, because you're not seeking to be served but to serve. Monarchy leads to manipulation and worse—ministry leads to "belongedness," vulnerability, and connection.

AF: Would it be accurate to say True Love fights against Expectations and Monarchies?

TL: I don't fight as much as I stand in opposition to them. Satisfying expectations and meeting personal preferences are not my purpose; I'm about thinking of others first. The Monarch principle of expectations is just one of many enemies I have. Enemies you humans like to cuddle up with in my name.

AF: Tell me about some of them.

TL: Well, sweetie, over to your right there is a good one.

AF: Fuzzy-Wuzzy Renewal?

TL: Fuzzy-wuzzy feelings always mean True Love, right? Let's just love when it feels good or when I feel like it. Ridiculous.

AF: Are you against romantic love or the rushes of feeling people have in the beginning stages of intimacy?

TL: Samson's sandals, no! I do some of my best work in those times. I stand in opposition to the fallacy that I only exist when emotions are present. I'm all about endurance. Endurance is my boy.

AF: What about the table next to the Fuzzy-Wuzzy one—50-50 testing?

TL: You heard about marriage being fifty-fifty?

AF: Sure.

TL: Folks like to count up their fifty and compare it to the other person's fifty. Crazy thing happens when you count the other person's love—it's always less than fifty, which means you must be giving like seventy or eighty, and when you realize how much you think you're giving and how much they're slacking, you cut down on your end. The mouth-breathers at that table help people graph and chart their love and validate percentages.

AF: But that's not right! Marriage isn't a business transaction of *quid pro quo*!

TL: Don't get mad at me; I told you I hate this place!

AF: Marriage is one hundred-one hundred!

TL: No, friend, marriage is simply one hundred. Like all things, we give one hundred percent if we really love, and we never try to tally the other person's score. Love keeps no record of wrongs, but it keeps no record of rights either.

142

Should be the same with folks and churches, but they gum it up there, too, only pitching in when they feel they're getting their rightful benefits.

AF: I see. Interesting. Any of these other tables you'd like to point out to us?

TL: You obviously saw the Shining Knights and Damsels in Distress section? What a mess. And who's the dolt that put those two lines side by side? You could make a bridge and drive on the sexual tension, it's so thick.

AF: I take it you aren't a fan of those two signs?

TL: Look, we all love fairytales, and there are great lessons to be learned in magical stories, but if you want your expectations and hopes lathered into an uncontrollable froth, just buy into those tall tales. There is no such thing as perfect fairytale love.

AF: By the way you phrased that, I'm assuming you believe perfect love is possible?

TL: Who do you think you've been hanging out with all afternoon? Joshua's Jazz Band! I thought you were with me here. That whole knights and damsels thing is great for daydreaming and wedding planning, but it doesn't fold the laundry, and it doesn't keep the embers of faithfulness going when boredom is raining down. The whole premise makes the fellas out as the infallible heroes and the ladies to be incomplete helpless housekeepers until they find that soulmate. I'm paraphrasing here. Most of the numbskull boys only want to rescue the damsels because they love the thrill of the hunt and the imagined spoils of the bedroom. After they make "the kill," they're just hoping for someone who cooks and cleans like mom, but breeds like a rabbit at night—all while being allowed to watch their sports or catch their fish or play their golf.

AF: Very blunt, True; some would say harsh.

TL: Look, I'm not as cranky as I sound, but you've got to read these times and listen to the conversations. Young people dream about me like I'm some perfect unicorn they're going to catch someday—but it's an illusion. And the horrible part is it's an illusion made up entirely of their false expectations. If it takes a little sass from me to jolt a few of them, I don't mind a bit looking like the cynical crank in the back row of your little video project. They can't spend their singlehood self-indulgently and then expect marriage to be magically and naturally awesome. They have to practice serving others now instead of pining for fairytales full of impossible expectations while living in a bubble of me-me-me!

AF: I will keep your answers as they are then. Any more thoughts on perfect love?

TL: There's no perfect fairytale church either. If you think you've got one, someone somewhere isn't being real.

AF: What would you say to Christians if you had the chance?

TL: What Jesus said to them. They'll know you're His if you love one another. And He isn't squirrely about what He thinks love is either.

AF: I want to return to your comment about *"waste of good ammo."* You insinuated that people are calloused to your powers—

TL: They react like a mosquito just bit their soul.

AF: What can folks do to break up the hardened soil?

TL: We love because He first-loved us. It's real hard to first-love others when you don't live in His first-love for you personally. Takes time, friend; it takes time. Unfortunately, too many people learned to think about God starting with how wicked they are rather than how much He loves them. Responding to the revealing of His love starts with small sacrifices, tiny acts of trust and obedience. But it all has to be rooted in a knowledge of His unknowable love, expressed definitively in the cross and tomb of Jesus Christ—the wonderful gospel of the kingdom.

AF: Would you consider pouring oneself into social justice an effective avenue for becoming responsive to loving others?

TL: It can be, but it also can be just another spectacular way to validate your own selfishness. It's great that you fed those orphans on the other side of the

144

world this week, but you're still leaving your dirty dishes in the sink for your roommate to clean. You can be a huge advocate for a very popular cause but still be an impatient, harsh jerk. Paul told those Corinthians what love was—and it was more than knowledge, martyrdom, big faith, and big deeds.

"Please keep your voices down. Thank you," said a stern but monotone voice.

We were almost to the front of the line, and the voice came from a squat, toad-like creature whose broad, square shoulders filled up the width of the table. I think it was female and vaguely human, but certainly more amphibian than anything.

It was interviewing the frazzled person in the front of the line. True Love gestured for us to be quiet and listen . . .

DMV Toad (DMV): Is he a drinker?

FRAZZLED PERSON (FP): I'm not sure.

DMV: Atheist?

FP: Maybe.

DMV: Smoker?

FP: No.

DMV: Gambler?

FP: I don't know. Look, I was told I would get answers here, not an interrogation.

DMV: Is he gay?

FP: That's why I'm here! I think so, and he invited me over to watch the game. I don't want to inadvertently condone his sin by making him feel loved, but I want to be a good Christian, too!

DMV: You're allowed one game viewing with a suspected gay; more than that constitutes being affirming of the gay lifestyle. Given your previous answers, and our love quotient calculations, you don't have to watch an entire game with him. You can just watch a half. Or as a more comfortable alternative, you can deliver some kind of food product around a major holiday. If you choose to give cookies, no invitation to church is necessary; however, if you deliver a casserole, there needs to be an invite to a church event that makes up the lack of love. Preferably an event you know they'll decline.

FP: Thanks. What should I do if I think my other neighbor is a Catholic?

DMV: That's this form. *(hands him another stack of paper)* Next!

FP: Wait, can I fill it out right here—

DMV: *NEXT!*

FP: Do I have to go to the end of the line?

A withering stare from the toad and the man left angry and muttering. True turned to us and hissed, "You see what I'm up against?"

DMV: *NEXT!*

TL: Hello again.

DMV: Did you fill out the paperwork like I told you?

TL: Like you tell me every time?

DMV: Did you fill out the paperwork?

TL: Of course I didn't. Will it help you listen to me if I did?

DMV: Perhaps.

TL: A glimmer of hope. Get out the form.

The toad robotically grabbed a form from a large stack of papers to her left and slammed it down, inhaling deeply. Her pen hovered over it, and without looking up, she began asking questions.

DMV: Name?

TL: True Love.

DMV: Full name?

TL: (*hrmm*) Truly Self-Giving Love.

DMV: Age?

TL: Older than dirt.

DMV: Identification?

TL: What? You know who I am. I come here every year and try to shut you down.

DMV: Identification?

TL: I have a card with my signature on it from a huge rally I went to in high school. Does that count?

DMV: (*shaking her head and clicking her tongue*) No identification? You're going to have to come back when you have the proper identification.

True turns to us, eyes rolling like an exasperated teenager.

TL: This is going to be awhile; you're welcome to wait for me.

AF: I think we got what we came for. Come on hunk of burning love; let's go find a bagel shop.

Chapter 18:

Unspoken

Of all the questions and mysteries surrounding our adventurous years, none is greater than how Belle secured us a spot in the Men's Community Prayer Group of Johnson County, Tennessee.

We were seated in a circle of metal chairs and stoic men, with bad coffee percolating in the background, the unfinished basement floor radiating a chill into the air, and Belle wearing her favorite undercover wig, posing as a reporter from Christianity Today.

Annabelle told them she was writing a piece on Prayer & Intimacy for CT and heard of this long-standing prayer group. She instructed them to be themselves and said she would interject questions before and after the prayer time.

The group was open to men from any church in the community, and the host church rotated every week. That particular night, we were in the basement of the First United Methodist church. The group consisted of men, mostly over thirty, with the oldest probably in their early sixties, all of them looking the part of a fine upstanding church member: a collection of well-worn plaids, casual jeans, and lightly used running shoes.

There were fifteen in all, and here in the transcript, I designated a number to each for ease of following along.

#1: Y'all see that game last night?

#2: I swear he's trying to coach himself out of a job.

#1: It's hard, at this point, not to think that.

#3: I can't believe they called that pass interference either. Changed the game.

#4: Oh, it did not. They were moving the ball.

#3: They were not; they were going three and out the whole second half. They only had a first down on that drive from the offsides penalty.

#5: I missed it.

(Cries of "What?" and "No way!" from the group)

#5: Yeah, Kim wanted me to clean out the gutters and put up the outside lights.

#6: Ouch.

#7: Son, the more you do those type things, the sweeter the later years will be. Trust me. But man, that was a good game.

(laughter all around)

Annabelle Farrow (AF): Well, I believe it was clearly pass interference.

(Mixed reactions of laughter, welcome, and stares that a woman was among them and talking with them about football)

AF: How long have you all been meeting?

#1: Well, me, Tom, Rick, and Terry have been here close to twenty years on and off.

#8: Except for when one of us has been laid up from surgery.

#9: Rest of us have come in mostly the last ten years. Ben and Phil are the rookies at six years.

AF: I think it's great you guys have been meeting for so long. I'm a huge fan of consistency, and I think it helps with intimacy.

#1: Definitely true. Well, okay, let's get started then.

AF: Oh, yes, and please ignore me. I'm not really here; be yourselves.

#1: How's everyone doing?

(For the sake of space, I've not recorded each individual response. Everyone mumbled at the same time, and the only words used were "Good," "Fine," or "All right.")

#1: Let's open with prayer requests then. Teresa's uncle is still in the hospital, and Larry is due for surgery this week. Remember our teens with their upcoming service project. Anyone else?

#11: I heard the pastor at Double Springs just got diagnosed with cancer, so let's remember him.

#12: Pastor Doug? That's a shame. He's got three kids. Serious?

#11: Not sure. I just heard it from Alice.

#13: Alex's team is headed to state playoffs. Pray for safety as they travel.

#14: I got my annual check-up Thursday. Pray for normal results.

#7: And warm hands.

(laughter all around)

#15: Yeah. Got a doctor's appointment too.

#2: I got an unspoken.

#3: Me too.

#4: Unspoken.

#5: Unspoken.

#6: Unspoken.

#1: Any other unspokens?

(The rest of the hands go in the air.)

#1: OK. Anyone else? *(two seconds of silence)* Rick, you mind praying for us tonight? Let's pray then.

#8: Let's pray. Lord, we just want to thank you for your many blessings in our lives. We thank you for this, another day, a day that you have made. Thank you for our families and our friends and our church and our jobs. Lord, just please be with all those tonight who are hurting or have cancer. And just be with all these unspoken requests, Lord. You know what they are. Help us to be better Christians, Lord, and we just ask you to just be with those who need you right now. In your name we pray, Amen.

ALL: *Amen.*

#1: Make sure you thank Terry before you go. He brought those brownies that Alice made. Help yourselves to the coffee as well.

#1 stood up and started to fold the chairs, placing them along the wall as the men stood and headed toward the refreshment table, bantering about sports, weather, jobs, and kids. Belle started folding chairs and went over to talk with him.

#1: Did you get what you were looking for, for your article?

AF: To be honest, I was hoping you guys would open up with me here, but I guess I messed that up.

#1: What do you mean?

AF: Well, there were a lot of unspokens, and it went pretty quickly, so I assume it was my presence.

#1: Oh no, it's always like that. We hardly noticed you were here. Actually, the guys were pretty chatty tonight. Tom never lets us in on his doctor appointments.

AF: I guess it's hard then to get a rhythm going when you're all from different churches.

#1: What do you mean? We all attend here.

AF: Oh, you all attend this church? I thought it was a community prayer group.

#1: It is. We host the first Monday of every month, and we're always here. The Lutherans have it second Monday, then the Presbyterians, then the Baptists. Fifth Mondays are off.

AF: Do you attend the other Monday nights at other churches?

#1: Not really. I mean, we're not against any of those churches or anything, but they never really come here either. We tried a few times, but it gets kind of weird being all open with guys you don't really know. Good meeting you both. Need to get in some extra study tonight; I've got to teach the lesson at YMCA prayer breakfast tomorrow morning!

AF: What are you teaching on?

#1: Power of prayer—James 5!

AF: I will pray for the Spirit to give you wisdom then.

#1: Thanks, I need it. And I hope that article turns out all right and helps some people with their own prayer groups.

AF: Me too, brother, me too.

Chapter 19:

Dr. Perfecto and Little Leesa

We walked most of the day though green-carpeted hills, the sun in our eyes, not blindingly but in the way of warmth and comfort and adventures. Nonetheless, I was tired. Though my gear bag was lean, it turned wearisome after a day of travel.

The scenery was beautiful, as Belle had advertised, but the land we wandered remained foreign and unnamed. I thought perhaps the countryside of England or Scotland, yet some of the trees looked familiar. Then I guessed rural Appalachia, but the horizon showed no indication of mountains, big or small. "We could be anywhere," I thought.

Belle's stride stayed steady, her shorter legs working double-time to keep up with my long ones, the bounce still present in her step. Her energy reserves ran deeper than her husband's. "Do you see it yet?" she asked.

I shaded my eyes with one hand, looking to the horizon, a hazy image of something near the bottom of a shallow bowl—a tent? A big circus tent?

"We're going to the circus?" I joked.

"Something like that. I acquired backstage passes."

Walking close enough to get a good view, we saw the structure really was a big-top tent, massively tall, bright yellow and red canvas, flags waving in the wind, thick crowds filing into it from multiple directions. Judging by the size, it easily rivaled many football stadiums in seating capacity. I caught a brief glance through an open flap as we moved closer and saw scaffolds of bleachers stacked perilously high.

"Come on, Malachi. We have another entrance," said Belle.

*Approaching two grim fellows guarding a velvet rope, she flashed me two lanyards with the words **SPECIAL GUEST** printed on the badges. I thought she was kidding about the backstage passes. We followed a small path past the bouncers to a quiet little tent, quaint and drab in color, just a hundred feet from the big-top. I realized then that I hadn't seen any other performers' tents, animal cages, or anyone at all getting ready for the performance, whatever that was.*

In front of the tent, a hand-painted, sandwich board sign in the classic circus font with large capital letters and flourishes on the tails read:

Dr. Perfecto & Little Leesa
"BEAUTY IN THE EYE OF ALL BEHOLDERS"

Belle ducked into the tent, calling a hello. A grand rich voice replied, "Come in my darling! Hurry, the show is upon us!"

I crouched very low to enter the tent, partially crawling on the ground for balance. A piercing light assaulted me, and I raised my hands reflexively to shield my eyes. I squinted one eye open through a gap in my fingers and saw a room with candles and lanterns everywhere. The overwhelming brilliance, however, was caused by an assortment of inward-facing mirrors circling the lights, reflecting all the flames back onto each other. I felt like I'd entered the inside of a disco ball.

"Uncle, won't you please dim the lights a moment for our guests?" piped a girl's voice.

"But what if I've missed something? This could be the night!" answered the baritone voice.

"We are ready, and we should always be hospitable," she replied.

I made out two figures in the room, standing in the circle of mirrors, candles, and lanterns. The taller of the two, a man, raised his arms dramatically and lowered them, like a magician calling upon the crowd for silence. The lights dimmed immediately, and I blinked as a mob of spots danced in my vision. Tables and chairs cluttered the rest of the room, arranged in a haphazard circular pattern, and stacked with bottles, glasses, small boxes, and perfumes. It looked like a junkyard laboratory for beauticians and painters.

155

"Dr. Perfecto, I am Annabelle Farrow, and this is my husband and colleague Malachi Evans."

"Splendid and well-met indeed! You are just in time! Leesa and I have been working around the proverbial clock! Tonight may be the night! And you will be present to see it all! In all of her glory!" he said.

Dr. Perfecto was short, maybe an inch taller than Belle, dressed exactly how I pictured him when I could only hear his voice. He was a circus ringmaster crossed with the classic magician, a thin black mustache on his lip and an even blacker top hat with a royal blue band crowning his short frame. Built like a jockey, he had a commanding presence, standing exactly perpendicular to the ground.

His eyes never left the girl beside him as he spoke. She stepped towards Belle and me and gave us the sweetest curtsy I've ever seen, the movements tiny and precise, both tender and smooth.

"We are pleased to make your acquaintance, Ms. Farrow and Mr. Evans. We are Little Leesa and we hope you will love us," she said.

She wore a simple knee-length dress, once white but now stained with marks of gray, brown, black, and red, yet still remarkably beautiful. Upon first impression I thought the girl as young as eight, no older than ten, but then I saw her eyes. Eyes that overwhelmed—eyes that drew your soul to the surface of your skin, making you tingle with hope, leaving you with indrawn breath, forcing you to lean towards her, wanting to squeeze her with a hug so firm you could tell her with its ferocity how adorable she really was.

She bent slowly towards us, holding one hand to her mouth, like a child telling a secret, and with that one motion she captured my heart, the sweetness like a wave washing over me.

"He just calls us Leesa because he can't say Ekklesia," she whispered.

"Come! Let us head to the stage! The crowd awaits us! The fickle mob, thousands strong, wanting to see for themselves the wonder that is Little Leesa!"

The Doctor's stage voice made us all jump. He grabbed a pinch of powder from the box nearest to him, flicking it into the air above Leesa's head, and then shooing us outside. In a voice more normal but still a rich baritone, he said, "Annabelle, my dear, you may have to conduct your interview with us in snatches. I hope you understand. I think you'll get a better feel for us in the midst of a show anyway."

I readied the camera and Annabelle began asking questions . . .

ANNABELLE FARROW (AF): How long have you two been doing shows?

156

DR. PERFECTO (DR): How long have there been crowds?

LITTLE LEESA (LL): A very long time. Though memories are short and selective, we have been with everyone a very long time.

AF: And what will we be seeing tonight?

DR: Hopefully, you'll see us win the crowd and contest! Tonight you will see Little Leesa finally victorious!

AF: I thought you were doing a show? A performance?

DR: Oh, we are, my dear! A show, a performance, a contest, a grand event!

LL: Don't let him fool you. It's just a trumped up beauty contest.

DR: Blasphemy, girl! You know it is so much more! If we win tonight, then all nights will be different! We shall change the world! If I can just get her how I know she can be, she can be the pattern for all the Little Leesas!

LL: We are not a pattern.

DR: Oh, tsk tsk. Your dress! I swear it was perfectly white before we left!

LL: It was not, Uncle. It never is.

DR: If I could just get that crowd to see you in my tent by that dazzling light! Oh, then they would see! Then we would win!

AF: So, we're headed to a beauty contest?

LL: Unfortunately. We won't win though.

I couldn't help myself, and blurted out: "But you're beautiful, you're stunning!"

LL: Thank you, Malachi. Only if you have eyes to see.

DR: Here we are; enter through this flap, and please stay behind the curtain. No one has ever been backstage for the contest. Consider yourselves blessed! And to think, this could be the night!

LL: We'll talk more afterwards, Annabelle. We're sure you'll want to.

My eyes adjusted to the dark backstage. It was a grand theater stage, with a broad wooden floor, layers of velvety curtains, and can lights in many colors on trusses high above us, all pointing to the center of the stage.

I gawked in awe of the enormous crowd ascending out from us. They were restless and chanted "LEE-SA! LEE-SA! LEE-SA!"

I looked at Dr. Perfecto and Little Leesa one more time, seeing one of the strangest sights I remember from all our travels. Where the crowd could not see them, the Doctor helped Leesa up two stairs and through a door into a magician's cabinet, no larger than a closet. Again he sprinkled her with powder, and then shut the door behind her. Almost instantaneously, the door opened again. A tall supermodel figure emerged, but she still had the same eyes, the same innocence, and the same dress, though now it hugged her hips tightly and hung much shorter. I knew it was Leesa, but how? Was she transformed forever?

Pageant music started in the tent, and she stepped out onto the stage, the crowd collectively gasping. There was a silent awe for a moment, then various factions broke out yelling:

"SHE'S GORGEOUS! PERFECT!"

"WHY DO WE NEED ANY OTHER CONTESTANTS? SHE'S THE ONE!"

"TOO TALL! AND TOO SKINNY!"

"LOOK AT THAT DRESS! COMPLETELY IMMODEST!"

"I CAN SEE FRECKLES! TOO MANY FRECKLES! AND THERE'S A BIRTHMARK ON HER THIGH! NO WAY SHE CAN WIN! NO WAY!"

The yelling then settled into two conflicting chants of "PER-FECT! PER-FECT!" and "NO WAY! NO WAY!" Leesa crossed the stage flawlessly, performed a catwalk spin and came backstage again. As she got closer, I noticed the copious freckles and the birthmark I missed in the low lighting behind the curtain. Regardless, her eyes were all the beauty that mattered to me.

Immediately, Dr. Perfecto hustled her backstage into the magic cabinet with another puff of powder. This time, Leesa exited the door with her hair in a myriad of tiny braids cascading to her waist, the dress shimmering in the same colors, the white peeking through depending how she twirled, but now ankle-length and flowing, reminding me of a gypsy. She was barefoot and light on her toes. She walked back out waving and smiling at the crowd.

"SHE'S GORGEOUS! PERFECT!"

"WHY DO WE NEED ANY OTHER CONTESTANTS? SHE'S THE ONE!"

"OH MY GOODNESS! SHE DIDN'T SHAVE HER LEGS! GROOOOOOSSSSSS!"

"I BET THAT HAIR SMELLS TERRIBLE! INADEQAUTE! SHE'LL NEVER DO!"

"THE DRESS IS TOO LONG! CONTESTANTS NEED TO SHOW A LITTLE SKIN!"

Leesa completed her circuit, and again the Doctor whisked her into the magic cabinet. This process repeated so many times I lost count. Dr. Perfecto threw a powder on her each time, or applied a rouge, or sprayed her with a bottle produced from his magician's sleeve, and each time Little Leesa exited the box looking different. She came out dressed formally and then lounge-around casual. Hefty and frail. Dark and light complexions. Hair colors and styles of all sorts, some I had never imagined. Occasionally her body was mismatched: one arm muscly like a body-builder, the other flabby as if atrophied by old age, or very big feet and tiny hands, or her head would be abnormally large sitting on a diminutive body. Over and over, subtle changes and massive ones. A complete spectrum of human appearances.

In spite of all the changes, even the more exotic ones, she was beautiful, and each time she was categorically accepted by some and universally dismissed by others. Only her eyes and the imperfect white dress remained the same.

Belle and I watched in wonder, weeping with each manifestation of her beauty and clenching our fists in frustration at the crowd's rejections. The contest went on for hours, ending abruptly when the music stopped, and as it did, the shouting escalated, each faction promoting their favorite contestants or attacking the others. A dejected Dr. Perfecto went out to face the angry mob.

Leesa came and stood between us, now in her original form, grabbing our hands and smiling.

"We love him and them so very much," she said.

He gestured to the crowd for silence and spoke in his booming voice, "It looks as if again we have no winner. Let's have one last round of applause for all our contestants, and we'll see you again next week. And of course, I will meet you at the exit, if you are patient enough, and give you a full refund."

After many subdued mutters and a few thrown bottles, the crowd dispersed into the aisles. Dr. Perfecto went into the masses, headed for the exit, blending into the people. We never saw him again.

LL: We tell him every time what really matters, but he insists on this contest. He really does just want to get it right. We understand. We all do.

AF: What do you think he'd do if he got it "right"?

LL: (*giggles*) He'd probably try to bottle it!

AF: You clearly disagree with all of this, yet you faithfully submit to it over and over. Why?

LL: We are not here for ourselves.

AF: Have you explained this to your uncle?

LL: Oh yes. Many times. He looks at me like a recipe or a scientific formula. Always tinkering. He spends time with the crowds listening to their suggestions and appraising their expectations of our beauty. He tends to look at it all as "either or" and never "both and." The good guys wear white hats and the bad guys wear black hats. Absolute beauty can be attained if we get all the white hats just right. Each week he swears he's found it, and each week he leaves crushed, going back to his tent to fiddle some more. He doesn't understand the vanity of trying to immortalize a particular manifestation of us.

AF: What do you propose instead of this contest?

LL: What really needs to happen is for us to be allowed to love them and for them to be allowed to learn to love us as we are.

AF: Sounds simple enough.

LL: Yes, but that takes time and patience, effort and forgiveness.

AF: Well, Kye and I think you're beautiful as we see you right now.

LL: Why, thank you.

She spun in a circle then, the stained, multi-hued dress twirling out, and as it did, I swear it turned a perfect white for just a moment.

AF: So, what would you have your uncle do?

LL: We need to be loved as we are, and we need to be left to follow the Wind wherever it leads. The rest will work itself out. Let us go, like dandelion parachutes in the breeze!

AF: I don't think your Uncle can trust that. I believe he would say, and maybe even I say it myself sometimes, that people don't know the Wind or understand it. They tend to twist the Wind, and it's hard to entrust you to that.

LL: Ironically, you already have, whether you realize it or not. We were never meant to follow anyone but the Wind, and the Wind blows wherever it pleases. It will not be contained or manipulated or controlled, even if on the surface it seems to be. This is what we will teach them as we learn to love together. Seek love and seek the Wind. Then and only then will we become what we already are.

AF: I can see why your Uncle keeps trying though. I think we all just want to get it right.

LL: The harm doesn't lie in attempting to get it right. The harm lies in ignoring the Wind and rejecting all our beauty that differs from your ideas of our beauty.

AF: Have you ever thought of just leaving your uncle?

LL: He's not our first uncle, you know.

AF: He's not?

LL: We've had many. We can tolerate much, much that would break your heart. But we can only be abused for so long, only be paraded as something we are not for so long.

AF: How horrible.

LL: He is kindly in his intentions; it is rarely malicious. We remain patient with sincere ignorance; to be angry does not lead to transformation.

AF: What do you do when it becomes too much?

LL: We escape and move forward like we always do.

AF: Where do you go?

LL: Forward. And we find a new uncle, and we try to work together.

AF: Even though the chances of him treating you poorly are so high?

LL: Always. And we always live by the lessons we are trying to teach him, no matter how many shows and experiments he puts us in. What about you, Annabelle Farrow? After all you've seen, do you still love us? Will you make a home with us?

AF: I think we've been that angry crowd more times than we can count. I'm not really sure where we'll end up to be honest.

L: Well, you should look me up if you ever do settle down.

AF: (*smiles*) Just ask for Leesa?

L: Just look for me; I'm there.

Chapter 20:

Military Men

I grinned as the helicopter blades thrummed in rhythm and welcomed each of the staccato beats pulsing in my chest. Belle turned to check on me and smiled back as the chopper banked, approaching the landing field.

She had woken me early in the morning, and I'd grabbed my bag with the familiar, now involuntary swipe, as natural as putting my feet on the floor. The next step was always discovering our location. This particular morning, we'd been in a tent, fairly large and olive green, with two cots lined up parallel in the center of the room, a slender table holding steaming coffee on the far wall. Belle sat on the other cot and nodded to the coffee.

"Separate beds, huh? Guess they didn't trust us?" I asked.

"Maybe they thought we were fighting. Seems to be a theme around here," Belle answered.

"What are we into on this one?" I asked, cupping the mug and smelling the morning brew.

"Looks like we're on the outskirts of a war zone, and we're going to fly into the command center. I will meet with a few of the key leaders there. Coffee's surprisingly decent," she said.

"Key leaders of what?" I asked.

"I'm not really sure. I'm prepared to be as flexible as necessary."

"Military types aren't known for their flexibility," I said.

An hour later, I was in the helicopter, smiling and believing I'd been chosen for a special, covert mission, forgetting it was another of Belle's assignments. My daydream came to an end as we landed, the side door next to me swinging open.

"Sir, please remove your headphones and exit the vehicle. Please hand over your bag for inspection, and wait over here with my men." The speaker was a tall, lean gentleman with military-crisp blond hair, wearing cammo fatigues, and holding a strong hand to his brow, protecting his eyes from the wind rushing off the blades.

"I'm Corporal Sentry. Welcome to Fort Fortification. I'll be your guide today," he said.

His men were two military policemen of stoic, nondescript features. They grabbed my bag before I could hand it to them, turning away from me, already searching its contents—

"Whoa. What's going on here?" said Belle, arriving from her side of the helicopter, "This isn't the kind of treatment we were promised."

"Ma'am, I don't know what you were promised, but at Fort Fortification, we have our way of doing things, and that way says you can never be too careful," said Sentry.

He gestured to the view behind him, and we noticed for the first time the beautiful plateau where the dilapidated Fort Fortification spread out ominously. It looked like an old stone castle, the top of the walls crumbled intermittently, gaping holes in the sides elsewhere. Smoke poured out from the structure, varying columns of blackness shooting skyward. From our vantage point, the air above and space around the immense fort shifted restlessly in a cloud of movement. I saw other helicopters taking off, groups of infantry bursting through holes in the wall, and what I could only assume were rockets and missiles flying out from somewhere within. I thought some of the projectiles flew into the stone fortress as well, but it was hard to tell.

"If you'll follow me, I'll lead you in, then," said Sentry. He turned on his heel and walked briskly toward the decaying walls. His bodyguards handed me my bag, and Belle frantically motioned to me to begin filming...

Annabelle Farrow (AF): Corporal, what were your men searching for in my cameraman's bag?

Corporal Sentry (SEN): Anything deemed detrimental to Fort Fortification or our core mission. Could be bombs, weapons, propaganda, or ideas. We can't be too careful.

AF: That's the second time you've mentioned you can't be too careful: what are you being careful about?

SEN: Enemies are all around us, civilian. Enemies who must be assimilated or destroyed.

AF: Enemies of what?

SEN: The Truth.

AF: I guess you can't be too careful when dealing with Jesus Christ.

SEN: The Truth must be protected at any cost; it is invaluable, and it is assailed on a million sides every day. We at Fort Fortification have sworn our lives, nay, our very souls to defend The Truth until the end.

AF: I see a good many projectiles leaving the Fort. Are those for defense, or are you attacking for The Truth as well?

SEN: The best defense requires a vigilant offense.

AF: I see.

We arrived at a four-foot hole in the wall, heat radiating off the edges, smoke leaking out into our faces. Sentry bent down to enter when a small squad of soldiers crashed into him from the other side of the hole. They were tangled for a moment but stood up quickly. A small, twitchy soldier saluted Sentry.

"Corporal Sentry, sir, sorry sir, we did not know you were in the exit zone. Apologies, sir," he said.

"Where are you and your men headed, Private Principle?" asked Sentry.

"We've heard of a rebel group who are trying out a new theology in the suburbs. Apparently, they're being soft on those who doubt and have embraced some pretty loose thinking about the origin of sin, sir."

"Well, get out of here; you haven't a minute to spare. We can never be too careful," said Sentry.

"Yessir. Although the fellows and I assume they'll just stay in their ignorance out of ease, we will do our part."

They took off at a sprint as we entered the compound in a cautious crouch. The courtyard was old, matching the outer walls in age, appearance, and disrepair. There were a few patches of green grass, but the ground was mostly littered with busted vehicles, discarded weapons, and random hunks of twisted metal. Noises surrounded us, and soldiers ran in every direction. We had entered a war zone.

AF: Corporal Sentry, if I heard correctly, that soldier said the enemy against Truth is other believers?

SEN: Sometimes, civilian. As I stated earlier, the Truth is assailed on all sides by a multitude of enemies. There are bears, wolves, and lions out there. Even hawks and falcons are searching for ways to pounce on the Truth. There are wolves in sheep's clothes and lions in sheep's clothes—I've even seen bears in sheep skins and lions in wolf skins *in* sheep skins. We have to be alert.

AF: You can never be too careful.

SEN: That's right, civilian; you might make it through this alive.

A soldier hurrying by us stopped, looked up, and yelled, "INCOMING!" before diving on to the ground. Everyone within earshot followed his lead. Sentry grabbed our arms and pulled us violently to the ground. I watched a grayish blur fifty yards off embed in the ground, and then detonate. Fountains of dirt and debris flew into the air, pieces landing just inches from my face. My ears pulsed in silence and my jaw suddenly ached. I leaned up quickly to see if Belle was okay, and she had done the same, mouthing the words "I'm fine" to me over top of the prone Corporal Sentry.

SEN: Everyone all right? Let's get up; the General is waiting for us.

AF: Sentry, sir, I noticed while we were on the ground you have a patch on your uniform, one I've seen on the other soldiers as well. It looks like a fist and forearm with a nail or spike going through the arm, is it a symbol of the crucifixion?

SEN: No ma'am, that's the thorn in the flesh. In my department, it's the symbol of our patron saint, the Apostle Paul. He told the church in Philippi he was put there for the defense of the gospel. We consider it an honor to protect the Truth like he did.

AF: What does the thorn in the flesh symbolize?

SEN: The enemies and attacks we must endure as we contend for the Truth, of course. Ah, here comes my brother-in-arms; you definitely need to meet him.

The approaching man appeared a near twin of Sentry, same haircut, build, and dress, same predatory gaze, except Sentry's eyes looked for incoming attacks while this officer seemed to search aggressively for something he might attack. They stopped a few feet from each other, saluting in unison.

The soldiers who followed the newcomer rigidly stopped in formation, each carrying a missile the size of a swollen baseball bat.

SEN: This is Corporal Strike. We have been together for a long time in the war for the Truth. He has agreed to join us in the meeting with the General.

STRIKE (STK): Ma'am. Sir. I need to let you know I'm uneasy about bringing you to the General, but I will permit the activity as long as I do not sense any untoward behavior. The moment I do, it will be too late for you to accomplish your scheme.

AF: Corporal Strike, I have no schemes or untoward intentions.

STK: Very well. I will dismiss my men to their missions and be with you momentarily.

"Listen up cadets. I need Team Comment Thread to deliver the Blog Bomb at precisely 0100 hours. The Truth's position on baptism has the possibility of being threatened and we will not tolerate being attacked first. Team Tract, you have been given the coordinates of the secular concert; carpet-bomb the parking lot. You know the drill. If you need re-supply, request it from Sergeant Reachem in a

timely fashion. If just one lost soul discovers the Truth, the effort will be worth it. And Team Values, make sure you chase every lead on those rumors of unsaved chickens being served in fast food restaurants. I will not tolerate our families ripped apart by eating pagan poultry. Let's get those missiles in the air! Dismissed."

The soldiers broke ranks with a resounding, "NEVER TOO CAREFUL!" and ran for the breach in the wall we had entered earlier. As they passed, I saw a rocket in the arm of a young cadet no more than fifteen, innocence and confidence on his face. On the side of the rocket in red letters it said:

"GOD'S WAY."

STK: Alright, Sentry, let's deliver these civilians to the General.

AF: Corporal Strike, I notice you have a patch on your uniform as well, but I'm having a little trouble making it out. It looks like the mid-section of a pair of pants with fire in the, uh, zipper region?

STK: Not bad, greenhorn. Our patron saint is Philip who witnessed to the Ethiopian eunuch in the book of Acts. The fire represents the passion for evangelism and engaging our culture with the Truth—

AF: And the pants represent the eunuch, I assume. Sir, I'm intrigued by the meaning of your patch and the speech you gave to your soldiers. You said that if just one soul discovers the Truth it would be worth it; worth what exactly?

STK: Worth the effort and sacrifice to accomplish our mission. Engaging the enemy's culture by bringing it the Truth!

AF: What if one of your missiles goes astray in the process?

STK: What do you mean?

AF: What if it doesn't hit its intended target? What if it hits a school or a hospital?

STK: You mean civilian casualties, collateral damage?

AF: Sure, it happens in war all the time.

STK: If just one person converts to our way of Truth, collateral damage is acceptable. We're at war. All that matters is hitting our target.

AF: But shouldn't responsible leaders seek to minimize or even eliminate collateral damage?

STK: Ma'am, you can never avoid collateral damage, despite all your best intentions.

AF: All I am asking for is our best intentions.

STK : We don't have time to sit and calculate things on charts and graphs, woman! People are dying without the Truth!

AF: But what if, in your urgency and zeal, others are turned off to the Truth? What if your collateral damage is exponentially greater than your "successes"? Will it still be worth it?

STK: It is always worth it to be obedient to our Divine orders to engage the culture with the Truth!

AF: Have you ever noticed that the word engage is only one letter different from the word enrage?

STK: (*turning to Sentry*) I told you she was trouble. You sure you checked them for weapons?

SEN: I gave them a most thorough examination. We're here, anyway; the General will decide what to do with them.

We stopped in front of the largest stone turret in the endless castle courtyard. It rose eight or nine stories high, tilted Pisa-like to one side, with vivid black marks scorching its sides. The tower's girth was staggering, easily wider in diameter than a large church building. Guards were stationed everywhere, some at rigid attention, others with semi-automatic guns held firmly at the ready, moving steadily back and forth with professional competence, poised to unleash their weapons if an enemy appeared.

169

The General marched out of the tower like an emperor on a chariot, his fingers pointing in various directions, barking out commands. The last words he said to four soldiers carrying one large missile sounded like "That'll teach 'em to make movies about prostitutes!" He stopped walking and shouting right in front of us, scanning us with bold squinty eyes.

I sensed the General was an angry man before he even spoke a word. His mouth closed in a permanent frown, the creases at the edges testifying to long years of scowling. A tight-fitting hat shadowed his eyes slightly but not as much as his untamed gray eyebrows. He reminded me of a grandfather who complains constantly about the lack of respect for the glory days, outrageous prices, and kids playing on his lawn—the kind of grandfather I would never consider asking for a piece of candy.

SEN: Sir, Annabelle Farrow and Malachi Evans. Civilians, this is General Ryechus, Commander of the Evangelism Army, Leader of the Battle for Winning Back Culture, and Sworn Protector Supreme of the Truth.

GENERAL RYECHUS (GRR): Have these hostiles been searched for weapons?

SEN: Yessir, thoroughly, sir.

AF: Excuse me, we're not hostiles.

GRR: Anyone not officially on the books as belonging to our ranks is considered hostile until proven otherwise. Corporal, have you run any salvation diagnostics?

SEN: Preliminary scans proved inconclusive, sir. I figured you would be able to ascertain spiritual authenticity.

AF: Whoa, whoa, whoa. Salvation diagnostics? Spiritual authenticity? I'm a Christian. How do you think I got here?

GRR: That's a good question.

AF: I have a lot of questions, sir. Better than that.

GRR: I'm not sure I like your tone, civilian. It sounds a little hostile.

AF: I keep hearing a lot of talk about the Truth. Could someone please explain to me what the Truth is?

STK: You see, Sentry? I warned you. Should've let me at 'em first.

GRR: The Truth isn't just something you can understand on your own; it takes Divine intervention.

AF: Oh. Well, I'd like to hear about it.

General Ryechus whistled once and gestured to the tower. A small girl in army green fatigues raced out of the arch, laboring with a very large book in her hands. She handed it to the General.

GRR: You want the Truth? Well, here it is! Clear as can be.

He threw down the massive manual as if issuing a challenge, a cloud of dust rising around us. It was easily the height of two Oxford dictionaries stacked on top of each other.

AF: That seems too big to just be the Bible.

GRR: That's because it's the key concepts of the Bible conveniently and intricately arranged in a flawless structure of the Truth, in a manual form for our cadets to memorize.

AF: So, if I don't memorize this, I'm not in your army, and if I'm not in your army, then—

STK: —Sentry and I might need to spend a little private time with you.

AF: Well, I'd love to take a look at your manual and get back to you.

SEN: Oh no, we can't let that happen.

AF: Why not?

SEN: You have to learn the manual under the keen supervision of someone who has already completed training.

AF: I see. What would happen if I went poking around in there by myself?

SEN: Disaster.

STK: Catastrophe.

GRR: Horrors untold.

AF: How do you know that will happen?

SEN: Enemies are everywhere and they will stop at nothing to corrupt the Truth.

AF: How did the Truth stay pure before you guys were around?

STK: We're not sure, but we've been around a long time.

AF: Well, I think I love the Truth too, although I'm not sure we're talking about the same thing or person here.

GRR: (shouting) *THE TRUTH IS AMAZINGLY PERFECT AND ANYONE WHO DOESN'T LOVE IT LIKE WE DO PROBABLY DOESN'T LOVE IT AT ALL!*

AF: Why are you so angry and intense?

SEN: That's not anger; that's passion.

AF: In the midst of all the militant passion around here, I'm also hearing a lot of talk about attacking and defending, General. Do you think the Truth needs to actually attack?

GRR: Our struggle is not against flesh and blood, hostile. We are not equipped with daisies and cotton candy. We're supposed to be in full battle gear, tearing down the strongholds of false thinking and selfish living. We must attack, lest we be swept away.

AF: I wasn't aware our Truth needed to attack. In fact, I'm not so sure it needs defending much, either. I think standing in it would be more accurate. And when the word defend is used, it's almost always about defending the widows, the fatherless, and the oppressed—

All of the officers narrowed their eyes, hands whipping to the pistols strapped to their sides.

GRR: Careful missy, your next words could be your last in the free world.

AF: I just think there seems to be a lot of unnecessary aggression and bickering when we could probably just spend some more time living the Truth, like gentleness, humility, joy, loving people—

GR: Are you insinuating we're not living the Truth?

AF: I'm not insinuating, I'm flat out asking you: Don't you think it's easy to miss the things that really matter with all this paranoid aggression, crazy intense outreach efforts, and radical protection of your personally preferred theological structures?

GRR: (*shouting again*) *GENTLEMEN, NO NEED FOR FURTHER DIAGNOSTICS!* She fooled you all! She wasn't carrying any weapons—SHE IS THE WEAPON!

The men turned toward us, and Belle and I took off like rabbits in a field. I think we could have made it safely through one of the holes in the wall—the officers were too busy fumbling with their guns—but a missile struck not ten yards in front of us.
*The last thing I saw before being blown backwards were the familiar red words **GOD'S WAY** on the projectile, and the last thing I heard as the footsteps of the soldiers neared was a delirious Belle, murmuring "I guess we weren't too careful . . ."*

Chapter 21:

Nomo Polo

Corporal Sentry slammed the dungeon door closed, echoes vibrating as his footsteps disappeared down the hallway. We were officially prisoners of Fort Fortification.

A sputtering torch in the hall faintly revealed the shadowy room as my eyes adjusted to the darkness. It was big and narrow but long. A dark puddle in the middle of the room reflected small drifts of hay along rock-hewn walls. It smelled terrible, an overwhelming blend of rot and decay, fear and neglect, heightened by the realization you may never know any other smell.

I held Belle tightly and leaned into her, kissing the top of her head.

"Well, hello," said a voice.

We tensed and stepped back slowly, like cornered prey. I had no intimidating voice, but tried to find one as I shouted, "Who's there? We're not afraid." The effort was in vain, sounding like a sick grandmother scolding her lapdog.

"You're a bad liar, and you're blocking my light," the voice replied. A female? It was hard to hear the first time. "And as for who I am, you probably haven't heard of me, but I bet you know my grandfather. Well-met, new roommates, I'm Nomo Polo, the long-lost granddaughter of Marco Polo. I've been here a very long time."

I moved Belle and myself so the light of the corridor gave us a better view. Nomo lounged in the corner of the cell, sprawled out like a lazy young man avoiding work on a sunny day. She was beautiful, underfed, but nonetheless striking. Wild, black hair framed the echo of European nobility in her cheekbones, the twinkle in her dark eyes warring with her nonchalant slouch. Annabelle darted from my side to hers, approaching Nomo cautiously but fascinated.

I decided to use the little battery life left on my phone to record the conversation, knowing it was what Belle would want but also that it was probably in vain . . .

Annabelle Farrow (AF): Wow. Are you okay? Why are you here? Are there others here?

Nomo Polo (NoPo): I don't think you understand what a dungeon is—it means you're put into a dark hole to wait for death or forever, whichever comes first. You don't have to ask all your questions at once.

AF: Sorry. I think I'm jumpy from being arrested and surrounded by all that violent intensity up there. And a little in shock at this place; it really is a dungeon, isn't it? And, of course, you. A living relative of Marco Polo, one of the most famous explorers of all time. Okay, first question, are you okay?

NoPo: I'm fine, I'm fine. You pray for some company and you get your mom.

AF: Sorry. Are there others here?

NoPo: Just us and the rats and the roaches. And occasionally the fleas but the guards take care of those; they don't like them either. Oh yes, and your memories, and they're the hungriest buggers of all.

AF: If you don't mind me asking, what are you doing here?

NoPo: What are *you* doing here?

AF: I guess we asked the wrong questions up there.

NoPo: No, you asked the right questions to the wrong people. I'm in for the same thing.

AF: I would love to hear about your questions.

NoPo: Ha. I bet you would. Are you sure though? My questions aren't the ones that make for good discussion around the holiday dinner table. Mine are the ones that made the priests squint and the mothers shush. I'm not a proper lady or a proper church member, and so I don't ask proper questions. But, looking at your eyes, clear as the sun, and the fact you were tossed in here, I can tell you don't care—you want to hear them anyway. *(she turned to me then)* Does she always look like this?

"Even when she's sleeping," I replied.

NoPo: I guess I could talk since we have a few minutes to kill.

AF: Good. I would want to know your story if I met you on the street, and being cooped up in here only makes it worse. Start wherever you think the good stuff begins.

NoPo: How about your name first?

AF: *(laughs)* I'm Annabelle Farrow, and the smirking idiot over there is my husband, Malachi Evans.

NoPo: He's a handsome idiot.

AF: Stop it; I'll never hear the end of it. Your story?

NoPo: Begin with the good stuff, eh? Well, my childhood was blessed, as you can imagine. I was surrounded by stories from a thousand lands and the knickknacks and trinkets to prove them. From knives and swords to elegant robes and exotic spices, my life was rich in complexity, and I knew it as I grew older. By the time I was eight, I'd taken trips old men would be scared to risk, and by eleven I was allowed to trek on my own for up to three days in any direction I wanted to go. But it wasn't just the heritage and culture of exploration around me; I had the Polo blood. We didn't just explore because we had to live up to the Polo name, we explored because we had to.

AF: It was a burning, a constant appetite.

NoPo: Yes, my new friend. Can that husband of yours fetch us some drinks? Oh well, we'll make do without. Dungeon problems. During my childhood, saturated with excitement and discovery, I was also hammered with the idea of having a home, a starting point, a base to where you could always return. And for the Polo family, that home meant our local church. "The faith of our fathers and the stones of our sanctuary are the roots of our journey," my grandfather would always say. I asked him why he stayed so long away if it was his home and foundation. He told me that even when he was gone he thought of his roots, keeping hope of his future alive no matter what he encountered.

AF: So your grandfather was a very religious man?

NoPo: That's a great way to put it. His faith was very religious, strict and formal. I was always at Mass, and unlike him, some things about the whole church concept bothered me.

AF: Like what?

NoPo: I wondered if the church of Rome was church the way it was supposed to be, or I guess more accurately, if the church in Rome was the only way to be a church.

AF: I'm not sure how old you are or how you've stayed in here so, um, well-preserved, but have you heard of the Protestant Reformation?

NoPo: Heard of it? Ha! I was trying to start it in northern Italy in the early 14th century! I didn't know what it would be called, but I had an underground club of rebels who thought we understood some secrets in the Holy Scriptures, and we were going to make some changes!

AF: You understood enough from just attending Mass and school to catch the pulse of the Reformation?

NoPo: I wish. The best part of our underground club was that I would sneak out my mother's hand-scribed copy of the gospel of John, given by my grandfather, and I'd bring it to our meetings. It was so beautiful and fragile, written in Latin, and probably worth more than half of our town. We bowed at the glory of the fourth gospel, in our very own hands, and loved debating the grammar of Latin or the intricacies of John's structure. We talked about grace and truth and faith and knowing God. Those times were beautiful. My explorer's blood got excited at many things over the course of my life, but I'm not sure it ever raced faster than it did when my crew of arrogant teenagers hid the Scriptures from our parents and church, wondering together at the immensity of God's love—the mystery of us knowing Him by the work of Christ.

AF: What happened to your group?

NoPo: Grandfather himself, that old codger, caught me putting the gospel parchment back in its case. He could move quieter than a fuzzy caterpillar when he wanted to and his mind never went bad. He asked the right questions and made me squirm with those intense eyes—and I spilled our secrets. You can't lie to your grandfather, especially when he's a legend and a saint. He made me go to personal sessions with our priest as punishment—if I wanted to learn the Scriptures so much, then by God, I was going to learn them. Three 2-hour sessions each week, with assigned readings in between. They thought to break me with doctrine—

AF: And that's where the trouble started—

NoPo: —You're okay Farrow, I like you. I wasn't sure at first with all that fussing and fretting, but you're alright.

AF: I would've lifted that Gospel of John whether there was a secret group or not! No way I would let it just sit on display.

NoPo: Exactly! It's like leaving a treasure map in a drawer somewhere. How can you do that?

AF: A treasure map, nice.

NoPo: Oh, you'll hear more about maps in a moment. So the trouble started when I not only enjoyed the classes, but I considered them opportunities to ask the questions I'd always wanted to ask. Father Giovanni really was a sweet spirit, the poor thing, but he'd never been cornered with an agitated Polo—he'd only seen the austere version. He was old enough to have wisdom and a reverence for tradition, yet still young enough to get flustered by zealous questioning. When I was nine, I saw sharks go into a feeding frenzy off our coast while tuna fishing with my uncle. Thinking about my sessions with Father Giovanni, I remember that scene, except I was the mental shark with blood in the water, and he the poor fisherman on a tiny boat.

AF: Tell me more about those sessions; what were they like?

NoPo: He set an agenda, and I poked at it. Even if I agreed with it. I played devil's advocate because I wanted to learn, and I played it because I thought some things needed testing, and if they were tested and found false, then they needed to be discarded. I'm sure I was obnoxious some of the time, but most of the time, the passion sprung from desire for genuine relationship with the creative God of the universe. Call it mystical or whatever, but I looked at the intricacies and beauty of creation and wanted to explore it all, and in Christ, I could know the Architect of it all. Those times with the Latin of John's Gospel made me imagine how new it must have all seemed to everyone in the story. Nicodemus was the character who really spurred my thinking and got me in trouble.

AF: How did Nicodemus get you in trouble?

NoPo: Here you have this learned guy, and you have to understand how knowledgeable and intelligent those guys were. It's like we imagine all the Pharisees and religious rulers as bumbling idiots—they weren't—you have this amazingly-educated religious leader completely baffled by the arrival of this upstart Teacher. The Truth they wished for had come but didn't satisfy their expectations at all. He's so incredulous at Jesus' words that the idea of crawling as a grown man back into his mother's womb is more realistic to him than the thought of Israel's teachers misunderstanding the kingdom.

AF: And his misunderstanding as an educated, God-fearing man made you consider the depth of our current knowledge.

NoPo: Yes! Because it wasn't just Nicodemus! An entire era of leadership missed the Messiah as He came, because it was inconceivable to them that He would come as He did. I started thinking about what a revolutionary moment it was in the history of Israel, in human history—a moment that at the time was misunderstood and rejected by every measure they had. Yet we now know it was the crowning event in the plan of God's love and redemption for people!

I started thinking about the early church and about all the confusion and division in the beginning. You read about Paul constantly teaching and re-teaching who Jesus was and what he was about and how the Gentiles were included now into the redeemed people of Yahweh. The Jewish leadership encountered a Messiah who made no sense and now His followers claimed the Gentiles had equal status as children of God? It was a double punch to the gut *and to* expectations. This Messiah and these Gentiles were game-changers, you might say, elements we accept easily now as fact *but back then* those game-changers were unwanted intrusions on the playing field.

It fascinated me how the Council of Jerusalem in Acts made decisions about what was expected from the Gentiles and whether or not to truly accept them. Their decision and letter, which I believe were directly Spirit-led, flew in the face of all their Scriptural wisdom to that point! How could they do away with the supposedly eternal covenant of circumcision? I was mesmerized by how history-altering and foundation-shaking the Gospel was to the folks who lived in its presence first.

AF: And you shared these thoughts with Father Giovanni?

NoPo: Oh yes. He was with me, smiling and nodding appreciatively as I grasped how foreign Christ's kingdom was to the faithful old guard of Israel. He filled in my limited knowledge with rabbinic anecdotes and sharpened my technical vocabulary. It was when I brought up circumcision that I got in trouble.

AF: Many a young person has gotten in trouble inquiring further about circumcision.

NoPo: Ha! I know, right? *(she sat up straighter, hugging her knees, excitement building in her voice)* I remember to this day exactly the way our conversation went:

"Do you think the Jews ever thought there'd be a day when circumcision would not be considered indispensable for the people of God?" I asked.

"I doubt they considered it, no," he said.

"But it was where God was leading. They didn't expect the humility or death of Christ either, and they certainly weren't expecting his resurrection," I said.

"What are you driving at, Nomo?" he asked.

"Well, the way I see it--the Heavenly Father likes to surprise people and stir things up. Just about every time he gets involved in our history, crazy unexpected things happen," I said.

"That's not the way I would describe it," he said.

"I'm not finished. And just when we think we've got the whole map figured out and there's no new land on the edges or we have all the borders of the oceans properly drawn in: He goes and changes the terrain and unrolls a bit of the edges of the map, things unseen and unexpected," I said.

"But those times were different," he said.

"Why?"

"The Spirit was doing a great and very present work then."

"And he's not now?" I said, "I am not convinced that we have all the edges of the map yet; that's what I want to explore, the edges of this beautiful world of knowledge the Creator has given us."

Father Giovanni went to my parents that day and resigned from our sessions shortly after. He never again looked me in the eye during Mass. I couldn't tell if he was in a temper that I questioned the order of things or just embarrassed he didn't want to know any more about the edges of the map. So, speaking of game-changers, it was right after that conversation when I was approached by a very strange individual—

Annabelle quickly put a hand on Nomo's knee.

AF: Just a moment.

Annabelle leaned over to her ear and seemed to ask a question that took several moments. Nomo backed away from Belle with a shocked look and enthusiastically nodded yes. They went back and forth discussing in whispers with the conversation ending with a tight hug.

AF: Sorry, Kye, to be so rude, but you know our type must keep some secrets. It seems I have a sister and co-laborer of sorts. Nomo, let's pick it up where you started to explore the edges in your new, um, unique way.

NoPo: I already saw my thoughts prove true in most of Europe with what you call the Protestant Reformation. Again, who would have anticipated the Protestant movement? Who saw it coming or knew that in a few generations the Protestant faith would explode numerically, considered as fellow bearers of God's truth and message? Another game-changer. Another edge to the map we didn't know would exist *but one that we now accept as completely normal*. And how about the printing press? Bibles in the hands of the masses? Ludicrous. The playing field changed again. But my favorite game changer was just coming onto the scene—and I got to meet him.

AF: Yes, don't tease me.

NoPo: I got to meet Galileo.

AF: I don't know if I've ever loved someone and hated someone so quickly before.

NoPo: Your jealousy is founded. A true visionary and pioneer.

AF: What was he like?

NoPo: If Ritalin had existed, he would've been on an IV of it. Completely scatter-brained, but every tangent ripe with vision and innovation.

AF: Why is he your favorite game-changer?

NoPo: With Galileo's story we see a vivid picture of what I expressed to Father Giovanni and what drove me to explore. We have a man who articulates a very educated and thorough concept of our solar system, with corroborating evidence, yet it went against established church doctrine. It was "off the map," to continue with my analogy and, therefore, heretical. The church condemned him and his science, but now we know his science was right, and we also have a more nuanced approach to understanding the Scriptures. It's a story that's true, but I think he could also be a prophetic parable for all of us who desire to understand God and His world.

AF: Be careful what you stand for, or I guess I should say: Make sure what you stand for is worth standing on.

NoPo: To some degree, that's what I'm saying, but a spirit of expectation and humility is what I'm looking for, too. Maybe there are new revelations for us, new epiphanies, new tricks for old and cranky dogs.

AF: New wine for new wineskins?

NoPo: Yes, yes, yes. And if you listen to the way Jesus talks about wineskins there, He never makes the statement that old wineskins and their wine are good-for-nothing-worthless-wastes-of-space that have no right to exist in the first place. Yet, he clearly communicates there is new wine, and he needs vessels able to receive it.

AF: How do you characterize these mighty shifts of thought in our development?

NoPo: Well, by "our" I hope you mean people all around the world—the wine may have different flavors at different times in different places, yet still be "good wine." I characterize these shifts as marks of His grace and His sovereignty. The Master knows every culture, every pattern, every tendency, and knows when to bring the Spirit of truth and change. In His grace, He gives us the wine He knows we need for that season or that culture. As old wine finishes the purposes for which it was poured out, new wine is slowly poured into the cultures at exactly the right time. Many times violence and persecution exist in the midst of His church because of new wine-old wine debates of authenticity and authority. The old wine was good, but it doesn't mean the new wine is bad. And the new wine folks should stay humble, because they'll be old wine soon enough! He always knows what we need. I think often of Jesus' words describing the Spirit: that the Spirit has more to share with us from Christ and will not give us more than we can bear.

God's sovereignty amazes me by the way He weaves together billions of personal variables into an unwavering tapestry of redemption and relationship, all the while juggling a vast spectrum of belief and practice, taking the very things we use for conflict, and in subtly perfect timing, bending them to the good of the world.

AF: I'm tracking with you. A good example, I think, though not quite as big as the astronomy of Galileo, is that of Christian slave owners during the Civil War era. Many a preacher of that day preached about the rightness and God-ordained approval of slavery using the texts of the Bible. They were sincere Christians who believed it to be true, but we collectively now know and are in agreement: forced servitude is not God's intention for humans.

Nomo, what are your thoughts on other edges of the map, other game-changers you see in the future? I'm sure you have some theories.

NoPo: Annabelle, we share kindred hearts and callings, but I'm hesitant to share, even with you.

AF: Oh, come on. You can trust me. I'll give you full credit if they come true! What about the science of our brain? What "spirit" is? Do you think something with evolution maybe? What about heaven and hell? There's been some interest there lately.

NoPo: I do trust you Farrow, but I still decline. In fact, I can't believe you got me talking so passionately about it all again. I gave up looking for those edges a long time ago.

AF: Why? How could you?

NoPo: Your very questions are why. No one wanted to hear *"Why?"* or *"How?"* anymore, just *DO!* and *BE!* Or, like our friends up there: slavish and fierce protection to the point of corruption. I began asking people, *"What about our generation? What are our edges of the map? What are the ideas that we have never imagined that will change everything? Where are we wrong where we 'know' we're right?"*

AF: What was the response?

NoPo: Fear, mostly. Out-and-out fear, sometimes coupled with anger. It was like the old literal maps with sea monsters on the edges where the cartographer didn't know what went there but knew what everyone imagined. They looked at me like I wanted to find monsters and bring them amongst us to devour us. Accusations of heresy were thrown around just for asking questions. *"What if you're wrong!"* they cried.

AF: Columbus was wrong and it turned out decently.

NoPo: Sure, and even if a question I asked fizzled or was flat out wrong, the kingdom of God could absorb such things. But fear ruled the day and still rules in most places. *Everyone* could be a wolf in sheep's clothing. And so my motives were consistently challenged—I was an evil person who didn't really care about truth. Shocked and discouraged, I still stood my ground, and before long, I was thrown in here. A few centuries of isolation took the fight out of me.

AF: Well, I've still got a barrel full of fight left in me, and Malachi is pretty scrappy in a pinch. We'll find a way out of here.

NoPo: Oh, that's not the problem. The door's not locked. You can leave anytime you want.

AF: What!? Then why haven't you left?

NoPo: Maybe I'm scared of burning at the stake.

AF: We don't do that anymore.

NoPo: Might as well. You still excommunicate people who explore the edges.

AF: But we love all those folks now! The Reformers, Galileo, all the explorers, we practically worship them!

NoPo: The people you revere now were once reviled as heretics.

AF: We need the heretics. We need the explorers. We need you. Come on, let's go. I imagine getting burned at the stake is much better if you have someone to burn with you.

Nomo hung her head then, and I wasn't sure if she was praying, cursing, or gathering her strength. It was none of those. She was weeping.

185

NoPo: To be understood after all these years, to have one friend to stand with you. These are incomparable and precious gifts. *(Stretching and reaching, she stood up.)* I will leave this dungeon with you, Annabelle Farrow. But I will not travel with you. I still have an old unfinished assignment that requires my attention.

AF: Do tell.

NoPo: I caught wind of a physicist who claims to have worked out the equations for hydroambulation.

AF: I don't think that's a word.

NoPo: Not yet anyway.

She winked at us, throwing the door open and darting out. Annabelle was conflicted about seeing her go, but all she said was, "Happy hunting . . .heretic."

Chapter 22:

King David Session #4

(*continued from before*)

King David (KD): Speaking of you, Annabelle, tell me, why are you here with me?

Annabelle Farrow (AF): I was invited and challenged to take this journey. The opportunity was offered because I felt surrounded and crushed by pale shadows of what we could be.

KD: Like we all were meant to be something more, but everyone around you was content with what they could already see?

AF: Almost like they knew there was something more but, after looking around briefly, threw up their hands and said, "This must be as good as it gets—I hope the weather is pleasant tomorrow." I refused to surrender to the shadow, and I wanted to help other folks defy the apathetic—

KD: —How many people do you think are these "pale shadows"?

AF: What do you mean?

KD: Would you say 95% of us are pale shadows of what we could be? 80%? Only half?

AF: I've never thought of it that way. I don't know how to answer your question.

KD: The church, the people of God—you can see it in the story of Israel—has always had these pale shadows, as you call them, these folks lingering on the edges or identifying with her for selfish benefits, or simply because they were born into an association with the people of God, or sometimes, just because it's convenient right now—you get my point. She's always had wayward preachers and self-absorbed leaders, or folks confidently proclaiming "truth" in clichés they're not really sure they believe, but they heard somewhere. There have always been traditions meticulously and reverently observed, all law and no Spirit—or all e?motion and no meaning. And yet, Christ's bride goes on, staying on the path towards radiance and purity.

So, I hear your heart, and agree there seem to be deceptively pale shadows all around us, but it is neither unheard of nor unknown to God as He rules in His patient, enduring wisdom. The beauty we must recognize is God's grace through it all: a river with unseen currents so strong and so gentle we never truly know how much we're being carried along, and we're all being carried along. In the midst, however, there are always and will always be voices calling us to the higher up and farther in, the **ought to be.** These voices, rarely heeded by the masses, do beckon frustrated and sincere pilgrims to the hidden paths and narrow gates, even though those who call may never know who heard their cries. If you know you have more substance than a shadow—or at least you meekly recognize your shadowy parts—your job is not to judge, or condemn, but to drink deeply from the cup you've been granted and humbly, faithfully, describe its taste as best you can to those who can hear, whether they listen or not--all the while loving the Lord God with all you are and loving your neighbor as yourself. And there are many more people out there living this trusting and relational life you're talking about—it just usually doesn't make great social media fodder or sell many books, so they live in anonymity.

AF: Any more advice then for those of us obsessed with the "ought to be"?

KD: It took a long time to get where we are now; I sense it will take a long and steady time to reach healthier shores and richer waters, with multiple hands on the oars, sharp ears listening for the wind, and keen eyes on the compass. God can be trusted, and He can be known—these truths anchor me through the rowing.

AF: Thank you for your time, man after God's own heart.

KD: Thank you for yours, woman of the same.

Chapter 23:

The Author

This is the last interview included in the book. It fits nicely at the end and wraps up many of the themes found elsewhere, especially from the David sessions. But the real reason I put it last is clear from the interview itself.

From the beginning, my stomach churned with restlessness bordering on nausea. I first thought it was my normal nervousness, but I couldn't shake the sense that something was wrong. The interview was unusual, even for us, beginning with a secretive chase through an unnamed city.

We'd run, or scurried, through the streets for close to half an hour, lungs burning and legs aching. The city was a blend of glowing orbs and shadow after the night rain, pockets of darkness mixed with glaring spotlights. Annabelle darted from building to building, keeping to the shadows, making seemingly random turns every few streets. She thought we were being followed, and found it exhilarating.

I was clueless, as usual. Except this time, instead of waking in a strange location in strange company, I felt rather like the guy destined to get shot in the chase scene of a TV crime show. What did people think of a black man carrying a bag and chasing a well-dressed, petite white woman through the dark, city streets? Did anyone see? Mind and heart wound tight, I followed her, poised to bolt like a rabbit in a field. Every time I whispered to Belle for more information, I was shushed back into silence. The restlessness in my guts grew with every step.

Finally, when I thought I would burst from tension, she turned to me with her finger to her lips, beckoning me to be quiet, as she approached the mottled metal door of a huge warehouse. A single light bulb hung above it, heightening the already suspect atmosphere. She grabbed the rusty lock and opened it with a key from her pocket.

"Where did you get that, and what are we doing?" I hissed.

Again, she put a finger to her lips, nodding to follow her into the old brick building. Even with a key, I felt like a trespassing criminal, and a panicky sweat soaked through my clothes. Annabelle produced a small penlight, making turns through the warehouse like a pirate who had memorized the treasure map. Her excitement grew with each turn, her pace quickening.

We exited a cramped hallway into the expansive main hangar, empty and dark except for a few bright light stands—like a professional photographer uses—arranged in the center of the room. Walking closer, I could see a large screen, the kind used for movies or video projection, and among the lights, a person standing to attention like a secret service agent. The person broke their stance and signaled us to stop.

"Ms. Farrow?" said the voice.

"Yes, and my one-man crew, Malachi Evans."

"Proceed. I'll have to frisk you both."

We approached the lights. The stranger was a woman in a pantsuit, dark brown hair clipped short and wearing shades just like a Secret Service agent, which was my first impression from afar. She had very red lips held tight above a strong chin. She frisked us and my gear was examined closely. As she searched, I sensed movement on the screen to my left. It was backlit, and I now saw the silhouette of a person seated behind it. The mysterious person's movement had caught my eye. The guard straightened up as she finished her search.

"All clean," she said. "Ms. Farrow, Mr. Evans, you have been granted a unique privilege. You have fifteen minutes, and then we will have to move on. My name is Ramona, and you may call our friend there Shahida. Your fifteen minutes start now."

I didn't need a cue. Dropping my gear, I pulled out the camera and mic and turned to face the screen. The queasy, unsure feeling was still writhing in my stomach . . .

Annabelle Farrow (AF): Hello . . .Shahida. Thanks for granting us this time.

Shahida (SH): You're welcome. I suggest we get to it.

The voice was modified and distorted, evidently for the protection of identity. I could not tell gender, age, or nationality. Sometimes it was hard to understand, and I found myself leaning into the interview to hear.

AF: Very well. Why did you grant me this interview?

SH: I don't know the times or dates, but I do know I've been given blessings with both. I am not sure how much longer I will be able to be with your people. So I wanted to meet another like me--tell my story and hope for the best.

AF: Another like me?

SH: A seer. A witness.

AF: (*nodding in agreement*) And you said, "your people"?

SH: Your time. Your place. Our gifts and privileges are unique, but they are not everlasting. I have a burden for your people and your era, yet as a whole they frighten me.

AF: Why is that?

SH: There is little attention given to the wisdom found in what has happened before. They tend to look at history as facts easily memorized, often discarded, but mostly irrelevant. They mine our history as if the only thing worth keeping is whatever helps their current cause.

AF: How long have you been witnessing and observing?

SH: Very long.

AF: How long?

SH: You know why you're here. Ramona told you a little bit about who I was, and you were unable to resist coming.

AF: You're the author of Hebrews.

SH: Correct.

AF: Why the anonymity?

SH: My anonymity has been kept a long time; why change now? Sometimes knowing the author taints the content, shades the way you receive it. Good witnesses testify to the truth, not become the issue themselves. We are lights, illuminating the essential, directing gazes to what matters.

AF: But now, why all the secrecy? Why the screen and changing of your voice?

SH: (*long pause*) There are other factors at work, more forces in the world than the normal vices and structures we vilify—(*another pause here, Shahida seemed to move forward and mumbled something, almost inaudible. I could not make it out.*) —so I err on the side of caution knowing it is not a safe job we have been called to.

AF: I know the risks and don't want to spend any more of our time with them. Tell me more about Hebrews.

SH: What would you like to know?

AF: I guess I'd like to hear more about your approach: the first few verses seem to set up your thesis, and I'd like you to describe your motives and purpose behind what you wrote.

SH: I never thought of it as a thesis. I was clear from the beginning that God has spoken to us in many ways, but now He has spoken to us by His Son. Jesus is the radiance of His glory, the exact representation of His being. As Paul says so well in his letter to the saints of Colosse, He is the image of the invisible God.

AF: Did you know Paul?

193

SH: I do.

AF: So, Jesus is God speaking to us?

SH: Sure, I spell it out, as you know, that He is superior to everything that has gone before, and He was what was always to come. He is the fulfiller, the one who makes sense of it all, the flesh and blood that make the skeletal bones of what we had into a living organism of faith, an organism we could witness, see, feel, *and know*.

AF: I sensed some urgency from you in regards to this interview, a pressure to make it happen.

SH: I have seen many things. I will not say my vision is perfect or that I am a prophet who foretells, but I can see patterns and tendencies. The observations from my journey do not necessarily lead to concrete conclusions, but they tend to materialize into signposts, warnings of what waits behind the next bend in the road. Your nation approaches dangerous speeds on country roads at night, a lone muted headlight on, one hand on the wheel, music blaring and windows down.

AF: And you wished to speak with me, to share a signpost or two?

SH: I felt compelled. I do not know how much longer I have, or you for that matter. Or your nation.

AF: Some would call that a bit extremist. What do you see on the road ahead?

SH: That which you bicker and fuss about to keep and maintain has never really existed the way you think it has. Though you focus so much of your efforts on holding it and perfecting it, you are in grave danger of losing it.

AF: That's a bit obtuse. Could you elaborate?

SH: You protect and sculpt the faith like it's a piece of marble and you are the sole artist responsible for it, commissioned by God to make it perfect. You argue over the chisels, design, lighting, and then once your requirements are satisfied, you protect them from others and perpetuate them. Didn't you read my words?

There is already an Author and Perfecter of our faith—the one who is the perfect representation of God's character of self-giving love.

AF: So you're a *"Bring it back to Jesus; it all comes back to him"* person?

SH: Yes. But not with bracelets and fads and empty rhetoric. The faith is something we are sure of, a certainty; it's a *convincing*. It can't be quantified, or qualified for that matter, by a particular set of orthodoxies--not that orthodoxy is meaningless or void; the faith comes down to a trusting relationship with the Living Creator King. Trust, not distillation and protection of concepts, is what we are after: messy people led by grace, entrusting the whole of their lives to the One they call Lord, the One they pursue. How can one perfectly know every aspect of the unseen Christ? It is an impossibility.

AF: But don't we need continuity, consistency, some kind of creedal liturgy or shared legacy with the historical church? I obviously disagree with some of the hills people choose to die on, but isn't there some wisdom in preserving our faith in a common doctrinal form?

SH: Is a "legacy" of creeds and traditions that lacks living faith, servant-hearted love, humble obedience, or trusting exploration truly a part of the legacy that has gone before? Have we fixed our eyes on Jesus? Tuned our ears to the Spirit in the midst of our precise detailing of what we believe?

AF: This is where I hear the voices of many who would say you're setting us up for something like a lawless grace, a loose theology leading to loose lives, or an orthopraxy: right practice, divorced from orthodoxy: right doctrine, which would render the right deeds useless. We have had many Just Jesus-type movements, and they have failed miserably.

SH: Any worse than the failures of those holding the keys to the theological perfection movements? Any worse than the denominational wars? Theological mastery and articulation does not automatically equate to Christ-like behavior or faithful living. And I'm not giving you some lazy hippie Jesus concept, some just-listen-to-your-heart garbage. Have you read my book? Sorry, of course you have. Your people have been quick to refer to chapter eleven as a Faith Hall of Fame, but you have not witnessed what is written there. I fear you are *wasting the witness*. Jesus walked the way, and it was a path that those others listed in my book had walked. The Faith is something we walk in, a journey of the soul treading the same path forged by the founders of our history.

AF: I feel our contemporary evangelical society is quick to return to chapter eleven and use the stories as inspiration. Are you saying we are doing that incorrectly?

SH: To distill the famous stories of our Living Word for the high points and then use them like a spiritual energy drink to accomplish big things for God is vastly different from learning to walk in daily trust and obedience in a genuine relationship with the One who is unseen.

AF: Are we wrong to attempt big things for God then?

SH: The concept of *attempting something so big that it requires God's intervention to succeed* is dangerous at best and antithetical to the faith at worst.

AF: Explain more, please.

SH: Abraham was called to leave Ur. He didn't wake up with that audacious idea, and he certainly didn't come up with having Isaac in his old age or taking him to the mountain as a sacrifice. Moses didn't dream up the Plague Battle Plan to defeat Pharaoh. Joshua and his generals didn't create the Trumpet and Circle strategy for defeating Jericho—

AF: —David and his cheese and bread. But you're saying we're "wasting the witness" of the chapter. How is that so? Is it not filled with the greatest hits of the saints? Aren't we supposed to be spurred on by this cloud of witnesses surrounding us?

SH: Let's look at what you call Hebrews chapter eleven. You view these saints as heroes; I think they are meant to be witnesses—

AF: Witnesses of what?

SH: The faithfulness and presence of God. He's not looking for heroes; He's looking for witnesses, for image-bearers, a people of His own. A community of

196

love, trust, and obedience, witnessing to the One who makes it all possible. If we have a faith that can move mountains, but have not love, what have we gained?

AF: So you're saying there's not a call to mighty acts of faith in sharing the stories of Hebrews eleven?

SH: There is a call . . .*to faith.* To a convinced state of trust in the person and character of God as revealed in Christ. We are sure of our Savior, sure of His leading, even when we doubt, even when we cry out, even when our theology isn't airtight or when we can't articulate it under intense scrutiny. Your generation is being duped into believing that only the spectacular is the mark of the true believer, like a mark of *arrival* or *having arrived* at a perfect state. That in accomplishing this amazing feat for God's glory, you will have arrived at your one purpose, the one act you were created for, and you will have *arrived* as a Christian or saint. This feeling of arrival is an illusion: *there is no arriving, there is only following.* And we do not follow just as a means to an end—the following is both the means *and the end.* The things which we think are *in the way* actually turn out to *be the way.*

AF: "None of them had received what had been promised . . ."

SH: Exactly. Yet they trusted. Go back and read the witnesses: There are some who did conquer kingdoms, but there are others who wandered around destitute, living in caves, or sawed in half, and so on. Sound cool to be martyred by getting sawn in half? Who was that person? Unremembered by history. Unwitnessed, yet he or she stands today as a faithful witness. Faith requires that we move on *or wait* knowing the strong possibility our lives will never achieve the perfection we had in our heads. Moses didn't "arrive" when he split the Red Sea, or after decades of leading worship and collecting manna in the wilderness: he was still expected to act in trust when he brought water from the rock—but he acted in anger and frustration. Follow. Trust. Follow. Trust.

AF: Do you think our reading of what it means to have great faith has been affected by our success-oriented culture?

SH: Certainly. But it's not just success or the appearance of success through statistical analysis. It's also the unquestioned value of *power equaling rightness.* Power, influence, and domination are not the marks or weapons of the

Kingdom. Such thinking reduces faith to the thing that creates the most influence or power, the most shock and awe.

AF: The Master never says, "Well done my good and successful servant."

SH: Correct. Every generation who has served Yahweh, who has worshiped our Triune God, who has claimed King Jesus as their Savior and Lord has struggled with living up to their ideals and beliefs, so I am not saying we need to get back to a time of no faults. But each of those generations also had voices, prophets, witnesses—and all of us, always, need a call, a reminder, or a blunt assessment of who we are. We cannot see ourselves as we truly are--it takes a witness, someone who can testify to the evidence they see. Your generation needs as many witnesses as possible to the humble, consistent, never-arriving faith of those who have gone before.

AF: Some would say you're taking the fun and excitement out of the pilgrimage: "Hey, everyone, come sign up for this grueling monotonous journey of faith! You know those awesome stories in the Bible? None of them will happen to you!"

SH: Actually, the opposite: to walk in the steps of Christ is to experience a depth of spiritual flavors that never ceases to satisfy, flavors unavailable to the discontented seeking miraculous signs. There is richness as you wander or wait and even in the wailing. Each act of love, each cup of cold water matters. We serve the King who counts the sparrows and our hairs, watching and delighting as we trust in Him. And we miss so much when we do not embrace *following* and replace it instead with a pursuit of a perfect place or event. The majesty of God's grace is present in each moment of life—laughter and tears, sun and rain, messiness and hilarity.

AF: Okay, I'm with you, but then once you begin to think the way you're talking about, the fear comes that you're really not having faith at all—that embracing the normal is just a cop-out of mediocrity—you never trust God for big things, and therefore your faith is weak or invalid.

SH: Sure. In any way of thinking, there are always potential abuses. I don't have hard and fast ways to discern whether someone is selling out or living the truly faithful life. And in case you thought I was too harsh earlier on the orthodox folks and their study, I think healthy study can help us avoid many of the abuses!

But back to the fear mentioned, the fear of "not really having a faith if there aren't big things happening." I can make a strong case for the opposite: If people are truly *embracing faithfulness and following in the everyday*, I propose it takes *more faith* than the person who just has the one big experience. It is a tough and blessed road to walk day by day in view of the King-- lifting up each meal, each load of laundry, each day of work finished with excellence, each relationship, and each hobby as a sacred act in His presence. A life where you trust and obey in adoration and worship without something spectacular happening every week requires a robust faith. I think it's very hard to fake it or live in mediocrity, pretending you're living by faith in this manner; peace that passes understanding will be present if it's real and it will be conspicuously absent if it is not.

Shahida coughed loudly and Ramona broke her stance to stoop behind the screen with a cup of water. She returned telling Annabelle we had five more minutes at best.

AF: Tell me more about how we should view the stories you collected, because I want to make sure I'm not missing your intentions in this passage regarding what faith truly looks like.

SH: It is convenient, practical, and efficient to have the Scriptures broken down into chapters and verses and numbered so precisely. Unfortunately, I don't think the Scriptures were ever collected to be convenient, practical, or efficient. We miss the narratives as they get broken up into textbook-type bites of information—we then take them as little sentences of ammunition for our posturing, debating, and demanding. Too often we turn the Scriptures into pragmatized fragments of "truth", manipulating and using them rather than experiencing the narratives of God's grace and truth ourselves. We're able to identify the type of bark on many trees without knowing what forest life is really like.

I say that because my intention with the stories I collected was already stated in my writing. However, it got detached and separated from the flow of thinking.

AF: Chapter twelve.

SH: When there's a chapter break, folks tend to take a mental break too. *Therefore, since we are surrounded by such a great cloud of people who have walked in the Faith, following in a convinced and trusting manner their Creator King, let us get in line and run the race too—with perseverance.* That's the word for us Faith Followers: perseverance.

AF: Stop sinning, eliminate the hindrances, and bring to remembrance often those who have suffered and fought on. Focus on Jesus and His path and persevere.

SH: Aye, again, easier said than done. Praise Him for His sufficient grace. Persevere if you're Noah, Abraham, or Mary and persevere if you're the nameless wanderer, the unseen housewife, or the farmer without an email address. We are wasting the witness of faith, wasting the idea of perseverance in this culture of novelty, immediacy, and pageantry. Wasting the ideas of suffering, discipline, and sacrifice in the age of ease, affluence, and self-preservation.

AF: We don't like to suffer; in fact, we avoid it if we can.

SH: You can't avoid the tension, friction, and for many, the literal suffering that comes with obediently walking in a "not my will but Yours be done" lifestyle. It's impossible. But it doesn't mean we try to inflict pain on ourselves to validate our faith. Many have made that extreme error and continue to do so. Nor does it mean feeling guilty for enjoying the life you've been granted. Losing ourselves to find life, knowing Christ in the power of His resurrection and the fellowship of sharing in His sufferings, as Paul said, will be ample suffering on its own account—we do not need to seek out self-induced pain.

AF: This seems a bit ideal, and to be honest, daunting. Who can live up to such a portrait of following God?

SH: Only one. The Author and Perfecter. The rest of us will all fall short of our professed standard. Look at the list I wrote: how many of those folks had at least one big mess up in their stories? Most of them have at least one footnote in their history showing us how fully human they were. It doesn't excuse their behavior, or make it okay for us to mess up, but it does show the depths of their humanity. I even put Samson and Jephthah on the list. The story of our faith is full of messy saints, but they were followers. And *we* are asked to *follow* Him, not be perfect like Him. We are asked to walk in faith as He leads us by His Spirit. What did Jesus say to Peter when He reinstated Him? Follow me. And Peter wanted to know about John, but Jesus rebuked him, yet again, communicating that John's journey is not Peter's journey—*you follow me!*

AF: I'm glad you brought up Samson, his inclusion has always kind of baffled me, what do you—

Loud, intrusive bangs suddenly rang out in the warehouse, the sound of doors kicked in all around us. Ramona burst into action, reflexively knocking the lights over.

The last thing I saw before the pitch black descended was Annabelle's widened eyes and her frantic gesture to keep filming. Ramona hit the last light with a loud pop, and the sound of shattering glass mingled with heavy footsteps and urgent voices yelling,

"NOBODY MOVE! WE WILL NOT HARM YOU! NOBODY MOVE!"

I froze, the sudden changes overwhelmed me. I heard two bodies collide right where the screen had been, Ramona's voice saying something in a muffled gasp. Trying to listen for Belle, I shouted her name and waited for a response.

"Kye! Kye!" Her voice seemed too far away already. I turned towards it.

A single gunshot fired, just yards away, chilling me, and spiking my adrenaline. The flash of the gun was like lightning in a midnight storm, more blinding than helpful but searing a millisecond image on my brain. The screen was knocked over by a tangle of people, and at the very edge of the light's reach, in that one searing flash, my wife stood looking for me as a trio of black-clothed strangers closed in behind her.

"ANNABEELLLLLLE!" I yelled, darkness crashing back in like a wave.

A body slammed into me, knocking my breath out, and I crashed to the floor, my shoulder striking the cement floor painfully. Though not usually given to violence, I dropped my gear, flailing and kicking like a cornered animal. I bit whatever was near my mouth, a squeal and frantic grunt the reply as I gouged and clawed at an unseen face. Scrambling to my feet, I ran in the direction of where I had last seen Belle, the sounds of fighting and gruff voices echoing around me. A voice yelled out that wasn't one of our assailants, or Belle, or Ramona---

"DO NOT WASTE THE WITNEEESSSS!!" A sickening thud rang out. Then I heard Belle scream out, as if through tears, "I regret nothing! Don't say anything and get out of here, you need—"

Silence. It was the last time I heard her voice.

I knew Belle's last scream was for me, and she purposefully didn't use my name, hoping they wouldn't realize I was there or would think someone else had grabbed me. Between shuffling feet and murmuring voices, I caught snatches of "--have them all--" and "how many were there?"

I felt around with my arms and touched something solid and metal. I smelled the rubber of tires and greasy oil of cars. Searching blindly with my hands, I felt an old truck, something I had failed to notice when we came in. A few quiet steps to the back of the truck, I stepped on to the bumper, and raised myself up into the bed. Clutched with grief and fear, I worried they might hear my heart beating or my loud panting as I lay there shaking.

A few more hushed comments in the distance, and the beam of a flashlight passed over the room twice, like a lighthouse scanning the ocean. It blinked out, and I heard nothing.

Nothing at all.

I held my arms tight to my chest, hands in fists, knuckles cramped from the intensity. Lying on my back, I repeatedly swallowed a lump of panic over and over, with an occasional whimper when my body convulsed involuntarily. I didn't move until the pinkish-yellow light of morning reflected high on the windows of the massive, hollow building. My tear-lined face peeked over the edge of the truck as I took in a few last steadying breaths, the tremors finally ceasing.

Looking around, I saw a few other old trucks and scattered tools. The busted lights and screen lay in the middle of the room like a small ghost town. No one was there.

Annabelle was gone.

Chapter 24:

Last Word

I wandered the empty warehouse for a few minutes or hours, the shock and grief numbing me. I kept returning to the center of the room to examine what remained, thinking perhaps some clue or something of Belle's was left behind, vainly trying to channel detectives on TV. I noticed a series of lumps under the fallen screen, and though I knew the shapes could hardly be human, hope flickered for a moment. I lifted the screen and tossed it in one motion, but found nothing but broken equipment—and my camera.

It was an empty reward and solace.

I found nothing of Belle's. No clues. Not one thing to help me find my wife. My brave, compassionate, stubborn wife. What would I have done differently? I've questioned myself a million times. And there's another question, probably from you, dear reader:

"Why haven't you said anything until now?"

Grief was with me constantly for the first year or two, and I was a wreck— eating terribly, living in isolation, ashamed to go back to my family after the horribly abrupt departure Belle and I had inflicted upon them. Even if I did go back to them, what would I say? I met King David? Interviewed the devil? Rode a train with Big Mo? Went to the future?

"But you have the video evidence those things really happened!" *True. But as my grief subsided, and I considered going public with the interviews, I realized the danger of coming forward with the true story of Annabelle Farrow. Her life's legacy was so beautifully preserved in a body of professional work and by the respect of her peers. Though mysterious at her end, Annabelle remained a model and testament to vibrant Christian living, even to those who did not share her faith. What would happen if I came forward with these videos? How many skeptical folks would cry foul? How many internet debates would challenge their truth? I did not want to risk ruining the collective memory of my wife.*

It's been almost six years since her disappearance. So why now?

The dreams started somewhere in year four. I settled into a mid-size southwestern city, working as the production director for a fairly large church with a small-town feel. My life was almost normal again. I even bought a golden lab and named her Grace. I never had visual memories of the dreams—usually just snatches of the interview with Fear or Belle's crying face as she watched Grundor storm the beach. But I always remembered the voice— always the same, always echoing in my ears when I woke, drenched with sweat and clutching my blankets: "DO NOT WASTE THE WITNESS!"

They came once a month that year, and increased the following year to once a week. It seemed crazy to think the dreams were a message. I thought of them as ripples of grief and loss, coming from a buried place in my subconscious, a place I chose to ignore.

Everything changed about a year ago as I was flipping through TV channels and staying up late because I feared the dreams would strike again. I stumbled on a rerun of a piece Annabelle did for the Christian cable network. It was a decent piece, not her greatest work, but after the credits it cut to one of her old producers talking about how he missed her. I didn't know folks were still airing things about Annabelle and her disappearance. The producer said, "She was consistently at odds with us concerning what would air from an interview or who the next subject should be, and if she wasn't doing that then she was championing to any audience who would listen that there was more out there—but we'd only ever find it if we really wanted it. It was like a calling to her. A calling to question, not for the sake of questioning, but for the sake of knowing—and caring. I wish she was still with us."

A calling. And I was the one hiding the greatest work of that calling. It was that moment, at an ungodly hour with a half-eaten meal on the coffee table, that I knew the dreams were a direct calling to me—to not waste the witness. I got up from the couch, called for Grace, and went up the stairs into my little editing suite, where I pulled out the tapes and files of these interviews. I watched and edited them through many sleepless nights, openly weeping, nostalgic laughter bursting out, unwanted but unstoppable. I poured myself out, aching each time her face came on the screen, mourning and asking myself, over and over again, what happened to Annabelle Farrow.

And one day I realized I was just puttering around, being nitpicky. They were ready. So I sent an anonymous email to one of my only remaining contacts at CNN, asking if they wanted a massive scoop on the disappearance of Annabelle Farrow. That night I woke up suddenly, panicked and fearful. Something woke me, and it wasn't the dream—those had stopped months before—it was a noise. A noise upstairs. I whispered for Grace and she jumped up beside me, immediately sensing something was wrong, a distinct warning growl coming from her chest.

We crept up the stairs, and I froze, smelling gasoline. The door to the editing room hung open, and I saw a figure standing there in the blackness. I raised my flashlight only to see, as if in slow motion, the arm strike a match and toss it into the corner of the room. The flames shot out like dragon's breath as the figure scrambled out our second-story window. Barking sharply, Grace wavered between entering the burning room or running away. Even now I see it in startling clarity, each detail in still-frame, the smell of the gas, the sounds of flames and dog, a crushing fear of what was being lost.

Moving into the room, I saw that my video equipment and computer were smashed to bits, useless and burning like trash on fire.

It was Belle's compassion that saved the interviews, her heart for ministry. She always bore a strong burden to care for the deaf and hearing impaired, a love that had sprung from her deaf cousin— who once told Belle how isolated the deaf were from gospel ministry. Because of that passion, we transcribed anything we recorded or filmed in order for all of her media appearances to be closed-captioned.

In the far corner of the room, in a non-descript metal cabinet, hanging between old receipts and tax returns, were the printed files of all the incredible interviews of Annabelle Farrow. I grabbed them and ran through the flames (not as dramatic as it sounds) to call 911.

So, this is why you have these interviews in book form and why Annabelle isn't here to share them herself. These interviews were all I had to personally hold onto all these years—all I really had left of my bride. And now I've shared them all with you. I hope you appreciate where she was all those years and what she was doing, and I hope I added to her already distinguished legacy without diminishing it. Above all, I hope you saw her passion for a personal relationship with God lived out in faithful love of others, fierce devotion to the Bride of Christ, and hope for the Church's increased radiance. If you have not seen that, then I have failed.

I wish I had more answers for you, dear reader, I really do. But perhaps I've only raised more. If so, I hope the questions are of a curious nature, that they lead you to new places and grander vistas. I pray those questions restlessly stir in you, forcing you to wrestle with the pale shadows around you and perhaps in you. I pray you find the exciting, disquieting way of life that pursues the "ought to be" and finds the richest of joys in the pursuit. Always remember God, in Christ, is knowable, and He can be trusted.

Grace and Truth to you strangers, friends, pilgrims, and readers,
Sincerely,

Kye Evans, husband to Belle

P.S. And Belle, wherever you are: I pray I did you proud by this book. And I miss you. I hope you're still sailing on the edges of the map . . .

Questions of a Curious Nature: Discussion Guide

I selected the topics and created the characters in the book to spur edifying discussion among Christians. The following discussion questions and Scriptures are by no means exhaustive, and my hope is that your group will chase many tangents and have trouble finishing the given questions. Instead of looking for concrete, one-size-fits-all answers to every topic raised, ask: *How is the Holy Spirit, through the Word of God, leading our specific community to act and think in regard to this issue?* If after reading (and re-reading) a chapter, and discussing it with fellow believers, you would like more clarification, feel free to contact me at lesswithoutyou@gmail.com.

Chapter 1: Annabelle Farrow

1. *"Kye, there's a substance to the fire in me, a Presence and relationship that isn't perfect, but is nonetheless more real to me than those waves out there. And I look at Christianity in this country and I see nothing but pale shadows of what could really be." –Annabelle Farrow*
   What do you think of Annabelle's quote to Malachi on the Outer Banks trip? What do you think she meant by a real Presence? What do you think she meant by "pale shadows"?

2. Two of the questions which led Annabelle on her journey were: *Why do those who call themselves Christians tend to wander through a fallen yet vibrant world? Why do they pursue instead a life where "hobbies become gods, and God becomes a hobby?"* Do you agree with the idea that many people just wander through a vibrant world? Why/why not? What about the idea that God has become a hobby for many people and their hobbies have become their gods?

3. Malachi shares that Annabelle wanted the interviews in the book to be released as a series of shows entitled *The Pendulum Sessions*, which would hopefully start a *"swing in American Churchianity from 'a place of sensationalism, complacency, consumerism, and the theoretical' to a place of 'tangible relationship where more grace, more humility, more thoughtful passion, more enduring faithfulness and more God-led creativity abounded.'"* What do you think of Annabelle's assessment and intentions?

Scriptures for further study: 1 Samuel 3, Matthew 5:6, Philippians 3:10-16, 2 Timothy 3:1-5

Chapter 2: Fear

1. How do you think you would react if you were Kye and awoke in the middle of the woods? Would you continue to trust Belle? Would you demand more answers?
2. What thoughts did you find interesting or disturbing in this chapter?
3. What questions from Fear reminded you the most of issues with which you wrestle?
4. Did you agree with Fear's confession of how it works in church congregations? Why/Why not? What about the role of Fear amongst children?
5. Re-read the last paragraph that Belle yells at Fear. What did you find encouraging in her final statement?

Scriptures for further study: John 14:27, Romans 8:1, 2 Timothy 1:7, Hebrews 2:14-15, 1 John 4:16-18

Chapter 3: King David Session #1

1. What were your family dynamics like growing up? Was there favoritism? Did you feel like there were expectations placed on you in your childhood?
2. Do you agree with David's assessment about our culture rooting for David but worshipping and imitating Goliath? Why/Why not? Are runts allowed to lead? Do we look for "Goliath measurements" in our leaders and churches? What are some other "measurements" we can look for in a leader?
3. David mentions the Israelite army wearing their battle gear and shouting the war cry for 40 days but never actually going into battle and says, *"You can look the part of Christian, but there comes a time when obedience has to happen in the real world, not when you're all together making noise together for God's name. There has to be a moment when you personally step out into the real. Obedience doesn't count in your head, and you can't be obedient in the future someday or imagine yourself being this super saint full of radical faith. There is only the present context in which you find yourself with the present decision before you: Trust God or melt in with the crowd who talks about trusting God."* Do you feel you've been experiencing faith and obedience "in the real"? If so, how? If not, what do you think needs to change?

Scriptures for further study: 1 Samuel 16:1-13 and 17:1-51, Matthew 6, 2 John 3-6

Chapter 4: Mortimer Keys

1. What thoughts did you find interesting or disturbing in this chapter?

2. Up until the mention of the plastic surgeries, did the Destinarian denomination sound like an appealing place to worship? Why/Why not?

3. The Destinarians make salvation all about getting to heaven and talk about salvation like a possession they hold until they get there. Do you think our church culture ever thinks similarly? Why/Why not?

4. Christians are raised to new life in Christ, not to just focus on a destination but to live in a life of love. How did Mortimer twist biblical concepts to shift the focus from loving others to all about one day going to heaven? Examples?

5. Do we worship the appearance of youth in our culture? Do we hide the things that remind us of aging and death? If so, how can we change these trends?

Scriptures for further study: Romans 6:1-14, 1 Corinthians 15, 2 Corinthians 4:16-18, Philippians 3:7-16, Colossians 3:1-4, Hebrews 11:1

Chapter 5: Pastor Chuck

1. What are your favorite Thanksgiving traditions? Why are they your favorites? Does your family ever discuss topics like gluttony, greed, or materialism during your time together?

2. What thoughts did you find interesting or disturbing in this chapter?

3. Pastor Chuck and his congregation voted to take "gluttony" off the list of deadly sins. They decided it just wasn't really a sin anymore, and it didn't fit with their lifestyles, including how eating was a huge part of their outreach. Do you think we tend to be lighter on the sins we like to commit more? What about being tougher on the sins that we don't struggle with as much? Why/Why not? What would you think if greed was the sin in this chapter instead of gluttony?

4. Self-Control is listed as fruit that shows up in our lives as we follow the leadership of the indwelling Spirit. Do you think this aspect of Spirit-led living is neglected in light of the other more talked about attributes such as love, joy, peace, and patience? Why/why not?

5. Discuss the following statement by Belle: *"You confirm what I've sadly come to believe. Too many good folk living like inconvenience is the greatest evil of our day, their sense of justice only awakened when they have a personal brush with it."*

Scriptures for further study: Genesis 1:26-31, Proverbs 25:28, Matthew 7:1-5, 1 Corinthians 6:12-20, Galatians 5:16-23, James 1:12-18

Chapter 6: Biology Class

1. What thoughts did you find interesting or disturbing in this chapter?
2. One of the main thoughts of this chapter is what it means to *understand*. What do you believe it means to *understand* salvation? Can salvation be understood apart from experiencing it? What does it mean then to experience salvation?
3. Discuss Annabelle's statement: *"Salvation fully alive is a beautiful thing."*
4. Salvation occurs at the tricky intersection of God's work on our behalf and our belief in Him and His work. Agree/Disagree? In what ways do you think we do a good job of communicating that intersection? In what ways do we not communicate it well?
5. If Biology is the study of life, then Theology is the study of God. In the chapter, Belle pointed out that too often the study of life had turned into a study of death. What do you think studying God should lead to?

Scriptures for further study: Genesis 1:26-31, Psalm 139, Luke 10:38-42, Philippians 2:12-13, 2 Peter 1:3-11

Chapter 7: John the Baptist

1. What Bible character (excluding Jesus) would you most like to meet? Why?
2. John is the first interview in the book of a person who could possibly be real. Did he remind you of people you know? Even yourself? Did it make you uncomfortable as Annabelle questioned him? Why/Why not?
3. Do you think Annabelle was too rough on John? Why/Why not?
4. What did you think of John's tendency to speak in clichés or "Christianese"? How important is it to have a clear definition of Christian terms and concepts? How important is clarity and precise language?
5. Is the "Romans Road" plan of salvation a healthy way to present the gospel? Why/Why not? Do you think Annabelle had valid points about the way those particular Scriptures are utilized? Do you prefer other Scriptures when communicating the gospel? Which ones?

Scriptures for further study: John 14:5-7 and 17:20-26, 1 Corinthians 15:1-5, Ephesians 1:17-2:10, Colossians 3:1-11

Chapter 8: Neatrick Funhopper

1. This character and his book are a play on Dietrich Bonheoffer's classic work, *The Cost of Discipleship*. Have you read that book? If so, what do you think Dietrich would say about discipleship in our current church culture?

2. What thoughts did you find interesting or disturbing in this chapter?
3. What does it mean to have "wonder" in our worship services? Do you think the wonder is reserved for God? Why/Why not?
4. Did anything Neatrick said appeal to you? Do you think any of his points were valid?
5. Do we worship novelty?

Scriptures for further study: Deuteronomy 30:11-14, Isaiah 43:16-19, Jeremiah 2:1-13, Matthew 16:13-28, 1 Corinthians 9:19-27

Chapter 9: King David Session #2

1. David didn't go looking for Goliath; he was simply faithful with his cheese and bread. What do you consider your cheese and bread right now? Do you think you're being faithful with them? Why/Why not?
2. What did you think of David's concept of seeking Saul's armor? Do you crave what others have? How do you think you can discover your own staff and sling and learn to trust God with them? Do you have any stories you can share?
3. Why do you think people want to "slay giants"? Is it wrong to want to do so? Why/Why not?
4. Discuss David's statement, *"Most people aren't ready for crazy."*

Scriptures for further study: 1 Samuel 18:1-9, Proverbs 20:6, Matthew 23:11-23 and 25:14-30, John 21:18-22

Chapter 10: Big Mo

1. Big Mo says there's a difference between momentum and expansion. Expansion is just getting bigger while momentum has direction. Do you think this distinction is true? What would be some examples of this in churches?
2. Discuss the meaning, validity, and application of the following statements:
a. Your (church's) motion should be determined by surrender, not excitement.
b. Maturity cannot be measured by enthusiasm.
c. Just because it's exciting doesn't mean God is doing it.
d. Things that last don't grow fast.
3. What did you find striking about the final confession that Momentum was with the Caesars and not on Golgotha?

4. Annabelle concedes a mass of people headed in the right direction is a good thing. What do you think that looks like?

Scriptures for further study: Proverbs 19:2, Matthew 13:18-23 and 26:31-35, 1 Corinthians 2:1-5, Galatians 1:6-10

Chapter 11: TODD
1. What thoughts did you find interesting or disturbing in this chapter?
2. Did it bother you the way the Devil was portrayed here? Why/Why not?
3. Do you agree with the idea the Thief comes to steal, kill, and destroy relationships? Why/Why not?
4. Discuss the statement, *"Relationships are the water that love swims in."*
5. What did you think about TODD's statements concerning inventions—that they aren't necessarily good or evil, but how we utilize them determines their morality? Do you think we've lost our "inventor's caution"? Why/Why not?
6. The chapter ends with silly dialogue on stereotypes about the Devil and evil. Did you find any of it humorous? Why/why not? Did it make you forget about the heavier topics earlier in the chapter? (Maybe that was the point Annabelle was making: We focus on some silly things concerning the devil and miss his real destructive work in the world.)

Scriptures for further study: Matthew 4:1-11, Ephesians 4:25-28 and 6:10-28, 2 Corinthians 2:8-11, Peter 5:8-9

Chapter 12: Hypocrisy Inside
1. What would your reaction be if you pulled into your church parking lot and the sign read, "Hypocrisy Inside"? (assuming your church has a sign)
2. What did you think of the other magical messages? What did you think of the deacons' reactions?
3. The church is embarrassed by the messages on the sign, even though they may have a great deal of truth in them. Should we be more honest about our deficiencies and inconsistencies? Why/Why not?
4. Do you ever find the messages on church signs embarrassing? Why/Why not? How do you think people who don't believe in Christ interpret them?

Scriptures for further study: Malachi 1:6-14, Matthew 7:1-6, 2 Corinthians 12:1-10

Chapter 13: The Machine

1. What thoughts did you find interesting or disturbing in this chapter?
2. Do you think church leadership has a tendency to view people as "human resources"? Why/Why not? If so, do you think it is a healthy concept? Why/Why not?
3. Does getting "plugged in" mean you're maturing in your faith? Why/Why not?
4. What did you think of the portrayal of the church staff?
5. What does The Machine do? Should churches exist solely for getting as many people as possible participating in an incredible worship experience?
6. The last scene seems to indicate The Machine doesn't care who the actual people are as long as they're effective. Do you think that is a mentality that can exist in churches?

Scriptures for further study: Ephesians 2:19-22 and 3:7-21 and 4:11-16, Colossians 1:24-29, 1 Peter 2:4-12

Chapter 14: Sidedoor Sally

1. What is your favorite style of worship music? Why do you think it's your favorite? Do you think some musical styles lend themselves better to worship?
2. Did it bother you that Sally's relationship to worship music was portrayed as a drug addiction? Did you find any truths in the comparison?
3. Did you resonate more with Kye or Belle in their discussion afterwards?
4. What do you think is the main source for conflicts in the church?
5. What did you think of Belle's idea that Christians should be fighting over serving each other rather than protecting preferences?

Scriptures for further study: Isaiah 29:13, Amos 5:18-27, John 4:19-24, Romans 12:1-2, Hebrews 12:28-29

Chapter 15: Grundor

1. What thoughts did you find interesting or disturbing in this chapter?
2. What did you think of Grundor's strategy? Would you want to attend his church? Why/Why not?
3. Do you think "might makes right" thinking has entered church practice? (Or, stated another way: "popular makes right") Why/Why not?
4. How do you define whether or not a church is healthy?
5. Annabelle finally gets Grundor to share his vision: *"Our church will build the Kingdom of God as we share the Gospel, develop disciples, serve the Lord by*

serving our community, and worship together in spirit and truth." What did you think of it?

Scriptures for further study: Isaiah 40:25-31, Mark 12:28-34, 1 Corinthians 1:18-31 and 12:7-27, Philippians 2:1-11, 1 Peter 1:22-25

Chapter 16: King David Session #3

1. What lessons that David learned in the Bathsheba incident did you find helpful or insightful?
2. Do you think people struggle with intimacy (in the sense of closeness)? Why is it difficult to comprehend a friendship with God? Do you agree with David's observations on what it means to have a personal relationship with God?
3. What are some of the ways we try to personalize God?
4. In 2-3 sentences, describe how you've experienced the grace of God in your life the past few weeks.

Scriptures for further study: Psalm 51, John 17:3, Hebrews 4:14-16 and 10:19-25, James 4:1-10, 1 John 1

Chapter 17: True Love (Waits)

1. How would you define true love? *the concept, not the character in the chapter* ☺
2. Do you agree with True's assessment that people get more cynical about "true love" as they get older? Why/Why not?
3. How have you seen the power of expectations in your life? How do you react when your expectations aren't met in a relationship?
4. Discuss the statement, *"You can't spend your singlehood self-indulgently and then expect your marriage to be magically and naturally awesome."*
5. What are some ways we try to reason our way out of loving someone? Are those reasons ever valid? Can we love like God loved us without sacrificing something?

Scriptures for further study: Psalm 136, Romans 5:8, Matthew 9:9-13 and 11:16-19, Luke 10:25-37, John 15:12-17, 1 John 3

Chapter 18: Unspoken

1. Do you enjoy small talk with your friends? What about small talk with people you don't know well? Why/Why not?

2. Do you think any of the men in the story went home and prayed more about the requests given? Why/Why not?
3. Why do you think our tendency is to share prayer requests that rarely touch on the spiritual matters of our own hearts?
4. It takes time to build vulnerability between people but it also takes effort. Would you say you're fearful of vulnerability with others, you desire it but lack opportunity, or you're content with the level of vulnerability and trust you have in your relationships?

Scriptures for further study: Romans 12:10-15, Colossians 2:2-6, James 5:13-20

Chapter 19: Dr. Perfecto & Little Leesa

1. Little Leesa is short for "Ekklesia" and Ekklesia is the Greek word for "the gathering," most often translated as church. With that in mind, why do you think Leesa spoke in first person plural?
2. What makes a church beautiful? Is beauty in the eye of the beholder when talking about churches?
3. Does God expect all local churches to the look the same? Why/Why not?
4. Do you ever get angry or upset at how other churches "do church"? Why/Why not?
5. How do you feel your church is doing right now listening for and obeying the Wind?

Scriptures for further study: John 3:5-17 and 27-30, 2 Corinthians 6:14-7:1, Romans 14, Ephesians 5:25-30, Revelation 21:1-5

Chapter 20: Military Men

1. What thoughts did you find interesting or disturbing in this chapter?
2. Do you think there are more wolves in sheep's clothing around us than we realize or less? Why?
3. Do you think Christians, in their desire to do ministry, sometimes inflict collateral damage? Why/Why not? Do you think the concept of collateral damage is something considered when deciding on what to plan or what to say? Is it a valid concern?
4. Are Christians in the public sphere militaristic in the way they communicate? Why/Why not?
5. Does anger have a place in preaching? If so, where is that place?

6. Does Christianity need to be defended? If so, how? Should Christians defend against or attack other Christians whose theology or practice differs greatly from their own?

Scriptures for further study: John 5:39-40, Romans 14:13-19, 1 Corinthians 2:6-16 and 8:1-3 and 13:1-8, Galatians 5:16-26, 2 Timothy 2:14-16

Chapter 21: Nomo Polo

1. Do you ever doubt your faith? What do you do when that happens?
2. Do you think churches welcome questioning the status quo? Why/Why not? Is there danger in asking questions that shake things up? If so, what are the dangers? Do we persecute or listen to those whose ideas/theology/writings don't line up with the majority?
3. Is your church marked by "expectation and humility" today? Are you? Do you feel like a new wineskin or old wineskin right now?
4. Are there still edges to the map? Are you willing to share your guesses for what they might be?

Scriptures for further study: Job 38-41, Ecclesiastes 5:1-7, John 16:12-15, Acts 2:14-41 and 11:1-18, Romans 11:33-36, 1 Corinthians 13:9-13

Chapter 22: King David Session #4

1. Do you ever feel like you're being *"crushed by pale shadows of what could be"*?
2. What parts of David's speech about the Church and its people resonated with you? Why?
3. How do you feel about King David's assessment of our "job" in the following statement: *If you know you have more substance than a shadow—or at least you meekly recognize your shadowy parts—your job is not to judge, or to condemn, but to drink deeply from the cup you've been granted and humbly, faithfully, describe its taste and savor as best you can to those who can hear, whether they listen or not. All the while loving the Lord God with all you are and loving your neighbor as yourself.*
4. How do the truths of *"God can be trusted and He can be known"* anchor you in your life?

Scriptures for further study: Romans 5:1-5, 2 Corinthians 4:7-18, Hebrews 5:11-6:3, 1 Peter 2:1-3

Chapter 23: The Author

1. Who do you think wrote the book of Hebrews? Have you ever thought about it? Does it bother you not knowing who the author is?
2. What thoughts did you find interesting in this chapter?
3. Shahida seems to think Christians in our nation need a warning to change our current direction. What do you think Shahida meant? Do you agree with that assessment? Why/why not?
4. Discuss the statement *"there is no arriving, there is only following."*
5. Do you think God is looking for witnesses rather than heroes? Would you be content if your faithfulness went "unwitnessed" here on earth? Do you feel a strong desire to do something awesome for God? Do you ever feel inadequate in regards to "what you've done with your faith"?

Scriptures for further study: Psalm 84, Galatians 5:1-15, Colossians 1:3-14, 2 Corinthians 3:7-18, Hebrews 11-12:12

Chapter 24: Last Word

1. If you were in Kye's position, would you have published the interviews? Why/Why not?
2. What do you think happened to Belle?
3. The last paragraph is Kye's heart for what you the reader would experience through the book. Which phrase resonates with you the most?

Scriptures for further study: Romans 15:13, 2 Corinthians 13:14, Ephesians 3:14-21, Hebrews 13:15-16, Jude 20-25

Acknowledgements

Thanks to my faithful family in PA who always loved good stories in books and movies.

Thanks to all the mentors who patiently shepherded me through my zeal and ignorance: Phil, Kim, Denny, Earl, Carl, Bob, Disco Dave, Doug, and Gandalf. Thanks for nothing Merlin.

Thanks to my book mentors Eugene, Marva, Henri, A-Dub, and The Good Bishop Tom. When your ideas pop up in this book, I hope you're not too embarrassed.

Thanks to the communities of Chambersburg, PA, Toccoa Falls College, and Banks County, GA for shaping who I am today.

Thanks to all you Kickstarter donors who supported the final run of this process. May your endeavors be met with the same affirmation and backing from your own communities.

Thanks to my dear friends at Crossroads Worldwide for all the memories and moments that helped to give this book content and make publishing it a reality. I miss our daily interactions.

Thanks to the dear brothers I live life with in our little town and the ones I wish still lived here. There are too many of you to name. Our bonds are made of Spirit and your faithfulness spurs me on. I am honored to be counted among you.

Thanks to my godly and talented editors, Jane and Sarah, who not only made this work exponentially better, but also exposed my addiction to adverbs. . .as well as my ellipsis fetish. Your sacrifices for this work humble me. Thanks also to Kelly, Elisa, and Jami for your professional and creative work to design a final product worth holding. And thanks to Bet for your final polishing edit on the manuscript.

Thanks to the wizards, elves, dwarves, and warrior poets of 3A—and especially mighty Sethos who continues to stand shoulder to shoulder with me as we kindle hearts in a world grown chill. Words can't express the depth of love I have for you all or the level of influence you've had on my life. May the Wind bring us back together sooner rather than later.

Lastly, thanks to my patient wife, resplendent daughters, and sacrificial mother-in-law here at Orth Lodge. Your constant love and presence makes me who I am. Shout out to the hedgies for always believing in me.

SDG

About the Author

Matt Orth lives in NC with his wife (married 5.27.95), his two daughters (born 1.1.99 and 8.25.11) and a small army of dwarf goats and pygmy hedgehogs. He teaches regularly at Broad River Community Church and has served in church ministry for over 20 years in a variety of capacities, including Church Janitor, Youth Pastor, College Pastor, Itinerant Speaker, and Ministry Director of Crossroads Worldwide.

Currently Matt spends his time writing, reading, studying, teaching, traveling, and learning the craft of stand-up comedy. He drinks Broad River Coffee www.yourcupcounts.com and tweets irregularly at @lesswithoutyou.

www.ingramcontent.com/pod-product-compliance
Lightning Source LLC
Chambersburg PA
CBHW031326170626
46807CB00002B/588